CW01638191

Savage ABANDON

SKY COPPOLA

Savage Abandon

© 2023 by Sky Coppola

No portion of this work may be reproduced or used in any manner without express written permission of the author. Exception for fair use, excerpt used in review and for editorial purposes.

This book is a work of fiction. Names, characters, places and incidents reside solely in the mind of the author's imagination or are used in a fictional manner. Any resemblance to any person, living or dead, is purely coincidental.

Editor:
Cover Designer:
Interior Formatting: Authortree

Trigger Warning

Some of the topics in this series might be upsetting or disturbing, and your mental health matters. I've compiled a list of trigger warnings for the entire series, rather than triggers for each book, because the books are not stand-alones. (Though I might add spin-off stand-alones at some point.)

Trigger warnings for the entire series include but aren't limited to: explicit sexual content, violence, gore, mental illness, animal deaths, murder, deaths of loved ones, extreme vulgarity, physical abuse and assault, torture, rape, human trafficking, mention of and flashbacks of child and teen abuse and rape, bullying, and drugs.

For questions about triggers or discussions about my books, feel free to message me on my "Contact" page on my website: https://skycoppolaromance.com.

A Note from Sky

Hello Reader Friend,

I enjoy hearing from my readers. Please feel free to contact me through my author's website at: https://skycoppolaromance.com. Or on my Facebook author page: https://m.facebook.com/people/Sky-Coppola-Dark-Romance-Author-Page/100078227946505.

Each of the books in this series ends in a cliffhanger. But through grueling trials along each character's journey, we get our happily ever afters.

I have most of the novels written for the entire series, with a few in the outline stage, but I won't leave you hanging. The series will be complete.

So grab a comfy chair, a mug of your favorite beverage, and I wish you a beautiful day slipping into the world I created.

Love,
Sky

Dedicated to those of us who love our heroes a little villainous.

"I will not let you go into the unknown alone."
—Bram Stoker

Three Rivers Ranch

Chapter 1
CARTER

WIND DANCE VALLEY, WYOMING

Sweat trickles from under my hat and drips into my shirt collar. I jam my shovel into the ground and stomp on the warped edge, the bottom of my boot pressing into the worn metal. The pointed tip grazes off an unseen rock beneath the earth's surface, sending shock waves through my arms.

"Damn it." I glance up for a breath of air.

The restless cattle shuffle in the nearby pasture, swishing their tails and bellowing hot air into the chilly April morning. I lean on the top of the shovel and swipe a hand across my forehead, looking over the grassy fields in the distance.

My black Quarter Horse, Bandit, grazes nearby, tied well away from this poisonous bush that grew out of nowhere and refuses to uproot.

A slight breeze ruffles the hair at my nape as I survey the herd of Angus beneath the sapphire sky.

The heifers look… ***uneasy*** this morning.

I squint through the glaring sunlight to pinpoint the source of the problem. It's calving season. Quite a few are close to giving birth, which can make any of these gals restless. It's not abnormal on a cattle ranch, especially one like ours—biggest ranch around, been in operation for decades, run like a well-oiled machine. The restless movements, the small steps, the way they're veering from a particular spot like they're spooked, tells me—

I freeze, fingers tightening on the shovel.

One of the heifers goes down.

Adrenaline races through my veins. I toss the shovel away and cross the thirty yards between them and me. I vault over the fence with a practiced move and head straight for the heifer straining on the ground.

Agonized groaning fills the air, coming from the prone form. As I draw near, the shiny black heifer kicks and raises her head, wide eyes staring at me like she knows I'm coming to help. I have to protect these girls if they have issues or their lives are at stake. I'm the problem solver who has to figure out what's wrong and be ready to help when the opportunity presents itself. The cattle can't afford anything less.

I can't afford anything else.

The heifer bellows again and lets her head fall to the ground. She's one of the young ones.

I drop to my knees at her hind end and examine her. The first calf of the season starts to emerge, wet-nosed, gooey, and...

Big.

Too big.

Damn it. I knew it. I ***knew*** this would happen the minute my fool brother, Tanner left the gate open and ol' Chuck—the biggest bull in our herd—took a turn at these young females.

Cattle birth on their own without any issues most times. Ranchers didn't invent biology. Nature's been doing its thing since the dawn of time without human intervention. But sometimes, it feels like humans are what cause things to go sideways.

My damn brother leaves the gate open, the wrong male gets in, and we get giant-sized calves from Chuck. Stuck calves suffocate... and even end the heifers' lives sometimes.

But this isn't anything I haven't handled before. After years of raising cattle, I've seen a thing or two.

I yank my cell from my jeans pocket and hold it to the sky. Where the 5G symbol should be—nothing. I don't get cell service out here, but it's always worth a try.

Shoving the phone back in my pocket, I lean away from the heifer's legs and rub her hip. "Guess I'm on my own. Because you're not gonna give me an option, are you, girl? Let's get your baby out."

Adrenaline pumping, I reach for the cresting calf and hope for a miracle. Losing even one calf hits hard when it's my job to save them, and losing a heifer is even worse.

"Not on my watch," I tell her, then slide my hands around the calf's forelegs to guide it to safety.

When the slippery ball of fur slides out, I grunt and breathe as hard as its momma. She scrambles to her feet after a while, and the calf takes its first wobbly steps soon afterward. Both miracles send a breath of relief through me, and I sit back on my heels.

Okay. This won't be bad.

My breath of relief ends at the sound of more lowing.

I'm on my feet and moving, the adrenaline returning. What the hell is happening out here? It's too early for this. The herd parts, and there's another heifer down. Another delivering early. Delivering big.

I don't waste time getting into position to help her guide the calf out, but this girl is more nervous than the first. She kicks and rolls. One hoof swipes my face, and I jerk back, but not fast enough to avoid the sting of a slash on my cheek. Hot blood trickles down my jaw, but I ignore it. Just another peril of being a rancher, which is exhausting and time-consuming… and mostly the biggest reason I don't have a love life.

Ol' Chuck gets more action than I do.

I'm wrist-deep in the flailing beast when a horrifying bellow comes from another heifer. I jerk to attention and look around for her, but she's lost in the herd, and I'm too busy with this one to go looking.

I know things are bad, but this is turning into an actual disaster. I'm in for some worst-case-scenario hell if several of these girls go into labor this morning and can't get their calves out on their own. If the first birth is any indication of what's to come, then the rest are going to be tricky, too. I hate to admit it, but I'm headed into full-on crisis mode.

Within an hour, I manage to pull three calves.

"This isn't going well," I grunt as I use my shoulder to push my hat up and wipe sweat from my forehead.

I hoped for one or two large calves and the rest of average size, but Chuck always sires these big-headed and wide-chested offspring. Of course, he had to be the bull to inseminate the heifers.

All in all, another life lesson about the problems that arise if you give in to your innate desires and impregnate something you didn't plan on.

I rub my sweaty neck on my shirt collar. Unfortunately, I won't be able to pull these births off on my own.

Why'd I have to choose to be the responsible son in the family? My younger brother runs off, chasing girls, and having the time of his life. Meanwhile, I'm here covered in birthing fluid, watching the herd in crisis.

It's in times like these it sure would be nice to have someone of my own to lean on; for her to offer support when times are tough. The love of a good woman when the world is against me... yeah, there's nothing like it.

No such luck around here, though.

I leave the field at a quick clip and make my way to my horse. After unlooping his reins from around the fence where I secured him, I mount up.

"Come on, boy. Let's go." I press Bandit into a full gallop, urging him to head home.

Bandit is one of the fastest Quarter Horses in the valley, and he blazes across the Wyoming landscape, making his way from the grassy fields to our ranch house with blinding speed as though he senses the urgency of our mission. He sure proves his mettle when the stakes are high.

Good thing, too. We have no time to waste. I press my calves into his sides to push him faster.

I need to get to my father right now.

No one besides Dad and me are on the ranch today. My cousin Dylan is picking up feed, and most of the ranch hands are up in the high-country running fence while the others are enjoying a day off in town.

Under the best circumstances, my father is a healthy cattleman, but he hasn't been well since the ordeal with Tanner. I hate asking Dad for help with his condition, but he'll have to assist however he can.

As we near the house, I ease back on the reins, and Bandit slows his pace. Before he even stops, I hop off and run inside.

"You up?" I burst through the side door and barrel into the living room. No answer besides the steady whir and click of the washing machine.

After searching Dad's usual haunts around the house, I find him asleep in his oversized leather chair beside the fireplace.

I shake his shoulder.

"Yeah? What?" He jerks and looks up at me with a confused squint. Deep lines mar the skin beside his dark blue eyes. His salt-and-pepper hair sticks up at odd angles from how he's been sleeping, like tiny bullhorns. "Carter? What's wrong?"

"It's the heifers. It's bad."

Dad sits upright, the recliner slamming back with finality. "What's wrong with 'em?" Despite the strength in his tone, there's a shake in his hands as he grabs his hat from the side table and shoves it on his head.

"A bunch of them are calving. The calves are big this time. They're in trouble."

Dad scrunches his face, still looking half-asleep. "Which bull went in with them?"

I don't want to tell him because I'm sure Dad will be the one having a calf when he learns the truth, but he needs to know. It might be the quickest way to get him moving if he can.

I lick my dry lips. "Remember how you and Tanner had that argument a while back, and he stormed out?"

"What's that have to do with the heifers?"

"Tanner didn't exactly stop to shut the gate. I hoped I caught it in time, but it looks like Chuck bred those heifers while he was in with them."

The news has the desired effect. Dad slaps his hands on the arm of the chair, now wide awake. "Why didn't you tell me?"

" I didn't want to get you riled up. I know lately, you've been—"

"Been fine." He cuts me off before I devise a polite way to say ***not too well.*** He uses the arms of the chair to jump up, but way too quickly. Before I can give him a hand, he stumbles and collapses, his hat rolling off to the side.

"Dad," I yell as his head cracks against the wooden floorboards, and a hollow thump fills the air. I bend and take his head in my hands to ensure he isn't bleeding.

He opens his eyes and shoves me away. "Would you get off me?"

He's always been a stubborn man, and though he refuses to admit it, he's been unwell for some time. But he won't seek medical treatment. ***Don't trust doctors***, he says.

He rests one elbow on the hardwood floor and props himself up, using the other to rub the back of his head. Only my father can take a tumble, hit his head, and still want to get outside. If the hard work and long hours aren't killing him, it's making whatever the heck is wrong with him worse.

He tries to reach for his hat. "Have the calves come out right so far?"

If things weren't so dire, between the heifer crisis and Dad's ongoing health issues, I'd chuckle at where his mind goes—how he ignores his health and only cares about the well-being of the animals.

"One came backward," I say, "but I got him out. Just big calves."

"How'd they look?"

I put his hat back onto the side table. "The calves are nice. The situation is not. Come on. Let's get you back into the chair." I scoop my hands under his armpits and yank him to his feet.

He uses me for support, grabs the arm, and then eases himself back into the seat. I sit him down, ensuring he's comfortable before I back away.

He rubs the ridge of his brow with tense fingers. "Tanner," he mumbles. "If he weren't so stubborn."

I say nothing. There's no sense in blaming my brother right now. We're all a little messed up this year for different reasons, and by the looks of Dad, he won't be able to help.

"The ranch hands in the high fields?" he asks.

"Yeah. For at least another week. I could ride up and fetch them back, but I want to get back out there."

"Where're your sisters?"

"Mina's off to the rodeo, remember?"

He nods.

"Your other daughter's married and lives in Colorado," I goad.

Dad's more than aware of Nora's whereabouts, and even though he's just taken a good thump to the head, I'm still going to give him a hard time. It's what I do.

"Right." He chuckles. "I know that."

"How about you call Will from next door?" I suggest. "See if he can lend a hand until Dylan and the guys get back."

"I ain't no damn secretary. I should be out there with you."

I know how Dad's mind works. He doesn't like having to sit inside, feeling useless. I need help. He'll have to pick up the phone if he can't get outside with me and pull his weight physically.

"Best get making those phone calls, ol' man." I tip my hat at him, then head through the side door to find Bandit.

I mount and get into focus mode as we ride. I can't think

about how Tanner's fuckup might cost us dead cows or how Dad's ailing health could affect our household. I can't think about the fact I'm going back into chaos alone—always alone.

"Come on, boy. Come on," I urge, and Bandit flexes and stretches with even more force. He's the fastest ever, but I still wish he'd move twice as fast.

By the time we get to the fields, and I take the briefest break to cool Bandit down, I wish I hadn't left. I stand, staring at the cattle like a witness at a crime scene.

What the hell am I supposed to do?

Two of the youngest heifers are flat on the ground, bellowing and panting. The herds' panic has grown more intense in the time I've been gone.

Help will come eventually, but the question is, how much damage will be done by the time the recruits get here? And how long will I be alone before they do?

I can stand and stare in panic. Or get shit done.

I set to work.

Hours pass. I focus on the cows, the following action, and keep moving. I don't think about what can go wrong. I don't think about how my muscles burn and my breath sticks in my lungs.

More heifers go down—more need help.

Mom, if you're looking down on me... now's the time.

As chemicals rush through my limbs, it's like the ground is pulled from under me... as though I'm falling through a cloud in the Wyoming sky and headed straight down with no parachute.

I blink once, then a second time, and another hour is gone. The air is rife with a potent mix of sweat, cow dung, and birthing fluid. Weak-headed, I drag myself to my feet and grab onto a nearby fencepost to catch my breath.

Where's my damn help?

Where the hell is ***anyone***, for God's sake? I know where my cousin and the ranch hands are, but I'm in a bind here. And the other guys out on the town? Why do they think getting their dicks wet is more important than these heifers?

Or maybe I'm just bitter I gave up my own girl for this life.

To hell with my conscience. It's not my guide today. I have pressing matters at hand.

I scramble toward the next heifer, my hands and clothes covered with blood.

It's about damage control now.

As I work my way through the moaning herd, numbness overtakes me. I move, doing what needs to be done but not fully conscious. The worst part is knowing that as much as I'm doing, it'll never be enough to save them all.

Chapter 2
DESTINY

I hold a needle in one hand and a sedated cat's abscessed ear in the other when the phone rings. And rings.

And rings.

I slap the needle onto the surgery table. "Oh, for Pete's sake."

I snap off my right glove, ripping it, then reach for the cordless. I glance at the clock on the wall. Megan, the receptionist, is on her lunch break. It's hard to hear over the animals' barks, yelps, and bleats in the clinic, but I try anyway.

"Hello?" I press the phone against my ear and squint as if that makes it easier to hear.

Taking calls while administering a shot, stitching up a wound, or attempting to drain an abscess of puss isn't the most convenient thing in the world, but things aren't going my way these days. The clinic is short-staffed, and I have to pick up the slack wherever needed.

"Doctor Destiny Hart?"

"Uh… yes?" I squint harder. Is this man just assuming it's normal for a doctor to answer the phone? Or is it someone I know?

Oh, damn. I hope it isn't another call from the student loan debt collectors. I've already made arrangements to mitigate payments, and the last thing I need is them calling my work and stressing me out more than I already am.

I'm unable to keep the suspicion from my voice. "This is Doctor Hart."

"Will Jenkins told me to call you, ma'am," the distant, gravelly voice says.

Will Jenkins? I rack my brain, struggling through half a day's worth of emergency visits, regular client appointments, and surgeries to place the name. Though there's a hint of familiarity in this man's tone, I don't recognize the number on the caller ID, and the voice only does a little to help me place who's speaking.

"Okay. May I ask who this is?"

"Name's Caldwell. Malcolm Caldwell."

My heart seizes. My fingers grip the phone and tension presses the hard plastic uncomfortably against the side of my head. I focus on the pain in my ear so I can't experience the agony in my chest.

This man can't be related to my ex-boyfriend, can he? There're lots of people with the last name Caldwell. Thousands. ***Maybe even millions.*** And perhaps only a couple dozen are directly related to the man who broke my heart.

This absolutely has ***nothing*** to do with ***Carter Caldwell.*** Does it? The urge to hang up the phone is strong.

"Doc, I have a situation at my ranch." Unaware of my inner turmoil, Malcolm continues speaking. "If I could have a moment of your time? Will told me you are hands down the best person for the job. Unfortunately, he can't help—he has some pneumonia issues with his cows."

I'm not entirely listening to the poor man's explanation. My mind is hijacked. I run cold, every nerve in my body rattling. Malcolm Caldwell's voice takes me to a place I should've long since left in the past. But I can't leave it behind. ***Ever.***

"Doctor Hart? You there?" Malcolm's voice cuts through the fog of my time traveling.

I try to pretend I'm of sound mind, while inside, I'm screaming. "What kind of situation are you talking about, sir?"

"You know how animals are." In his thick drawl, he sounds as if he's actually sorry to have to call me.

Each word brings back flashes of Carter. It's incredible how much of him I hold on to, even now, and each time he crosses my mind, I tell myself he doesn't deserve to linger in my dreams.

But he does anyway.

"I know you're busy, Doc, so don't be afraid to tell me to go to hell if you can't help, but my heifers are in trouble," Malcolm goes on, a bit of chagrin in his voice. "Chuck, my biggest bull, got in with them, and they're all coming up on their due dates, and some are having a heck of a time trying to push their calves out."

I get it. Sometimes unfortunate things happen to livestock. They're constantly putting ranchers in a bind at the wrong time, doing things their way. But rather than attempting some kind of empathetic ***hmm*** to let him know I'm listening, I stand with Carter's face in my mind.

"I can't have them suffering, ma'am. My son's doing the best he can, and I'm—I'm not well." Malcolm's voice breaks.

That pitiful sound is enough to snatch me out of the past.

Knowing there's a field of suffering animals weighs heavy on my conscience. This is the reason I spent so much time and money going to veterinary school in the first place. I can't turn my back on animals in need. And from what Mr. Caldwell is saying, these heifers are in serious need of help.

The clinic is full of every imaginable call today—horses needing health certificates, five goats needing their CD&T shots, and half a dozen dairy cows who need to be inseminated by five o'clock this evening, on top of the regular small animal visits. It's a lot of work, but as challenging as it all may be, Doc Jones can handle it with the help of his assistant while I attend to this emergency, I'm sure.

Damn it. Why am I such a bleeding heart?

"I can wrap up and head over in about an hour," I find myself saying. "Is that okay?"

"The sooner, the better, Doc."

"I'll be there as soon as I can. Where do you keep your herd, Mister Caldwell?"

"Three Rivers Ranch. I'll send you the address. I have them penned off from the rest. Once you get here, I'll show you where to go."

My heart sinks as soon as I hear those three words.

Three Rivers Ranch.

My worst fears slap me in the face. Carter mentioned that name before, I'm sure of it.

I give Mr. Caldwell my cell number and tell him I'll watch for his text. He sends me the address a few seconds after we get off the phone. I stare at it, contemplating calling him back and telling him I won't be able to make it. I could say the clinic caught fire. Both grannies are already in the ground, but I could use a family death excuse, couldn't I?

Nah, I'll go to hell for that.

I resume treating the cat on the exam table.

I don't know if I can handle running into Carter, just being honest. Seeing him might be enough to undo me. ***Again.***

But maybe... if there ***is*** a chance he lives at the ranch, perhaps it'll help me get him off my mind? Maybe I can break this spell he's had on me for the last ten years?

I gently finish up with the cat.

Maybe I'll go and rub my success in Carter's face. I want him to experience the sizzle of knowing I never needed him by my side to accomplish my dreams after we promised to stick together.

Okay... I'll go. But wait... I'm doing it purely for the sake of the calves. This isn't about the possibility of seeing a particular man. And there's a good chance Carter might not even be there. Even if it is his family's ranch, there's no telling where he lives. He could be anywhere. Could be married with thirteen kids.

I ***want*** him to be married with thirteen children. It'll be closure. Even though the fleeting thought of him building a family with someone other than me still cracks my heart open.

Doc Jones is occupied with a pregnant Dachshund in one of our five sterile exam rooms, his coppery head bent low over the dog's bulbous belly with his stethoscope pressed against her short red fur.

I stick my head past the door and catch his attention. "Can you and your assistant handle things while I run out on an emergency? Calving situation a few hours away."

He's going to grumble. It's coming. It's shaping on his thin lips. Okay, this is it—this is the excuse I can use to avoid Three Rivers Ranch.

I'm sorry, Mister Caldwell, but my boss can't spare me right now.

But Doc Jones peers at me over wire-framed glasses, looking unfazed. "We can handle things. We always do."

A small part of me hoped he'd argue, tell me ***absolutely not***, and force me to stay. Or hell, maybe even offer to handle the emergency himself. But he aged out of the heavy traveling years ago, content to run the clinic while I do the gallivanting.

I swallow my astonishment. "Okay. Well then... I'll update you as soon as I can."

On the plus side, a chance remains that my mother will shoot this down.

I call her to explain the situation, careful to keep that cursed last name off my lips. The last thing I need to do is invoke Carter Caldwell within my parent's hearing range.

"It's a good job, but it means I might not be home for a few days, Mom." I hold my breath for her reaction.

"Okay, honey." Her tone is distracted. I hear the splash of water in the background and dishes clinking in the sink. "The extra pay will be good. You can put it toward your loans. Climb that ladder of success."

Of course she's supportive. Mom wants me to achieve my dreams, and we've discussed the sacrifices necessary to get me to where I need to be in my career.

"It means you're holding the fort down," I warn her in one last-ditch effort to get her to give me an out. "Several days, at least. Think you can keep everyone fed until I get back?"

"You know I will, honey. Stay safe. Call us later."

I hang up the phone and make a face. Well, now I have no excuse. Everything's in order. The only thing left is to pack my supplies, get in the truck, and drive.

I make a mental list of things I need. Tons of gloves, disinfectant, my bag of medical gear, calving supplies, water, hat… I glance at my clothes. The jeans and plaid top I wear over a T-shirt are okay, but I need my heavy-duty boots. My shoes around the office won't last more than ten seconds out in a cow field.

I keep a bag in my vehicle with spare clothes and toiletries for emergencies like this, so I'm set there.

I search under stacks of papers on the desk for my keys but come up empty-handed. Crawling under the desk next, I look for any sign of shiny metal that might be considered a key to the old red Chevy parked out front. I bang my head on the underside of the desk and groan out a terrible curse word as I pull myself off the floor. Grabbing my jacket from the hook by the office door, I glance around again, flip the lights off, and leave.

Gathering everything only takes about ten minutes of racing around the supply room. Luckily, I don't need the keys to throw stuff in the truck's bed, so I knock out the packing while waiting for Megan to return from lunch.

I walk into the reception area just past one to find my receptionist restored to her seat. She's leaned back in the creaky chair, her blonde hair in a ponytail of tumbled curls and her black eyeliner winged like a celebrity on the red carpet. Her attention is focused on the magazine splayed over her knees instead of the blinking phone, clearly keeping someone on hold.

"Hey, have you seen—"

Megan doesn't even look at me, but her hand appears, dangling the keys from one of her orange-painted acrylic fingernails.

"Megan, you're a lifesaver. Where were they?"

"You left them on the counter this morning." She sounds unamused and snaps her chewing gum.

Shoving the keys into my jacket pocket, I tap my knuckles on the counter to draw her attention. "I'm headed to Three Rivers Ranch for an emergency. I might not make it back until tomorrow or even the next day. But Doc Jones will take over the rest of my appointments until I return."

Megan sits up, dropping her pink Chuck Taylor high-tops to the floor as she tosses the magazine down and meets my eyes with a look of intrigue on her tanned face. "Three Rivers Ranch? That's the Caldwell place, right?"

My stomach clenches at the mention of the name again. "Uh, yeah. I think they're the family who owns it." Again, I keep it generic to avoid getting into this. "Look, I gotta go. Grab that call on hold, will you?"

"The Caldwells are billionaires." Megan ignores me, leaning over the counter, raising her pencil-thin eyebrows, and then waggling them suggestively. "They have more money than the entire state of Wyoming put together."

I roll my eyes. Billionaires? Really? This may not be the same Caldwell family. I remember Carter looking well-to-do but not snobby, and… not like other people from my past who had money and flaunted it.

"Megan, I need help finding my Muck Boots. Could you check if they're in the back room, please?" I could go, but she'll find a way to follow and keep talking about the Caldwells.

"They aren't back there." Megan shrugs. "I just cleaned before lunch. Did you check your truck?"

So much for my distraction. "They might be out there. Yeah. Okay—"

"Do you think they have a pool?" Megan sounds like the person who writes the gossip articles in the magazine she's reading.

I ignore her. "Thanks for your help, Megan. I'll see you in a couple—"

"I bet they do have a pool," she squeals. "And probably a tennis court. Maybe even an elevator!"

"To the tennis court?" I ask sarcastically.

"I bet that place is full of priceless works of art and marble floors and—"

"They're regular people like you and me. Don't let money go to your head." I sling my bag over my shoulder. "Text me if you need me. I probably won't get cell reception most of the time, so just be aware."

"Got it, Doc. Be safe." Megan waves goodbye and returns to her magazine while the caller on hold waits.

The midday sun is high but not too hot this early in the year, and the warmth feels good on my face as I walk to my truck. I load the last of my stuff in the cab, then look behind the driver's seat. ***There are my boots.*** By the night's end, I'll most likely be covered from head to toe in mud and afterbirth, but the less that ends up on my jeans, the better.

My mind wanders back to Megan and her excitement over the ***Caldwell billionaires.*** Where'd she hear those rumors anyway?

When we were together, Carter paid for everything and drove a fancy Silverado. But a billionaire? That's out there... though I guess it could be true. I never made it to their ranch because we were in Texas and busy with school and... ***fucking.*** Lots of fucking.

I did know his family were from Wyoming, but Carter was long gone before he got a chance to invite me to meet any family. When he never called again, I realized I knew him less than I thought, so maybe they do have all those things Megan mentioned.

Maybe Carter hid more from me than I ever knew.

But to be fair, I can say the same about myself.

In the silence after shutting myself in the cab, I waste a few minutes checking my phone, looking over my supplies, and doing my best to delay the inevitable.

Leaving.

Making the journey to Three Rivers Ranch.

I worked hard to move on from Carter, but now, sitting here on the verge of heading toward the unknown, I can't deny my heart is racing at the possibility of seeing him again. Even the idea of meeting his family after all these years oddly excites me.

But what if they're a bunch of rich snobs? What if they don't even know who I am? Did Carter ever tell them about me?

I slump against the bench seat and take a deep breath. The cyclone in my stomach is having a field day. How am I going to get through this while acting professionally?

What if Carter sees me and runs the other way? And… well, what if he is indeed married with thirteen kids?

Damn it. He really could be.

Why do thoughts of him still profoundly affect me like this? It's embarrassing. It's like I'm young again, and ***not*** in a good way. Naïve. Inexperienced. I wasn't smart back then.

Maybe there's a way I can avoid speaking with him. Maybe I can drive straight to the field where the heifers are penned and get to work.

The more I think about it—nah. Big house, fancy ranch, upper-class family… I can't do this.

No! The word explodes in my mind, shutting down all the circling worries.

First of all, I have no confirmation this ranch is connected to Carter. And even if it is, that doesn't mean he's joined the family business.

Secondly, I have to think of the heifers. ***Focus.*** This is about the animals, nothing more. Not about the Caldwells or the wealth they ***may*** or ***may not*** have. And ***definitely*** not about Carter… whether he's at the ranch or not.

I resolve to stay as dedicated to my work as possible, no matter what happens.

I turn the key in the ignition, and the Chevy starts. There's no way I'm not going now. It's an emergency, and I need to think about the bigger picture.

Get a grip, Destiny Hart. You're a cattle-saving genius.

I place shaking hands on the steering wheel, knuckles turning white.

Cattle-saving genius. One with a big, big secret that'll change everything if Carter finds out.

Please. Please don't let him be there.

DRIVING UP THE LONG DIRT DRIVEWAY TO THE RANCH, I spot the mansion-of-a-house off in the distance in front of a huge mountain range. A greenhouse, a chicken coop, and what I imagine are stables and other outbuildings for the livestock dot the land around the house. And beyond that is a decent-sized lake, a stream, and a substantial fancy-like structure near the lake that looks like a venue with a nice parking lot and beautiful patio. There's another stable, several cabins, and—that looks like another house up there on the knoll. Beyond that is nothing but wide, rolling green hills and valleys.

I drum my fingers on the steering wheel, eyeing my surroundings as if seeing this land will assure me if Carter lives here or not. But Wyoming is a vast state. It's too big of a world for this road to lead me to where I don't want to go.

The GPS directs me to the main house, where I park, turn off the engine, and take a short moment to breathe before stepping out of the truck.

As soon as my boots hit the gravel, something is set into motion I can't stop.

My heart thuds in my chest as I go to the front door, eager to get to work but beyond nervous about who may be waiting on the other side. When I reach to ring the bell, my hand jitters. It's that extra cup of coffee I drank this morning, I'm sure. But my heart tells me it's something else. Something like the thought of seeing the sexiest man alive matured and settled.

The door opens and...

It's not Carter, but a handsome man looking to be in his mid-fifties. He smiles, though his blue eyes are lined with pain. His face lacks the rich color I expect of a man in the sun on a ranch daily. As soon as I have the thought, I remember he told me over the phone how he isn't well.

I resist the urge to study this man's face, seeking a resemblance to Carter. I'm here for work. Nice and professional. I'll be safe keeping my thoughts on the cattle, thank you very much.

I greet him with my widest, most convincing smile. "Mister Caldwell?"

"Doc Hart?" He steps onto the log-and-stone porch with an outstretched hand, leaving the front door open. "Thank you for coming, ma'am."

Somehow, as his grip swallows mine, he's gentle and firm at the same time. His plaid flannel shirt is well-worn, nearly fraying at the elbows, and his boots look like they've seen some serious work in their time.

"Not a problem at all, sir," I say as his big hand releases me. "I came as quickly as I could. I recall you're not well, but can you show me the way to the heifers?"

The briefest tightness to his lips and eyes tells me he doesn't like to be reminded of his current physical state. "My nephew just got back from town. He's going to take you out. Let me get him."

I smile. "Wonderful."

For a spine-tingling moment, I think he's about to say

Carter's name, and I want to turn and make a run for it. Far, far away from here. But then he turns slightly. "Dylan?"

I glance over Mr. Caldwell's shoulder for a peek inside the house. A custom-built log and stone home with twenty-foot ceilings, stone tiles, and hardwood flooring. From what I can see from my place on the porch, the place is decorated with brown-and-white cowhide rugs, antlers, and Western decor. I can't remember the last time I've seen a place this magnificent. I'm not sure I ever have.

There may be some truth to Megan's tall tales about the billionaire Caldwells.

"Uncle Malcolm?" a smooth voice calls back from inside. "She here?'

"We're on the porch, Dylan."

A tall, broad-shouldered guy appears through the open front door with a black cowboy hat in hand. Like his uncle, Dylan wears a dark-blue flannel shirt and worn jeans with his boots.

"Dylan McClintock." He shoves his hand out with a huge lopsided grin. "Pleased to make your acquaintance, ma'am."

"The same, Mister McClintock. I'm Doctor Hart." I shake his hand. "And I'm ready when you are."

"I like your dedication, Doc. It's sure needed around here. Come on. I've got you a horse ready. You do ride, yeah?"

"For almost as long as I could walk."

We share a laugh, and he motions me forward before following me down the front porch stairs. He has a true-blue swagger that immediately puts me at ease.

Dylan has saddled a bay gelding for me, and after I collect my bag from the truck, he takes it up on the saddle with him. I mount the gelding, and we turn the horses to head to the fields.

My companion edges up beside me, and I notice the hint of worry behind his baby-blue eyes for the first time. "You aren't afraid of a little speed, are you, Doc?"

"I'd only be afraid if we weren't in a hurry."

Something like relief smooths his brow, and he urges his horse into a gallop. I follow suit.

It's been quite a while since I've ridden all out like this, but I fall into the rhythm as if no time has passed. The wind whips my ponytail behind me as the strength of the gelding beneath me sends the thrill of adventure up my spine. I cling on and let the freedom run, my sights set on what lies ahead.

As we approach a grassy area where the heifers are, Dylan slows his horse, and I do the same. My gaze lands on a man and two women huddled around one of the heifers on the ground. The sun splashes on them, bouncing rays all around, and I can't get a good look at their faces.

We dismount. Dylan takes the horses to cool them, and I move to the group on foot.

"Hey," Dylan calls as we close in. "Calvary's arrived."

A tall, lean woman with shoulder-length glossy-brown hair and mint-green eyes, and a younger, auburn-haired, blue-eyed girl turn to face us. They're both standing over the downed heifer, sweaty and sun-drenched, blocking my view of the man tending to the animal.

"Hello, everyone. I'm Doc Hart," I offer when Dylan doesn't immediately introduce me. Then, as we draw close, I toss the two women a wave. "I'm the vet Mister Caldwell called to help." My voice catches as the cowboy on the ground turns in my direction.

I prepared for nervousness, but I'm not prepared for how my pulse races like I just downed too many Red Bulls. My arm trembles so severely that I almost drop my bag and sweat beads on my upper lip. Then, my mind goes blank, leaving me useless and rooted in place like some bumbling cartoon character.

The cowboy's jeans are dirty from kneeling on the ground, and his shirt is covered in blood. His short black hair pokes out roguishly from under his black hat. His face is handsome and rugged, those whiskey-brown eyes as fierce as ever. His chiseled jaw bears the five o'clock shadow of a man working too hard to shave.

He's older, but I know that face well.

Kneeling at my feet is my ex-sweetheart from my university days.

The man who ghosted me ten years ago and never looked back.

Carter Caldwell—in the flesh.

Chapter 3

CARTER

Nothing has stolen my breath like this moment. Right here, right now.

Sunlight pours behind Destiny Hart like a halo or divine touch from the heavens. She's as beautiful as ever; as if ten years haven't passed since I last held her in my arms.

This perfect, sexy, intelligent woman was mine once—before I walked away from her.

What in the actual hell is she doing here—other than haunting me like a goddamned ghost from the past?

"I'm the vet Mister Caldwell called to help." Her resounding words melt into silence as my gaze locks with hers. I'll always remember her voice.

Thoughts of us together crash over me, threatening to unman me. Her dark hair. Her clear skin. Those deep doe-brown eyes that always call to me, begging me to satisfy and claim her.

I read in her gaze how much I've fucked up. She's blocking me as coldly as if we're strangers.

But there's ***nothing*** unfamiliar about this woman or her body. I know every inch.

When I don't move or say anything, Lara clears her throat. "We're glad you're here, Doc." My best friend gives me a look like I've lost my mind. "Carter, you wanna catch her up to speed here?"

Lara's pointed statement snaps me out of the past. I get to my feet, filing through all the different things I could say in greeting. ***Hello. I'm sorry. I miss you. Can I ever make it up to you?*** But my silence drags two seconds too long.

"I understand things have gotten pretty tough with your heifers," Destiny says.

Beneath her stern expression, questions seep from her eyes. Questions only I understand. These are the same questions my soul has tossed around for years.

With answers only I know.

Air catches in my throat as her presence rips open places I've struggled to bury deep inside.

I'm standing, staring like an idiot, instead of saying any number of the words at my disposal. Behind Destiny, Lara gives me one of her patented ***pull-yourself-together*** looks.

But I know nothing of substance will come out when I square my shoulders and open my mouth. "Welcome, Miss Hart." I manage. That's a place to start, at least.

One of Destiny's dark eyebrows quirks. "***Doctor*** Hart."

A smirk tugs at the corner of my mouth.

Oh yeah, she's not done with me.

"Well then..." I step up and lock onto her flashing eyes. "***Hello... Doctor Hart.***"

A flicker of impatience crosses her face. I hold my hand out, ready to shake, but her fingers grip her bag tighter. I've always loved her sass.

"Easy," I whisper, softening my eyes. "I haven't taken up biting out here in the wild." Just a touch of a smile plays on my lips. "It's good to see you."

A heifer's loud bellow tears into the silence between us, which sets Destiny free. She goes from spurned lover to confident vet in a second. Her determined expression says this is her business, and I'm nobody.

Nobody.

I never thought I'd be a ***nobody*** to Destiny Hart.

"Excuse me." Already pulling on a pair of gloves I didn't

even see her slip from the bag, she slides between the heifer and me, turning her back with incredible poise.

My eyes lock on the jut of her hips in her tight jeans. She squats behind the birthing heifer, and I remain still for a few seconds before I clear my throat and step out of her way.

Destiny examines the huge calf emerging from its momma's back end, experienced hands sliding over the heifer's rump as she appraises the situation. Then she sits back on her heels and pointedly looks past me at Lara before pointing to her supplies bag.

"Grab the chains from my bag, please?" she says calmly. "This one's too slippery to get a good grip. Its shoulder is stuck."

Lara jumps into action. After a brief dig through Destiny's bag, she brings the birthing chains, and Destiny hooks the calf's two legs.

She turns her brown eyes up to mine, with a cool glint shining in them, and hands me the ends of the chains. "I take it you know what to do?"

Her tone forces me to get my act together and focus on the moment. I drop to my knees and begin birthing calves. This is suddenly the easy thing to do. More challenging is being at Destiny's side.

Liquid flows out of the heifer, covering my arms to my elbows as the calf's head pops out. After scrambling in the dirt and pulling for several minutes, the big calf slides out. The little fella lets out a huge bellow.

Destiny turns to me and shrugs one shoulder. "Well, you've done ***something*** right."

Shit, maybe I deserve her flippancy. I've done a lot of things wrong.

Memories of Mom's death rush me like a stampede of cattle.

Wrong or not, leaving Destiny was the only option back then. When I lost Mom, I lost myself. Numbness and a kind of internal death overtook me. Months later, when I emerged from the fog of grief, I realized I'd also lost the only other woman in my life. It was too late to go back. Too late to apologize.

I chose the ranch as my escape and buried myself in work to forget this woman.

Now here she is, looking at me with cold eyes. And we couldn't be farther apart. We're in separate universes now. She's on a pedestal, staring at me like she's battling anger and indifference.

And indifference has the lead.

I glance at my hands, unable to wipe away the blood and sweat and also unable to utter a word.

Destiny's gaze darts around the group. "Let's break up."

I think her wording is purposeful.

"Dylan," she addresses him like an old friend in a way that sends an irritated, possessive anger through me, "could you take the girls and find the next heifer we need to help, please?"

My cousin flashes her that shit-eating grin he uses to snag girls. "Sure thing, Doc."

He's getting punched in the nuts later.

But even stranger is the fact Destiny chooses to group up with *me*.

"Come on, Caldwell." She gets to her feet. "Our next patient awaits."

She heads across the field, but before I can follow, Lara snags my arm and yanks me back. "What's going on there?" She glances at Destiny's retreating back. "And why are you looking all dopey?"

I stare at her but don't respond—I don't know how to. Then my cousin Juliet joins us, looking slightly unsettled, and raises one auburn-colored eyebrow.

Lara punches me in the arm. "That's her, isn't it? Destiny, your college girlfriend?"

I swallow and let my gaze slip from Lara to follow Destiny's bobbing ponytail. She's already halfway across the field. If she's noticed my absence, she's unbothered by it.

"That's her," I say softly.

Dylan sucks in a surprised breath while Juliet studies the doc with thoughtful, narrowed eyes as if she's trying to place if I ever mentioned Destiny to her.

Lara gives a low whistle, then motions for the other two to follow her. As they walk off, presumably to do Destiny's bidding, she smirks back at me. "Talk about fate, my friend."

"Hmmm," is all I say because... fate? Ha! Maybe divine punishment.

I go after Destiny, trying to figure out her angle. She chose to pair up with me for a reason, which has nothing to do with ***wanting*** me at her side. Is this when she eviscerates me? When she asks me all the questions I'm not ready to answer?

Why's our reunion here? Why now?

Those questions lodge in the nooks of my mind as I follow her. My years of hiding at Three Rivers Ranch, cowering in the dark, are over.

She's here, and she's going to break me for hurting her.

But instead of laying into me the moment we're alone, she points to one of the heifers. "Not bad, this one," she says, tone even and unbothered.

How is she so calm? I'm coming out of my damn skin.

"I think she'll birth on her own," she goes on, oblivious to the effect she's having on me. "Pick up your boots, Caldwell and find me one who needs help."

I lead her further around the herd, scrambling for clever words, trying to come up with ***something*** that doesn't sound fake or scripted. Before I can form something genuine, she stops and shoves her bag against my chest without even looking at me.

She smells like something sweet, like vanilla, but with a hint of spice beneath it. Cinnamon whiskey, with a touch of honey, and a night sky.

"Hold this."

I latch onto her bag, and she digs out a fresh pair of gloves.

I have to say something. Anything. "Thanks for coming today."

"No thanks necessary." She cuts me off with a sharp glance, keeping her straitlaced composure. "Just doing my job."

She's not cracking. I like the assertiveness—I don't remember that as seasoned from our university days. It's sexy. But I hate that it's directed at me in a way that won't let me in.

"I got into all of this mess because—" I tip up my hat with my free hand, then hook my thumb toward the back pastures. "My ranch hands are up—"

"In the high country, running fence," Destiny clips. "Your father told me."

Hmm…

A veterinarian. ***Doctor*** Hart now.

Back at Texas A&M, she had big dreams of becoming a veterinarian. Pride puffs into my chest at her accomplishments, even though I have no right to it anymore. She's looking at another half-birthed calf with all the determination of a champion, and I almost see the wheels turning in her beautiful mind.

I step over to her. "Need help?"

"Never." She smiles saucily, those brilliant dark eyes meeting mine just long enough to let me know the ***never*** stands for more than just right this minute.

She never ***needed*** me before, either. But she ***wanted*** me back then.

Life was good in those days. We let loose, made memories, and enjoyed being carefree before we made the journey into adulthood, loaded with responsibilities and hardships. I thought it would be like that forever.

I shove my hat back and wipe away sweat. "If you need a break, let me know."

She lets out a small laugh. I can't place if it's humor or sarcasm. "You think the calves are going to wait for a break?"

Oh, it's sarcasm, all right.

I wipe away more sweat with my bandanna. "I suppose not."

She gives me a dismissive glance. "Let's continue, okay?"

We pull more calves, falling into a silence that's equal parts comfortable and uncomfortable. I work beside her, every moment heating as time passes. Every inch of my body is aware of her presence, like she's still mine. Like I have a claim on her.

Some heifers have already birthed before we reach them, but Destiny eyes them anyway, checking for complications and administering medications if any need it. She works with a professionalism I never had the chance to witness. Now she wears that confidence like a superhero's cape.

She's moved on, grown up, and thrived in life while I've spun my wheels since my mother died.

At a pause in the action, while we chug water by the gate, I find the courage to say, "Congratulations, by the way."

She finishes her swig of water, then crosses her arms, fingers wrapped tight around the plastic. "What do you mean?"

"What do you think I mean?" I ask to throw her off. When the hard glint returns to her eyes, I rush on before she can respond, "congrats on becoming a veterinarian. That's what you always wanted. Ever since we were together."

The reminder of our past falls between us and grows like summer heat over the hills. I'm inundated with images of us together—sweet and X-rated—and suddenly, I need a cold shower.

"Wow..." Destiny's eyes widen in mock surprise. "Didn't expect you to bring that ancient history up just yet."

My stomach clenches as I realize how much she sees us as a thing of the past. As if she's completely forgotten what I meant to her while I do nothing but remember how much she means to me.

"I'm happy for you."

"I'm happy, too." She looks me straight in the eyes as if to emphasize how thrilled she is with her life now.

Without. Me. In. It.

We assist and monitor the cattle all afternoon. Some calves have their legs and noses sticking out, waiting for us to pull, while others are breech or just taking their good ol' time before something else goes wrong. By evening, we've scaled through a fourth or so of the heifers.

It's something. I'll take it.

My eyelids droop, my joints ache, and I smell like dirt and something metallic. I desperately need a breather, but I'm not the one to suggest we take a break.

Destiny strips off her gloves as our latest survival story wobbles away on new legs. She shoves the gloves in an exterior pocket on her bag, then tightens her ponytail, taking a deep breath. "They're lightening up a bit," she says. "It might be a good time to rest and grab some food. What do you think?"

I meet her eye, shocked she's asking my opinion. "Whatever you think, Doc."

It's a great idea.

Her expression doesn't hide the tiredness creasing her brow. Her dark hair is wild, sticking out of her ponytail. Sweat stains the fabric around her breasts, soaks through her shirt, and trickles into her clavicle area. She swallows, and I love the little gulp in her throat.

Damn, I want to kiss you.

We step beside each other, heading across the pasture to where Dylan, Lara, and Juliet are gathered at the fence, looking as dusty and drained as we do.

Warm rays of the setting sun slice into the valley below, painting the sky a gorgeous hue of red. I watch this sunset every day, but today is different. Even as it makes me battle with regret, it's still damn nice to have Destiny here.

As we join the others at the gate, Lara waves. "Juliet and I are about to head back for the night. I'm going to stay the night." She looks past me. "Destiny, you should come with us and rest. It gets freezing out here. The men will handle it, and if they need us, they'll come get us."

Destiny politely bows her head. "I appreciate your kindness, but I should stay."

"Okay, then." Lara nods. "We'll return in the morning with fresh supplies and food."

"Tent's ready, cuz." Dylan claps me on the shoulder. "I'll take Lara and Juliet home, then bring dinner back."

"You're leaving, too?" I clench my jaw, uneasy about being left alone with a force like ***Doctor Destiny Hart.***

"Can't let these lovely ladies ride home in the dark, now, can I?" Dylan inclines his head in their direction. "Plus, I'd like more than a granola bar. Wouldn't you?"

"Yeah, yeah." I agree, but my heart pounds furiously. So loud I'm sure everyone can hear it.

The girls bid us a good night, then head into the twilight to where the horses are grazing. Leaving me alone.

With my ex-lover.

And with all the ways I've hurt her.

Chapter 4
CARTER

The sound of Lara and my two cousins galloping away fills the growing dusk around us. Silence falls with a presence I hoped to avoid.

I steal a glance at Destiny and swallow a lump of nervousness. I try not to stare at her, but my eyes switch back and forth, finding new things I want to take in. Memorize. If I lose her again, at least I'll have the memories.

There are drops of sweat beading on the side of her cheek, making her hair stick to her face. She shifts on her feet and gives me a sideways look. "So… there's a tent?"

"Uh, yeah." I try not to choke on the words.

Destiny. Me. In a tent.

Alone.

I'm tempted to call Dylan back before she can murder me in cold blood. Or before I do something stupid like try to seduce her.

"But you can have it," I rush to add. "The tent, I mean. I'll stay outside. I won't—you know, ladies need their privacy and all that."

She's watching me with a bemused detachment, one corner of her luscious mouth turned up, and I'm glad my awkward word vomit has given her a reason to smirk. How am I supposed to survive out here with her? And how does she seem so unaffected while I'm losing my damn mind?

"I have an idea." Amusement is in her tone. "How about we just clean up and sit a while?"

I turn on my heel to lead her to the tent and stay a couple of steps ahead, hoping she doesn't notice the redness rising in my neck.

I'm a fucking idiot. After a few hours in her presence, I've turned into a seventeen-year-old fumbling moron mooning after the prom queen out of his league.

Dylan's raised the old canvas tent under a lone oak tree several yards south of the gate. A pile of firewood waits not far from it—a campfire, unlit—and a Coleman electric lantern sits just outside, next to a plastic-wrapped package of bottled water.

I swoop down to grab the lantern, turn it on, then hold open the tent flap for Destiny. "After you, ma'am."

She brushes past me, looking around the space with undisguised interest. "Can't say I've ever seen a tent tall enough for me to stand in before."

I'm pretty sure she's being sarcastic again, but I smile, playing along. "Top of the line."

She sets her leather satchel on one of the three cots side-by-side, eyeing the giant pump bottle of alcohol-based sanitizer by the door. "Is there somewhere to wash off, or are we relying on hand sanitizer?"

"The river isn't far. It isn't warm this time of year, though."

I don't expect her to jump at the offer. Only a few would. The water is freezing.

"It'll work," she says. "I'm hot anyway."

I can't stop from responding with an internal ***you sure as hell are, baby***. And she'll be even hotter naked, bathing in the river—something to look forward to.

Seeing her satin flesh, her curves—and God, she has them—won't help me relax or feel better about our situation stuck out here in a dirty cow field, though. If anything, it's going to make the tension worse.

"Let's wash off before Dylan brings dinner." I still hope to see those curves of hers one way or the other, but I keep the eagerness from pulling in my voice. "Did you bring a change of clothes?"

She nods, ponytail bobbing. "Back at the truck, but we aren't done for the night."

I bite my tongue against the inclination to suggest she could go naked.

"We've got some spares." I edge further into the tent to grab the bundles off the cot behind her. They're men's clothes, but she can roll them up and make do. We'll be getting them messed up, too. Because she's right—the night isn't over.

As tall as the tent is, it's cramped. Stepping forward to reach the clothes puts me close to her. Really close. Lacking anywhere else to go, I loom over her, unsure whether I should excuse myself or physically nudge her out of the way. Instead of scooting over, she stands her ground—shoulders back, chin up, eyes squinted in a wordless challenge.

We're an inch from touching. One deep inhale will press her breasts against my chest and send a wave of her soft breath over my exposed throat. Even with the dirt and muck, I still smell her sugary scent. Feel the warmth spilling off her body.

A moment passes between us, and neither of us moves. I can't be sure, but I don't think we're breathing. It's just tension between us you could cut with a knife. I imagine all the things I want to do to her. Just close this small space between us, pull her into my arms, and take back what used to be mine right here in this tent. I want to crush my mouth on hers, grab her ass, and grind against her.

She might even let me.

Or maybe she won't.

Perhaps she'll shove me away, give me a word lashing, and never get this close to me again.

I resist the urge to touch her and take in a sharp breath before gesturing to the cot. "Uh. Clothes. Shirts. There."

Her lips twist up in a bemused grin. "You're a regular wordsmith nowadays, Caldwell."

I clear my throat. "I don't do a lot of talking out here."

"That's where you're going wrong, then. Cows make great listeners. And they don't judge you for being an asshole."

I chuckle at her blatant insult. I lean toward the bundle, conscious of how I brush against her, my blood turning into a raging river inside my veins. I carefully pretend I don't give a shit how my chest slides against her perfect breasts or how the back of her hand grazes my thigh.

But she notices. I hear the catch in her breath.

I scoop the clothes off the cot, and my cock responds like she's just waved a flag of surrender. If I don't get the hell out of this narrow space, she'll know it, too.

"Come on, Doc." I sidestep around her and head outside. "Let's get you cleaned up for round two."

The sun is long gone over the horizon, and the sky is a twilight purple, dotted with the night's stars. There's a light breeze, but nothing too startling. We pick our way down to the river and focus on our footing. It's easier to watch for cow pies and hoof holes than to acknowledge we've been thrown together like this after a decade of radio silence.

Goosebumps rise on my skin as we near the water. I'm thinking of the last time I saw her wet flesh. ***If I don't get this shit under control.***

"Is it safe out here?" Destiny's voice breaks the silence.

For the first time since arriving, her tone is tinged with uncertainty. Hearing her reminds me of the younger Destiny, sometimes shy, so I'd hold her hand or wrap my arm around her to offer reassurance.

Since I can't now, I go for humor. "Of course it is." I assure her with a grin. "There're no piranhas in this region." I don't know how the statement forces its way out of my mouth, but it makes Destiny laugh, so it's worth saying it.

And I know why she's laughing. Once, we went on an excursion to the aquarium, and I spotted a weird-looking fish with razor teeth. ***Pygocentrus nattereri***—that's what Destiny called them. She told me horror stories about their capabilities and how they go for the fleshy parts first. Gave me a damn fright, and she teased me about the man-eating fish for days afterward.

Under the moonlight, her face is softened—but I don't need moonlight to remind me of all her various curves and valleys. Her rosy cheeks, deep brown eyes with extra-long lashes, full pink lips, her full breasts—I could never forget her.

I blink and force my gaze past her to the river. "C'mon. Wash up. I'll keep watch."

She reaches for the buttons on her top shirt. Her fingers move, unhooking each pearlescent button from its hole. I watch the two panels fall away, revealing the soft wings of her collarbones and the way her breasts strain against her T-shirt.

I stand transfixed. I should turn away but physically can't. I look like a complete fool, staring at her when I just said minutes ago that ladies need their privacy.

Get it fucking together!

Destiny lifts her gaze from her shirt and frowns. "Maybe some of that privacy you promised?"

"Sorry. I, uh… I'll be over there if you need me." I gesture vaguely off to the right, hand her a bundle of clothing, then head up the path. Angling behind a tree, I lean against the rough bark and push my hat up to let the breeze lessen the heat rolling off me.

Damn. I lick my salty lips. Damn.

I remember us together… her warm skin, her vanilla-and-honey scent invading my senses. I yearn for her fingers to travel over me, for her mouth on mine, for all the things she used to do to me.

I tip my hat back further and swipe my palm across my face.

She's ***supposed*** to be with me. Everything should be right between us. She should be in my arms, in my bed, in my home. ***Our home.*** That was the plan from the moment I met her. Claim her, marry her, and bring her back to Three Rivers Ranch.

And I fucked it all up.

The guilt plagues me, reminding me that no matter how much I want her, I'll never deserve her again.

After what seems like forever, rustling comes from the bushes, and she steps onto the path. I stiffen at her nearness, aching to pull her into my arms.

"Hey there." She rolls up the sleeves of the borrowed sweater. "I had to keep my pants. Yours were too big."

I don't even know what she's saying. I swallow hard as she wets her lips.

"You finished?" It's a rhetorical question, but I ask to have something to say before I get an erection.

"No." Destiny raises an eyebrow. "I'm still in the river, cowboy."

She unseats me with seemingly no effort. "I'll, uh, wash up now."

"Don't wade out too far," she says in a singsong voice. "You never know what exotic fish might live in that river."

The sound of her saucy laughter follows me down the path, and heat flares in my cheeks. No woman has ever affected me as she does. I push through the bushes and go down to the riverbank, where I strip and wade into the water in my underwear. I move out further and stand, gazing at the moon.

Moments before, she'd stood in this very place, naked and dripping, the river rushing over her body the way my hands used to. My cock pulses at the memory, and I splash cold water over my skin, cooling it from the branded-hot memory of Destiny Hart.

I'm stuck between remembered desire and a bone-deep ache at how much I must've hurt her. Remorse knifes through me. I want to bring a smile to her face like I used to.

I need her forgiveness. But I'm not sure there's any left in her to give. I toil with the idea for several long moments while hearing the light splash of the water around me. Will she forgive me? Maybe. Will she forget? Never.

Minutes later, somewhat clean and dry, I return to where I left her. At least the smell of calves and blood doesn't burn through my nose anymore as we make our way to the tent.

Back at camp, I rummage through the supplies bag, remove extra blankets, and hand Destiny one. "In case you're cold."

She tosses it on a cot, then settles on the edge. "I'm good, thanks."

I move further into the tent, gripping the bag of supplies in one hand. "Mind if I sit?"

Her gaze darts past me to the sliver of night sky outside. "One of us should keep watch in case any heifers start having problems."

I sit on the cot across from her and put the bag down. "I'm sure we'll hear if something starts happening out there."

Destiny rummages through one of her bags, rubs some lotion on her hands, and makes herself comfortable, crossing her legs beneath her. The pose reminds me so much of when she'd sit on her bed like that while we studied.

She pointedly ignores my presence.

To make her pay attention, I say, "How'd you end up out here?"

She rubs the lotion onto her forearms and eyes me silently.

"I'm just curious," I add. "I don't see you for ten years, and then you show up on my ranch with a vet bag."

She stares at me as if I'm from Mars, giving me all the necessary answers. She doesn't want a reminder of how long it's been. If I bring it up, I better be ready.

"In case you've forgotten, you were the one who disappeared. I shouldn't even be having this conversation." She shakes her head and looks at her bag, busying herself with something I assume is an excuse not to make eye contact.

I want to throw that bag out of the tent.

She's been calm and collected. Hardened and indifferent.

But I'm hoping for a shift. "Dylan should be back with some dinner soon. You want a snack until then?" I rummage for a granola bar and offer it to her. Our fingers linger a second too long as she accepts it.

"Thank you." She pulls her hand back, looking down at the bar.

Okay, if this is a small gesture at smoothing things, I'll run with it. "You look really good." I swallow hard. "You've achieved your dreams. I'm happy for you—damn proud. That's what I what I want to say."

What I want to say is, ***I regret what happened. Ever since I left you, I spent years living in circles. And this guilt… it's eating me alive. If you choose to hate me, I understand.***

I want to say—***I'm sorry for everything.*** But when I open my mouth, the guilt and unworthiness living in my private recesses hold me back.

Destiny avoids my gaze and bends low over her bag. "When your father called me today, I didn't know I'd be coming to your ranch. Since I never got to meet your family, I could only make a guess when I heard the last name." There's a pause before she looks up, and her eyes harden again. "I didn't want it to be you."

Her final statement sinks in like a gut punch.

I'm still kicking myself for hurting her and throwing our relationship away for vengeance. But there were reasons outside of my control back then.

"There was so much happening." I look at the ground as I speak, my palms resting loosely on my thighs.

"Right." She blinks several times fast. "You had to leave. Of course." She interlaces her fingers, clasping her palms together in her lap. "Look… you want to know how I ended up here? I got a job. Simple as that. I got my veterinary license, and I was looking for jobs all over the country. I just so happened to get hired in the one state I dreaded. Back here. Your state."

I cock an eyebrow, wanting to remind her it's her state, too

—she's from here. "That's something, though, isn't it?" I try to make light of it and bring a smile to her face.

She crosses her arms and shifts her butt. "What're you talking about?"

"Kinda like your name—Destiny. You're destined to be here."

"Oooh." She makes a dramatic roll of her eyes. "Give me a break."

"Now wait. I know it's stupid." I chuckle. "I just can't help but think—with you ending up here, getting called to my ranch and all. Don't you wonder if that's supposed to happen? Maybe we were meant to cross paths again." My voice is low—my heart hanging off my sleeve.

She stares at me as if I've lost my mind. Maybe I have. What am I even trying to do with her? Thinking that playing with the idea of fate will get her to accept she's supposed to be with me again?

"None of that is real," she tosses out.

She's so adorable with her hair sticking out of her ponytail. I bite the inside of my cheek so I don't chuckle or tease her.

"You believe that?" I ask. "I mean, of all the places, we're here, together." Wrong word. Entirely the wrong word. "I mean, working side by side."

"It's a job I'm staying at until the birthing is finished." Her expressionless face gives nothing away, her voice as cold as it is empty.

The note of finality isn't lost on me. So much for mending fences.

I stand abruptly and say, "I'll be outside for a while. Let me know if you need anything." That's all I manage to get out before losing more nerve. I tip my hat and exit the tent.

I'm a coward.

I'll never be able to claim what I genuinely want until I man up and apologize for the past.

A dull throb settles in my temples, and the cold air creates goosebumps on my skin as I walk into the night. I glance toward the two ranch houses in the distance, barely twinkling so far away under the night sky, and curse Dylan for not returning sooner.

It used to be easy to talk to Destiny. The words flowed, no matter what was coming out. But now, there's a lot of bottled-up energy brewing beneath the surface.

What's she thinking now? Is she ashamed of me? Or worse —maybe she doesn't care anymore?

Before I can settle too far into my sullen thoughts, a commotion arises in the field, one of the heifers moaning like she's in trouble. One long, pained bellow spurs me into motion, and the tent flap opens aggressively. Destiny shoves her way out in response to the animal's cry—the expression on her face is one of raw instinct.

I push my emotions into the far recesses of my mind so I can slip into birthing mode. One of my ladies in trouble is the only thing capable of keeping me together, so the timing is fortuitous. I toss Destiny a flashlight from the pack sitting outside the tent, and she's already moving at a quick clip as she catches it. I kick myself into gear to follow her into the dark.

Our two flashlight beams dart between resting heifers and startle a few as we seek out the troubled gal. We find her, thanks to her cries, and crouch beside her. All the tension from our prior conversation is gone, buried under the weight of purpose.

"I wonder what's wrong, girl?" Destiny eases her hand into the heifer, her eyes unfocused as she gropes around for the calf. "Let me just...."

She moves, pulls, and guides the baby into a suitable birthing position. Two hooves finally slide free of the momma, and Destiny is only slightly winded as she wraps her hands around the calf's ankles.

"Come on, baby. You can do it," she whispers to the calf and its momma simultaneously.

Leaning over Destiny's warm back, I slip my arms around

her sides to grip the calf's forelegs with her. We pull slowly and steadily downward until more of the legs emerge, allowing the contractions to do their work. When they stop, we slow, and when the heifer pushes again, we pull. Destiny rubs the heifer during the difficult contractions, murmuring to her soothingly.

For several long minutes, we work like this, our bodies moving in tandem, and I feel the strength in Destiny's body against mine. Her voice reverberates through me when she speaks, and her hair tickles my face, but I lean in, holding her without holding her, taking what little I can get.

My brain flashes to my job, the calves, the ranch, my inheritance… everything I've drowned myself in over the years to force Destiny out of my mind. But the moment she showed up at Three Rivers Ranch, all of that was wasted effort.

Nothing will ever rid me of this woman.

Nothing will ever wash away this blood between us.

Together, we pull the calf into the world. The baby slides out, and we release him.

"Good job, momma," Destiny says breathlessly, climbing to her feet and away from my arms. She slips away so quickly you'd think my touch burned her.

The exhausted heifer lies motionless but seems to enjoy Destiny's attention. After a few minutes, she regains strength, scrambles to her feet, and licks her baby with her long abrasive tongue.

Destiny smiles warmly. "She'll be all right."

I don't know what comes over me. Maybe it's the softness in her gaze as she stares at the momma and baby. Perhaps it's just her being in my presence, reminding me of everything I've always wanted and everything I gave up.

But I wrap her in my arms.

At first, it's awkward and weird. Her body doesn't fit against me, not like it did while we were working on the calf. She feels like hard edges, immovable and uncomfortable—a fish out of water.

A piranha.

But then something changes. She sinks against me, burying her face in my chest and wrapping her arms around my waist, returning the embrace.

The scent of honey and something floral from her shampoo wafts to my nose, and a rush of familiarity washes over me. All the hard edges vanish into the night, and she's warm and pliant against me. It's as familiar as the breath in my lungs. I'm catapulted back to when she was naked in my arms when I could press close against her flesh and taste her skin. To when we belonged together, and we fit together.

The heat from her body joins mine. My breath hitches. Her waist is curvy under my palms, and I get lost in the sensation of having my hands on her at last. After talking in the tent, I admittedly lost some hope. She'd clarified that this was just a job and dreaded coming to my ranch. She didn't want my excuses... she didn't want me.

But right now, I'm torn. I can't help but continue to lean on fate. The way we fit together. And it's like no time has passed between us.

Suddenly, someone clears their throat behind us, and we break apart.

Dylan stands on the other side of a few meandering cows. He raises an inquisitive eyebrow in my direction as he saunters over to us. "Everything okay here?"

I glance at Destiny, who studiously avoids my gaze.

"We're good." I go for ambivalence even as my heart's beating out of my chest. "Difficult birth. Doctor Hart was amazing. Just caught up in the moment. Nothing like a good birth."

Dylan snorts. "You got that right."

Destiny gives me a small smile but turns to my cousin. "I had adequate assistance."

Even though she doesn't say anything to give away what she's feeling, she seemed to open up to me during those fleeting moments.

Dylan shakes his head, clearly amused and well aware he's out of the loop on something. "There are tacos by the fire. Why don't you two grab a bite?"

Destiny thanks him and hurries in the direction of the tent. I can't help but think she's trying to escape. But before I follow, my cousin latches onto my elbow and pulls me to a stop beside him.

"Hey. You expecting visitors?" he asks. "There's someone at the Big House. A vehicle I don't recognize."

"No. Uh, I mean… I don't think so." Unspoken worry etches itself in my mind. I shift my shoulders, wondering if I should take the time away from the cattle to check on Dad. Rarely, Dylan doesn't recognize a vehicle, and something in his tone tells me there's concern he's not voicing.

It could be Will stopping by to see my father, or Tomas, our neighbor worker, looking after the horses. Both men are known for putting in the extra effort to ensure Dad is okay and that Three Rivers Ranch is running smoothly these days.

And hell, Will has more trucks than he knows what to do with, so there's a good chance Dylan wouldn't recognize the vehicle.

The more I think about it, the more I talk myself into it being Will. That's the only thing that makes any sense.

Another heifer moans nearby, drawing my attention. Dylan and I exchange exhausted grins and then move into the crowd to find the laboring girl.

Destiny returns, shoving a taco in her mouth as she weaves toward us, and all thoughts of the stranger at the house disappear.

Something that shouldn't happen.

Chapter 5
DESTINY

We work and wait through the night, fueling up on Dylan's tacos in the empty moments between births. By the time the sun tinges the horizon a deep pink with the promise of golden rays to come, we're limping and dragging, and my eyes are desperate to close. My brain is mush. I haven't been this exhausted since veterinary school, when I stayed up all night cramming in as much studying as possible.

Carter tosses away some gloves after the most recent arrivals—twins being bathed by a tired but proud momma. Sweat rings the collar of his undershirt, a testament to our hard work.

"You hangin' in there, Doc?" he asks me.

His tone is casual, but his gaze isn't as our eyes meet. Every question feels loaded. Like he's asking about so much more than if I'm hanging on or need another taco.

"I'm good," I say with what I hope is a dazzling smile. Unfortunately, a twitch in my left eye reveals my lie, but I don't think he notices.

Even though this isn't my first rodeo—metaphorically speaking—staying up through the night to partake in so many births is surreal. Bringing so much new life into the world is profound, and all the more so because this time, I did it beside a man who used to be a large part of my life. I loathe him in some ways. How can I not? He stomped on my heart. He hurt me.

I toy with thoughts of our past. How can I want to spit fire at him and find bliss in his arms at the same time?

I shake that. It's just the memories coming to haunt me. My body is eager for that comfort, but my mind knows the risks that come with it. ***You don't want that pain again. You're better than this.***

"You want another taco?" Carter asks.

I fall back onto the seat of my pants, stretching out my aching legs as I peel off my bloody gloves. "If I eat another damn taco, I'll lay down right next to Bessie here and sleep till evening."

I taste the seasoned meat in my throat and feel it burning in my chest. I need a TUMS, but I don't want to leave the cows long enough to find one.

"Deena," Carter says.

I toss the gloves—inside out—at my medical bag. "Beg your pardon?"

"Her name's Deena," Carter clarifies. He gestures toward her shoulder. "See that little star-shaped white spot? My baby sister, Mina, named her."

"And you remembered?"

He shrugs with a boyish grin.

And it's like I'm seeing Carter for the first time. All the rush and excitement. The heat. This particular glimpse of a man who loves his baby sister enough to remember the name she gave to a heifer in a herd of hundreds. Again, I shake it off, irritated with myself for letting it mean more than it should. He remembered the name of a heifer, not some extraordinary feat.

That small detail opens a door of warmth inside me, though. I force myself to tamp it back because the warning bells leave no mistake about what lies ahead—nothing but tears and suffering.

Good, my head is keeping my heart in check for once.

I break the spell by shifting eye contact. "You want some water? I'm parched." I fold my legs, get to my knees, then stand so quickly that a rush of dizziness flows through my head.

"Oh. Uh, sure. Yeah, thanks."

I leave him sitting on the ground next to Deena and her new twins and head toward the tent to snag a couple of bottles.

Carter… he never goes down without a fight—like saving these calves. When there's no hope, and we're on the verge of giving up on some of them, he swoops in with renewed energy to tackle the birthing issues right beside me.

When we first met in Texas, I fell in love with his big heart. Now I'm watching that same man with that same big heart save these animals, and my chest swells with longing.

Does he realize how hard I had to work to get where I am today? How hard it was to make my dreams happen after he left… after the ***way*** he left. If only he were a jackass now. If only he said all the wrong things. If only he'd let me hate him.

But he's still himself, with all his quirks and good nature, which makes him leaving me all the more confusing and painful.

I grab onto the top board of the fence, hike a leg up, and climb over it instead of using the loud, clanging gate and waking Dylan, who is taking a turn at some shut-eye. I hit the dirt on the other side with a little stumble, then meander to the tent.

Carter misses me and says only half of what he wants, I can tell. But I can't push him to tell me everything—all that's in his heart.

It won't undo the decade we've spent apart, either. All the things he doesn't know. It'll only reopen wounds that've taken me years to close. This situation is awkward enough, and bringing up the past will only make it worse.

I'm swaying on my feet, and it takes Herculean effort to keep my eyes open. Even blinking is hard—I'm afraid I'll fall asleep whenever I do.

Dylan is stretched out on the dirt next to the dying campfire, his hat perched over his face as he sleeps. I tiptoe past him and cringe as the plastic crinkles on the package of water bottles, but he's so out of it that he doesn't even move.

Back in the field, Carter kneels next to another heifer, his handsome face drawn tight. Then, finally, he looks up long enough to take the water from me and opens it. "I think it's another one with twins."

Exhaustion makes me want to turn and walk away, but duty calls. I sit the bottle down and kneel beside him. I pull on some gloves, then ease my hand inside to check before I make any bold claims. My arms are like mush. My muscles are weak and heavy. My body aches in every place imaginable.

I want to close my eyes, but the heifer bellows me back to reality. She twitches, trying to escape my examination but too tired to make any headway.

With a big sigh, I say, "Judging by their size, I think she's going to struggle."

I glance at the last heifer who birthed twins. She lies with her cleaned calves near the fence, all three looking much better.

The scent of blood hangs in the air, magnified by my tired senses. Each inhale makes me dizzy and nauseous, and there's no telling how long I'll last before I throw up or pass out. I force my eyes open, wanting to slap my face.

Carter follows my gaze. "What's this make? Four sets of twins?"

I nod. Rising to my knees, I struggle to get the right angle and move my hand around to take stock of what's happening with the heifer. A nose touches my fingers, and beyond that, a hoof. But I don't feel the other hoof. "Hmmm."

"What is it?" Carter's face is lined with tension, and the tautness in his shoulders tells me he's on high alert. "Whatever it is, we can fix it."

I smile at his determination.

On one of our first dates, we went jogging and encountered some terrified meowing in a storm drain. Carter barely fit into the passage and risked his life to save the little tabby that had fallen down there.

Watching him save calf after calf, regardless of how exhausted he is, reminds me of that man. My Carter. My brave soldier sacrificed his well-being for his animals' sake. I know he's had a hand in every birth and death on this ranch. It's what a rancher does.

But he's ***not*** my Carter anymore. And no matter how well-matched we were, our story's over.

After he left Texas, I spent years yearning for him. Eventually, the longing was replaced with coldness until I left my old apartment to escape the memories haunting me daily. Some things, though, make it impossible to forget.

Storm is one of those things.

Shoving away my thoughts, I tell him, "I feel her contractions, but she isn't pushing. You'll have to pull the first calf as I push the second out of the way."

He gets on his knees beside me. "Can you tell which is which?"

I'm all too aware of the warmth seeping through his blue jeans as our thighs press together. His big hand slips beneath mine.

"Yeah." I latch onto his fingers and guide him gently into place, trying not to think too hard about how close he is. How nice it feels to hold his hand. "Got her?"

"Damn it…" He grunts, his gaze unfocused and his fingers probing. "I can't… I can't tell if I have front or back legs or… even whose legs."

Every time he moves, the mournful lowing from the heifer intensifies, making it difficult to concentrate on what I'm feeling. Stress creeps into his eyes, and he darts a glance at the animal, almost like he wants to apologize to her.

"Hey." I press my palm over the back of his hand. "We've got this."

Our eyes meet, and then he nods. Some of the urgency eases in his expression. "Yep."

He gets a grip and braces.

I lean in, arranging my body beneath his to get a better hold of the calf. "Okay. Pull," I say.

Carter grunts, and his muscles tense. I shove against the second baby, keeping it clear of the birthing passage as he lodges the first through. Within seconds, the momma joins the battle, pushing as Carter pulls. She keeps pushing until a hoof appears. Then another, followed by a nose.

"Damn it," Carter snaps, but there isn't anger in his voice. Just worry.

The baby's head has begun to emerge, and its blue tongue hangs out of its motionless muzzle.

We both pause for a moment and take in the scene—a horrible one to see at a time when only life is supposed to be happening.

"Let's get it out," I say matter-of-factly, and we both renew our efforts.

Carter's palpable worry, while sweet, also irritates the fire out of me.

Where was that worry when he disappeared from my life without much explanation? He returned home because his mother had passed, but he never reached out afterward.

Ever.

Carter can give this heifer and baby all his devotion but couldn't be bothered to explain anything to me? Where was he when I needed him? I needed him, but I wasn't important enough, apparently. And I'm not now.

The tears start to return, but I decide to blame the exhaustion. I'll never let him see me weak. All he needs to witness is the woman who picked up her broken pieces and put them back together.

Burning anger stokes at my core. The way he left—leaving more behind than he even understood.

The heifer isn't pushing anymore. One after another, the contractions roll over her, her belly undulating but without progress. I focus on keeping the other calf out of the way while

Carter pulls downward on the first and keeps his pressure steady.

"C'mon..." he says with a pained huff. "C'mon..."

The word becomes a mantra, a soundtrack. His voice and grunts get louder, and I keep doing my part, praying that the calf will come out with enough time to save the other.

Carter doesn't give up. He pulls until the calf slides out.

I scoot out of the way. "Okay, get the other one."

Without hesitation, he starts working on it.

My movements must be quick and perfect if the first calf will stand a chance at living. But first, I have to clear its airways. I can't always have life, not in my field of work. Sometimes, I have to challenge death to win.

I wedge open its slick muzzle and sweep my fingers inside, checking for blockages, then I give it a few good thumps to see if it'll start to breathe.

As I work, I think about what it means for life to be in such a delicate balance. It can all change so quickly, can't it?

I tried moving on when Carter ghosted me. I went on countless dates, giving other guys chances. But none of them measured up. I compared them all to the standards Carter set. I couldn't help it.

He showed me a world beyond what I thought was possible. Our relationship was filled with everything I wanted—passion, great sex, friendship, and excitement. There was no way I could be in another lukewarm relationship, so I stopped trying after a while.

I haven't been in love again. But, of course, Carter doesn't know that. And I wonder whether he's met someone else. For all I know, that could've been why he left in the first place.

I rub and thump the little calf like I'm trying to bring my own heart back to life, and I'm almost ready to start digging for tubing when it begins coughing.

"There we go." I rub some more, relief flooding me as it starts breathing. It's a strange mix of euphoria and terror, ending with a deep understanding that this is what I'm meant to do in life. Who I'm meant to be.

Then Carter and I are sluiced with fluids as the second calf finally slides from its momma. It's wet and looks surprised to be here, and I can't blame the little guy.

Carter looks at the first calf, who's panting but growing stronger by the minute. Where his and my sides are pressed together, I feel his warmth, and the tension seeps out of me.

He reaches to pat the calf on top of its wet head. "You're a godsend, Destiny."

We exchange grins, our gazes meeting. This camaraderie is... natural.

And it terrifies me.

Carter gestures to the heifer, who's still on her side and eyeing her wobbling babies like she hasn't a clue what to do.

"She's no help," he jokes.

"I'll check her." I'm glad to have something to do, so I don't focus on how much I enjoy this time with him.

"I'll watch over the calves while you do that."

I hand him a couple of cloths from my bag so he can clean their noses better, then I kneel beside the heifer to begin my exam.

With this new life, I'm reminded of Storm. Her birth. How my world changed when she came into it. I was tempted to call Carter plenty of times to tell him about her, but my pride stopped me—and he never reached out, either.

"How's she looking?" Carter asks from beside me.

"Good. Just tapped out.

Anger grows in the pit of my stomach again, pushing the longing and nostalgia to the side. Why should I even care about Carter Caldwell anymore? After I finish my job at his ranch, I'll head out without looking back. And yeah, it'll be hard to leave, but I've dealt with the pain of our parting before. I can do it again.

The heifer gives an exhausted bellow, then stands on shaky

legs. She shoots a wild glance back at me as if to say, ***snap out of it, you fool.***

"Easier said than done," I mutter to her under my breath.

In the following calm, we check on the heifers who have already labored. Some of the calves are trying to stand. Some of them are walking around, curious about the outside world. And the tired mothers draw them in close, giving them full baths with their sandpaper tongues.

"This one is in great shape," Carter says to a robust ball of black fur with the cutest ears ever. "Beautiful calf."

I smile, glad the heifers and their offspring are doing well. I found myself at my limit many times, and if it hadn't been for Carter's strength, I'm afraid I would've given up.

The first set of twins we delivered are doing fantastic. When we draw closer and the calves stray from their momma's side, she makes soft noises to call them back—little fighters. I smile as my hands unconsciously trace their way across my belly.

I think of Storm again.

Damn it, Carter. You should've fought for us.

He has his back turned, and I force away tears.

Why didn't you?

The hurt is present, but I'll stand tall against the onslaught of tears. He'll leave me hollow again, and I'll be stuck with pieces of my heart. And I don't have the strength to put it back together again. I've worked so hard to get to where I am now. It's not worth losing my grip on everything I've put in order.

I shouldn't let myself be fazed by his presence, jokes, or powerful body. I don't need him in my life now. All he and I have are memories. Sometimes I think our time together was never real, like we were yesterday's dream that turned into a nightmare.

When we leave the heifers and make our way toward camp for a break, my joints ache, my back hurts, and I'm starving. I'm ready to have one of those tacos I swore I'd never eat again. As we exit the gate, I turn toward the steady thump of hooves galloping nearby. Through the morning light, two bay horses race over the knoll.

Lara and Juliet ride up with breakfast for us all, including egg sandwiches, apples, oranges, coffee, a ton of granola bars, cookies, bottles of water, and packets of electrolytes.

Thank goodness I don't have to eat a taco.

Lara hands me a warm traveler's mug of coffee with a smile in her green eyes. "Here you go, Doc. It'll warm your insides." She turns to Carter. "Hey, were you expecting anyone to stop by your place? We saw an SUV parked on the hill."

Carter pauses, sandwich halfway to his mouth. He squints at Lara, then at Dylan, concern tightening his brow as he cocks his head.

Dylan unwraps his sandwich. "Sounds like the same vehicle I saw last night."

Carter looks at the two women. "Did you see Dad on your way here?"

Juliet shakes her head.

Lara looks thoughtful. "That's not abnormal, right?" she adds gently, pushing dark hair behind her ear. "He's not been well."

Carter shakes his head. "I need to go check on him—"

"I'll check on him when I return to get lunch." Lara stops him before he gets too worked up. "I promise."

"Yeah, you know the old man will pitch a fit if you leave the heifers right now," Dylan says. "People come and go all the time around this place."

"Yea," Carter mutters.

"We'll check, Carter," Juliet adds. "Don't worry."

Lara casts her eyes to mine next as she sits on the log beside me. "You've done great work, Doc."

I want to hate her. I want her to be the stereotypical best friend who wants something more with Carter, whom I can turn up my nose at just for the hell of this situation. But my time in her company has shown that's far from the truth. She isn't afraid to get her hands dirty and truly cares for the animals. That alone endears her to me.

"Thank you." I smile. "And please, call me Destiny."

She returns my warmth with a pleased expression. "Call me Lara, then." She holds her long, slender arm out to shake my hand, her nails neat and manicured with French tips. "I'm the next-door neighbor. I grew up with these guys."

Juliet raises her hands for high fives from both her cousin and me. "Job well done. You haven't lost any, have you?"

I return her gesture, though it takes a lot of energy I don't have. "Not one."

"We had a few close calls." Carter flashes a smile at me. "The Doc handled it like a champ. We probably would've lost a few without her quick actions."

His compliment sends warmth to my cheeks. Maybe I'm set on leaving and never looking back, but I'll never turn away from a compliment when it comes to doing what I love. I tip my mug of coffee up, and the liquid goes down the wrong way. I sputter while coffee comes out of my nose. My choking stops the conversation for a minute as all eyes land on me.

"You okay?" Lara passes me a water bottle, and I accept it, mouthing a thank you.

My face and throat heat. "A little tired." I bite the remainder of the sandwich from my wrapper and try not to cause any more stares.

"I don't know how you do this for a living." Lara nods. "You're a miracle worker."

I chuckle. "One who needs a hot shower."

I'm about to announce my intention to leave when Carter steps beside me. My gaze lingers a little too long with his as I take in his eyes and chiseled jaw—my favorite parts about him. From beneath the sweat-soaked fabric of his shirt, I also make out the shape of his muscular chest.

Unconsciously, I lick my lips.

Oh, damn. My silent battle continues. Head against heart. Only my body is now involved, too.

Fuck.

Chiding myself does little to help the fluttering of my pulse and the heat building between my thighs. I can't let myself be overtaken by desire. I need to focus on finishing my work so I can return home to my parents and Storm.

The people I love. The people who ***didn't*** leave me.

Chapter 6
ATLAS

I have two rules in life. First, keep your distance from others and secondly, never let your guard down. Because in this world, every motherfucker is in it for themselves. You live and die alone.

And I'm fine with that.

"I'm giving you a last chance to speak, Tomas." Sweat trickles down my neck, but I keep my expression firm. Unmoved.

The ranch hand stiffens as I walk to his heap of flesh piled onto the floorboards of the shack. He wouldn't be in this situation if he'd returned home instead of making his rounds to check the damn horses for the Caldwells.

Now he is.

I can't fault his loyalty. But we're at war. And war has casualties.

Tomas didn't know what hit him when my men grabbed his skinny ass and dragged him up to the hillside shack overlooking the Caldwells' ranch house.

I perk, my muscles flexing in my back and shoulders at the waft of Tomas's blood filling the air.

While some people are addicted to drugs, alcohol, gambling, or sex... I'm addicted to the scent of life—and I prefer it leaving the body of some people. Especially when it's the blood of my victims. I obtain pleasure in seeing a person's light snuffed from their eyes. It reminds me I'm alive, and if I'm alive... I'm winning.

And how many people have I killed?

Far too many. And yet… not one related to the Caldwells.

Damn shame.

I adjust my gloves, crouch, and point the tip of my knife against Tomas's cheek. There's something beautiful about disfiguring a person's face. It makes them imperfect in a perfect way. It allows me to leave a mark, a memory of our time together. Time they'll never forget.

Tomas lets out a groan. He's just the help… a good, hardworking man. But he might have the answers I need, and I'll do whatever I must to get them.

His legs are beaten, and blood drips from his forehead, nose, and mouth.

Bruised.

Broken.

Aching—yet still alive.

"Tomas." I draw a streak down his face with my knife, tearing his flesh.

He screams, then bites his jaw tight.

"You're a smart man, Tomas. I need you to tell me where Tanner Caldwell is."

"I—" Tomas chokes out. "I don't know."

"Why are you so loyal to your master? What's he done for you? He doesn't care about you. You're his dog."

Finally, the pathetic look leaves Tomas's face, and a darkness settles over him, shadowing his eyes and hardening his jaw. I've seen the look before. He's trying to fight.

"A loner like you will never understand." He eyes me with a harsh gaze. "And I'm sorry for you."

"You're going to die. You understand that, don't you? And for what?"

"If you're going to kill me… get it over with." The words come out a bloody mess.

I don't understand why someone with no connection to the

Caldwells would go to such a radical extreme when this could all be over so quickly if he spilled what he knew.

"Does Malcolm owe you anything?" I ask. "Did he offer you money? Citizenship?"

Tomas inclines his bleeding chin, his brown eyes cold and dull. "He's family."

"So… citizenship?" I grin. "Dogs ***do*** love their master's boots."

That can't be it, though. What use is citizenship if he's dead?

"Are you not a dog yourself, hombre?" His entire cheek of peeled skin is red and gnarled, but his eyes light up like it's Christmas morning at the chance to spew something courageous at me.

"If I were a dog,"—I lean closer, breathing on him —"***hombre.*** Would I hunt like a wolf?"

Tomas coughs up some blood. "It's an illusion you have."

I slide my knife into his shoulder.

It's custom-made. Titanium. Sleek and sharp, but with a jagged tip to tear the skin from the inside, and he's experiencing every twist. The only sound in the shack is my knife ripping into his flesh, and the muffled grunts of pain he's trying to pretend he doesn't feel.

"This is your last choice, Tomas. Tell me where Malcolm is hiding his son."

He spits on my boot, his eyes starting to swell shut. "Go to hell."

"I suppose, then, I'll see you there. Your wife, too… and… daughter."

His eyes fly open, change, then die inside.

Got him.

With newfound confidence, I say, "I'm curious how they'll look carved up, begging on their knees—"

"L-leave them alone."

There's a twisted satisfaction when I get my victims to break. A surge of pleasure, dopamine rising that floods my brain with so much elation… for one moment. Then it's gone just as quickly, and I'm left drifting into my imagination, wondering when I'll get the surge again.

Tomas's eyes fill with hate. "I don't know where he is," he tells me through battered lips. "The family hasn't seen him, either. We'd know. We'd see him."

Tomas isn't going to talk—or he ***truly*** doesn't know. I see it in his eyes.

No one knows where this damn kid is hiding!

My boss, Don Renaldo Moretti, assigned me this job because of my reputation for sniffing out anyone I'm tasked with locating. He numbered Tanner's days. And yet, I'm out of my element here, longing to get this job over with so I can be free of this place altogether.

Where the fuck is this kid?

I stare at Tomas with visible disappointment. All this for nothing…

Tomas begs me with his eyes. "Are you going to hurt my family?"

"It depends on if I deliver Tanner to my boss after I speak with Malcolm." I shrug. "I'm not interested in hunting anyone's family. I only need Tanner. Then I'm gone."

As Tomas's blood leaks onto my boots, I stand and clean them against his pant leg, then drag his limp and bloody body outside and tie him against the shed that overlooks the Caldwell house in the valley below.

I pat his shoulder a few times. "You'll get a front-row seat to your master's death."

"Bastardo," he grits through ragged breaths.

I chuckle before making my way to where Marcello and Rocco are set up, watching my boots as I walk. There's still blood spatter all over them.

When I get to the Escalade, Marcello nods. As the tech expert of the group, he can crack any code and hack just about anything.

"Boss." He nods. "The house is ready."

After lighting a cigarette, I take an inhale. It calms me while I bask in the silence of the dawn emerging over the mountaintops in the distance.

My right-hand man, Rocco, steps beside me. "There's only one person in the house... Malcolm Caldwell. Tanner and Carter's father."

Malcolm likely won't tell me where his son is. If I were in his shoes, I sure as hell wouldn't, but it's worth trying.

I take a long drag, preferring the smell of smoke to the surrounding nature. The smells out here are enough to choke a man, a strange odor that sticks to me wherever I go. "Any news if the fucker is still in Chicago?"

"Nah," Marcello says. "No sign of him in Chicago or anywhere else."

"You think the papa will tell us where Tanner is?" Rocco asks.

"Hmm." I crush the remainder of the cigarette on the bottom of my boot, then place the butt in a zipper pocket of my coveralls.

The cold morning breeze blows against my hair. I thought I knew cold growing up in the slums of Chicago, but it's ***absolutely fucking nothing*** compared to Wyoming. It's vacant and brutal here, with land stretching for miles without a single building or person.

The longing for Chicago hits me like a throat punch. I already know the first thing I'll do once I return. I'll enjoy a glass of neat Scotch and some—I don't know—***chicken marsala***. I don't ***fucking*** care what it is, so long as I'm out of this freezing Wild West shit and not hunting a cowboy who killed my boss's son.

The wind picks up, making my jaw clench. Nothing but cattle, horses, clear, dark sky, and open land as far as I can see.

I turn my thoughts to the Caldwell family and my plan for them, steeling myself. "Follow me."

Rocco and Marcello turn up their collars, adjust their caps, stiffen their backs at my command, and fall in line.

My gaze never leaves the ranch house as I approach the front entrance, moving through the pasture swiftly and quietly. A gentle breeze feathers through the wild grass, muting the sound of our boots upon the soft earth. We stop before we get to the wraparound porch. I signal, and Rocco bounds up the steps, rings the bell, and gives two knocks.

"Who's there?" a rough, masculine voice says from inside after a minute.

Rather than answering, Rocco knocks once more. Slower and louder.

It's strange. People living in the country don't have peepholes or cameras. They open the door to see what or who might greet them. In the city, you'd be setting yourself up to be robbed or worse. There's so much trust here. And I plan to use it to my advantage.

"I said, who is it?" the voice barks from the other side of the door.

Without warning, the door is swung open, and I'm met with the barrel of a shotgun.

My men react, pointing their guns in return. Rocco stumbles backward off the porch and regains his place next to me.

"Hold," I command, throwing out a hand to keep them in check. I control my breathing. Focus. ***Focus.*** Because all of my senses are trained on this man, ready to kill—and so are his.

Malcolm is a tall and broad cowboy, maybe in his mid-fifties. He's wearing a flannel shirt and a pair of dark jeans. His hair is pulled back under his hat, eyes narrowed. He's got large, rough-looking fingers, and his skin is tough from doing hard work for years. He looks like he's been plucked right out of a Western film, and I know better than to test these old fuckers.

"Who the hell are you?" he grits out.

He could kill me.

I've had close calls with death, but I don't move because this won't be where I die. There's an innate knowing sometimes that goes along with this job. And this isn't my time to go.

Despite the clear and present threat, I stand my ground. "They call me Atlas."

"The hell you think you're doing on my property?" Malcolm bellows.

"Word of advice." I flash him a crooked smile. "That's not a good idea, that shotgun."

"You won't be telling me what's what on my land. What the hell do you want?"

"A wolf picks up a bloody trail." Then, with a lazy smile, I test him. "Shoot and see what happens."

The atmosphere is tense with each passing moment. His jaw works.

"What do you mean?" His hands hold tight to his shotgun. "And I ain't asking again… what do you want?"

The suspense is thrilling. Pumps my blood. The itch starts again. The need for another surge. Another high. "I'm looking for a boy who has unfinished business with my people."

"That right?" Malcolm's eyes narrow. "And where exactly are ***your*** people?"

I don't answer.

"City people." Malcolm snorts. "Could've guessed it from the new shoes. Watch your feet, my friend—plenty of horse shit out there."

I briefly glance down at the combat boots, not comprehending his meaning, and when I look up, there's a half-grin pulling at his lips.

I regain control. "You want to know what the boy did to get a million-dollar price on his head?"

"Quit your yapping and spit it out," he snaps.

"He killed a man's son."

"And who the hell is this murdering boy you're talkin' about?" Malcolm asks.

"Tanner."

I digest each of Malcolm's expressions. His pupils widen before decreasing, slipping into camouflage. It's all I need. Tanner is his son, but Malcolm doesn't know about Lorenzo.

Malcolm clears his throat, his fingers tightening on the shotgun again. "Is that right?"

I feign ignorance. "You know him?"

"Don't know him."

Too quick.

I flash a smile. "You sure about that?"

"Get off my property."

We continue to square off, seeing who'll give ground, and I admit, Malcolm is brave for keeping his child safe. I've always envied the recipient of this quality. If my parents had protected me, I wouldn't live in darkness, bathed in other people's blood. Sometimes my own…

But this is my job. I kill those who cause others pain—those who hire me to do so. Or I kill those who cause me pain. And this cowboy—showing off his love for his kid—is causing me pain.

I'll have to use other tactics because ol' Malcolm the cowboy isn't budging.

"All right." I take a step back, preparing to back away. ***At least until I make it up that hillside.*** "Stay safe," I goad. "Take care of your health, old man."

I back more, sensing his gaze on my head as I turn, my men beside me.

Malcolm is there, rooted in place, waiting for the right or wrong gesture.

That's where we differ. I'd have killed me.

But Malcolm has honor; probably told his entire life that doing the right thing is always better than doing the wrong something.

Lucky for me, I understand no such restrictions.

Finally, my men and I make it up the knoll, breathing hard from our climb.

"Hand me the detonator," I breathe, removing one of my gloves.

Marcello places the remote into my hand as I face Malcolm Caldwell's house. I gave him a choice. He wasted it.

This may bring his son out of hiding. And the more I cause the Caldwells to suffer, the happier my boss will be.

I press the button, and the massive structure explodes into an inferno.

My men howl with glee as the explosion illuminates the entire valley. I stare at the flames, curling my fingers into a fist. This is it. The big bang, I need to get their attention.

I'm here. I'm not going anywhere.

As I head to the Escalade, I give Tomas a pointed-finger gesture, but his eyes fixate on the burning house, his face bloody in the firelight even at this distance.

"See you around," I throw at him. "And if you see Tanner… tell him Atlas Lupo is searching for him."

With my back to the blaze, I'm an actor in an action flick. And I *love* how this blockbuster plays out.

Chapter 7

CARTER

A blasting bang resounds in the valley and through the entire ranch, the air hissing a warning—a premonition of danger that raises the hairs on the back of my neck. The field of black heifers scatters in all four directions, their little fur-ball calves fighting to get out of their way and run on their new legs.

The vibrations shake my bones. Whatever follows that blast is nothing but bad news. An evil claw lodges in my gut and twists.

My life is never going to be the same.

My gaze turns to the rising mixture of dust and smoke billowing from—

No!

Not the—

Not our house.

From about two miles away, a burning inferno rises from the place I call home.

The blazing fire licks into the sky, and my stomach drops. I can't think or move, my boots rooted to the soil. What the hell is happening? Has a gas line exploded?

No. No.

My father is inside that house! Memories flood my mind violently as if my head already accepts the worst.

The fire rises against the dawn. The dark red—almost black

—flames dance and puff like a mythical dragon, consuming anything in its path. My heart rips apart.

Ground yourself. Think. Dad needs you.

I barely hear the screams of Juliet and Lara as they yell at each other over the roaring blood in my ears. The girls huddle together and crumple onto the grass like paper dolls. Destiny runs to hold them, and they stare into the valley, their faces stricken.

Dylan gives me a crazed look and shakes his head.

Breaking out of shock, I run for Bandit and hoist myself into the saddle. I look over my shoulder, and the fear in Destiny's eyes is there, evident and burning. I can't let her anywhere near this.

"Stay here," I yell.

There's a brief look of defiance, but she breathes out and nods in understanding.

Dylan follows me, and we gallop toward the blaze as fast as the horses will carry us. The two miles to the house is usually a breeze, but now, it's like we've ridden for hours—days.

Are you dead?

The fucking house blew up. It's in fucking flames. Of course, he—he—

But I can't let myself think about it. Dad must be alive… somehow. He's survived so much. He's a great oak. Resistant. Strong. Unmoved. Maybe he escaped. Perhaps he went out to check on the horses. Tomas always comes around, and they have coffee and talk about horses and cattle.

I have to cling to something, or my sanity will slip before we reach the Big House. And if I know one thing for sure, it's that Malcolm Caldwell is the toughest man alive, and if anyone can get out of that inferno, it's Dad.

I urge Bandit to speed up, desperate to reach the house. He's at his limit and breathing wildly. I hate to overwork my horse, but at the moment, nothing else matters. Nothing. Every minute of delay comes at the expense of Dad's life.

Just get to the damn house.

I imagine my father with a logical explanation as to what happened, waiting for me, huddled somewhere outside. I have to believe it.

The throbbing in my head increases with the speed of my thoughts and Bandit's hooves. But that doesn't measure up to the pain squeezing me, the raw fear of not knowing what's happening, of not knowing if my father is alive. A painful grip attacks my skull and chest at every flash of thought, forcing quick breaths out but not back in. I'm strangled. I'm riding the damn wind, yet I'm weighed down and use everything to keep going.

I've lost Mom. I can't lose Dad.

Renewed bitterness rises as I think about possibly losing both of my parents to horrendous accidents. I go numb. The low groan from my chest vibrates to my throat and forces its way out of my mouth in wails.

I urge Bandit even faster.

I yell out as we cut through the bracing wind, but the sound is lost to the onslaught of air and the horses' thundering hooves. ***I can't lose Dad. I can't lose Dad,*** I chant. The pain in my chest expands with every gallop, bursting into thousands of fragments.

Instinct takes over, drowning my ability to think. I want to run into that fire like a mad bull.

"There," Dylan shouts through the insistent throbbing in my ears, pointing to something on the horizon. "Look."

I follow his direction and spot a black SUV on the road above the Big House. I blink slowly, taking in the image. Is that the same vehicle Dylan and Lara saw?

I should've checked it out. I should've done something. But, unfortunately, I was so distracted by Destiny that I let my better judgment disappear. Regret burns inside me as I turn Bandit in the direction of the SUV and ride straight toward it.

Three men dressed in black coveralls, gloves, and caps rush

out of the vehicle. The tall man in the middle reveals a long, slim gun and a wide grin.

Growling in anger, I don't halt. Instead, I'll trample these bastards head-on.

The one on the right points his gun at the sky and pulls the trigger. The blast reverberates through the air. He looks straight at me as he shoots, warning me.

I pull Bandit to a halt just shy of them, the shot ringing in my ears, and Dylan stops beside me. The men back up, climbing into the Escalade for cover. One lowers the back seat tinted window, and I meet a pair of piercing steel-gray eyes.

I lock on those eyes, wanting him to see the fire in mine. I want him to know whatever is going on, they've messed with the wrong man—the wrong family.

Are they the ones responsible for this? ***Why the hell would you blow up my house? Who the fuck are you?***

"Carter?" Dylan's voice snaps me out of my thoughts, and I break my gaze away. "Uncle Malcolm is more important right now." He reminds me, turning his horse and riding toward the burning pile that was my home only a few minutes ago.

I turn to the vehicle to see the window closing and the men pulling away. I'll find them again. Whoever they are. But now I have more important things to attend to. I direct Bandit down the slope and gallop for home, catching up and passing Dylan in seconds.

The inferno blazes under the morning sun. The thick smoke creates a fog that envelops the entire valley, and I pull up a corner of my shirt to cover my mouth. Tongues of fire shoot into the sky, the roar, crackling, and spitting of wood filling my ears. The hot air is incredible, blistering my skin and invading every part of me. Sweat gathers on my arms and my forehead and pours down my face.

When I reach the house, I sail off Bandit and race toward the fire without a second thought, adrenaline rushing.

"Dad?" I choke out.

Smoke hits my throat, heavy and thick. I cough hard, then inhale in an unsteady gasp. My chest burns. I can't see through the char as I run into the middle of it all. Memories flood me, all the things I won't experience here again. Everything lost in a matter of minutes. My eyes start to water.

Dylan grips me hard by my shirt and pulls me back. "No, Carter!"

"Dad is in there!" I break loose from his grip. My legs give way, and I go down hard on my knees, the smoldering heat everywhere at once.

What do I do? Call the fire department? ***What's the point?*** The house is gone. They could do nothing to help us now but stand here and share in the experience. I could call Sheriff Parker—would he be able to help?

What the hell is happening?

"Dad!" I shout again, this time louder.

My breath comes out ragged. I cough again, breathing in the toxicity. My mind is growing hazy, and it's getting harder to think the longer I stay within the fray of the burning house.

But I can't give up yet. I fly to my feet and run around the pile of blazing-hot rubble, barely noticing the heat, my earthly possessions around me turned to ash. I run, frustrated and confused, listening for a sound, anything from Dad other than the drone of consumption.

"Help!" a faint voice calls over the raging fire.

At first, I don't believe what I think I'm hearing. It's probably my mind deceiving me, hoping for evidence of finding my dad alive.

"Help!" the voice comes again. It's low, drained with fatigue, but I hear it. It's there.

I trace the call to the back of the house and sprint across the yellowing yard, holding my arm up to protect my face from the roaring heat. Racing to the drainage ditch behind the house, I spot a glimpse of red plaid underneath a pile of rubble. My heart smashes.

"Dad?" I holler with all my might.

"Carter." The voice is faint.

My heart gives an enormous tug at the sound of his voice, at the knowledge my father is alive. I call back toward the front of the house, "He's here! Dylan. He's here!"

Dylan bounds over as I fly into the ditch and jumps in after me. Boards, rocks, and dirt cover Dad almost entirely, pressing him to the ground. As we remove the debris, bit by bit, I see he's bleeding everywhere, covered in so much dirt and blood we can't tell where he's injured. His head, his neck, his shoulder.

Dad's blackened clothes are torn to shreds, and he's sprawled in a grotesque position. My gut clenches, but I'm relieved he's alive, even though there's still a sizable boulder pressing down on his legs.

"What happened?" My voice shakes.

Dylan struggles with the boulder, and I grip Dad under the arms, ready to pull him out the moment Dylan lifts.

"Three men knocked on the door," Dad pants. "One of them named Atlas." His voice warbles, his lips barely moving. "After they left, I went out the back door to spy on them," he rasps. "I was about to climb the hill when the house exploded. The force of it picked me up and blew me into the ditch."

He coughs, and I rub his shoulder, ready to wail in relief. But, instead, I bite down on my trembling lip at how lucky we are he's not dead.

"They're gone now," I say to ease his worry. "Dylan and I saw them leaving."

"Carter?" Dad grips my arm. His eyes search mine, worry lining his face. "We need to find your brother."

"Let's get you out of here. Then we can worry about Tanner." I drag him out.

Dad's legs are cut up, black and blue, and caked with blood. This could still end badly if he doesn't get medical attention soon.

"No, y-you don't understand... we need to find your brother." Dad coughs. "He's in danger. They want him. They were here for him."

I try to piece the puzzle together but end up confused. "I'll find him, Dad." I turn to my cousin. "Let's get him out of here." We lift him out of the ditch and carry him to the potting shed, where the smoke is less severe. I prop him against one of the outer walls and kneel beside him. He starts to breathe a little slower but makes the sounds of someone in agony. Someone who's survived too many punches in this life.

"Get him a bottle of water," I say to Dylan, and he jogs into the shed.

When it's just the two of us, I look into Dad's eyes as intently as possible. He's having difficulty focusing, but he holds his gaze on mine.

"I'll find Tanner, Dad. I promise." I have no idea what's going on, and I need answers fast. "But you have to tell me everything."

Chapter 8

DESTINY

Carter, you better stay alive.

The air is electric as Lara, Juliet, and I take in the billowing fire in the valley.

Thick black clouds of smoke rise and stretch across the morning sky. The smoke corrodes my nose and throat, my eyes watering, and my skin itching. I've never seen a fire like this. It's not how they portray it in movies or on the news, that's for sure. Instead, it's terrifying, filling the air with raw, powerful energy.

The explosion was unreal, like a shotgun going off beside me. The deep, loud boom shook me to my core. We were celebrating the calves one moment, and now we're faced with destruction. Everything important to the Caldwell family was lost in seconds.

The temptation to rush after Carter pounds in my head, but I can see him yelling at me to stay behind. I don't want to listen. I never want to listen. Since when do I take orders from Carter? But the more I watch the fire, the more I see Storm in my head. A reminder I have to stay put.

Compared to the hell in the valley, it's tranquil here. Little white flowers amid the tall grass blow softly in the breeze, contrasting with what lies below. I take a deep breath, trying to focus on the beauty, but find it impossible with the smoke looming, drawing closer with each passing second.

What if Carter doesn't come back?

"I can't believe this." Lara balls her long fingers into fists.

"What the hell is happening? We should do something. Not just stand here."

Juliet's long auburn hair spills around her shoulders as she paces and looks at Lara. "Do what?"

"Something." Lara shoves a hand through her hair. "We should've checked on him, Juliet. We should've checked."

I pull myself together, walk over, and snatch Lara by the shoulders. "You don't know what happened. We don't know anything right now."

"It could've been an accident or something," Juliet murmurs.

"I don't give a damn what caused it. What about your uncle being inside the house?" Panic leaves Lara's face red and splotchy.

Carter's father. My heart sinks. My expression must give away the dread because Lara quickly turns on me.

"So stop trying to calm me down!" Lara begins again.

Carter has already lost his mother—I can't imagine him losing his father, too. I want to be down there with him, helping to look for his dad's body. But, instead, my anger eases, replaced with empathy. It's times like these when the past doesn't matter so much.

Another loud bang sounds in the distance, and I jerk hard.

"Something's wrong," Lara's eyes flash, and without another word, she starts forward, like she plans on walking right down into that fire herself.

Juliet and I grip her as she attempts to go, holding her close. She fights us with a strength I didn't see coming, and it takes everything between Juliet and me to keep her still.

I shake her shoulder. "You can't go down there."

But Lara isn't listening. She lets out a strangled sound, fighting to tear free again, but gives up after Juliet and I won't let her go. I hug the two women, giving each support while we wait for Carter or Dylan to provide us with an update.

"Should we call the sheriff?" Juliet drags out her cell and pecks buttons. "There's no fucking reception."

"They probably called already." I don't know the right thing to say. "All we can do now is stay strong. Stay here and keep safe."

"I don't want anything to happen to Uncle Malcolm," Juliet whispers.

I want to respond sensitively. "If he's anything like Carter, he found a way out." My words relieve her, even though I'm not sure I believe them myself.

"What's even going on?" Lara mutters again.

My mind goes back to the explosion at the park in Texas. There were no answers to that, either.

Squinting, I see a flash of Carter racing around in the valley. I hate this. I want to go. Want to move. I place my hands on my hips and start pacing. I've never been good at standing still. But if I race into action and something happens to me, what about Storm?

I relent and sit on the hill with the girls, holding onto them. Our horses stand a few feet away, their large brown equine eyes reflecting the horror. I continue to watch for sightings of Carter and Dylan, imagining the desperation and urgency they'll be experiencing.

Carter's entire life has just collapsed.

Taking a deep breath, I look at the sky, focusing on a small patch of blue that hasn't been blotted out with smoke. Little pieces of ash float around, almost like it's snowing. I remember watching a show on TV about wildfires in California. Entire towns burned in the blink of an eye. What if the flames fan out? Will the Caldwells lose their land, too?

I grab some soil. It hasn't rained for a few days, and the grass is dry. Most of the pastures are a reasonable distance away, but it would take only one strong gust to send the fire right up here. I was looking forward to going home and getting some sleep after being out in the fields all night, but now I won't be resting for a long time—none of us will.

I pull my knees up and rest my hands on them, watching the raging fire. It will take an entire lake's worth of water to put that out.

After sitting restlessly for what seems like hours, I can't watch the devastation anymore. The ash and smoke have worsened, and I would like to know if we should move to even higher ground. I check on the horses, stroking the bay's neck and whispering reassuring words to him. Horses have a sixth sense about these kinds of things. They know danger before we do, so if they begin acting differently, I'm taking that as my cue to get the hell out of here.

The smoke gets thicker, and it's harder to see now. What is it like for Carter down in the valley? He has common sense, but I'm afraid of what his desperation might lead to, trying to save his dad. I know what lengths I'd go to save my parents.

I don't know what moves to make. But whatever they are, we'll need to make them soon. Just then, one of the heifers behind us lets out a bellow, and I whip my head around, eager to be of use and to have something to focus on. She's flat on the ground. I move slowly toward her, mentally and physically exhausted, but I have a job to do.

Returning to the cattle after Carter's home exploded might be insensitive, but this isn't the time to be sensitive. I have animals to save.

I close my eyes and enter my element, shutting out the chaos around me. The heifer pushes and strains for a while. Then, finally, Lara and Juliet come to assist, and we wait some more because sometimes it's all you can do.

I use the girls' assistance, trying my best to distract them.

"Really big head." I grunt and wallow on the ground with my face smashed against the heifer's back end.

Lara laughs, tearstains streaking her cheeks. "That's what she said."

"Eww!" But Juliet looks like she's caught between tears and laughter as well.

"Everything's definitely going to be okay if Lara just made a ***that's what she said*** joke," I tease, still trying to lighten the mood.

I grip the calf's two front feet and pull downward. The heifer pushes. I meet her rhythm and keep pulling, guiding the calf out. Lara helps me with a leg.

"Good grief." Juliet throws her mass of auburn hair behind her. "Petition to make epidurals for cows."

We all give a little chuckle, then fall into focusing on our work. The process is slow, but eventually, the last leg emerges, and we help the calf onto the ground. Then, we move back and leave the heifer alone, and soon she's licking her baby and has long forgotten us and our silly jokes.

I collapse somewhere on the ground beside Lara and Juliet, and we watch the smog covering the morning sky. I glance back at the mother and calf. Something about a new life gives me a sense of calm in the chaos around me.

"Good girl," I say over to the heifer. Then I curl up in the fetal position on the sun-warmed earth and close my eyes. "Everything's going to be okay," I whisper, more to myself than to anyone.

But is it, Destiny? Is it really?

Because it's not okay in that valley. Because besides my father, the only other man I've ever loved is in a death trap, which will move us further apart than ever.

Chapter 9

CARTER

Acrid smoke chokes me, the gray fumes irritating my eyes. My house is a dark pile of rubble.

What used to be my family home, filled with decades of memories, is reduced to nothing as the orange hue of sunlight reflects off the giant pile of ash. We wait at a safe distance in the pasture, where I'm shuffling around, trying to figure out which wounds to put pressure on, while Dad makes uncomfortable grunts.

"I'm fine," he snaps. "Still breathing, aren't I?"

I push my hat back and cock my head. "Barely."

"Leave the fixing to the professionals, will ya?"

I roll my eyes. At least he's got his spunk. But the more I think about all the little moments that made up our relationship, I sink into myself.

I almost lost you today.

The thought must be visible in my eyes because Dad hits the side of my arm. "I know what you're thinking." His gaze turns stern. "I'm not dead. Don't worry about me."

That's not going to happen. He can't expect me to be okay after all this. A couple of thugs is one thing. A house explosion is entirely another.

"Now… about Tanner," he says.

I need some clarification. What does my brother have to do with any of this? "What'd those men tell you?"

"Those guys. Their leader, I think… he wants—he wants

Tanner. He's looking for him." Dad sends me a grim look. "That's what all this is about."

Inside, rage boils, lashing out for blood. There's an army building in my soul, needing to take down whoever wronged my family. "What do you mean?"

"Someone wants him dead." Dad is breathless and shaky. "I've seen that look before. The one in this man's eyes... He's not going to stop."

My father has never been this shaken, and it's not something I enjoy seeing. "Can't Tanner live without being a problem wherever he goes?"

Dad looks down but doesn't fight me on it. "He's your brother."

"You almost died," I remind him, not wanting to break his unwavering loyalty but at the very least make him understand when I find Tanner, it won't be pretty. "Even his absence at the ranch is wreaking havoc."

Dad licks his chapped lips. "They said something else."

I study him, waiting. "What else?"

"They said he killed another man's son."

I swallow the dry lump in my throat.

"They're out for blood and sending a message," Dad continues gravely. "If we don't hand Tanner over, they'll do worse."

"It's hard to hand over a ghost," I grumble.

Dylan crouches beside me. "But who are those guys?"

"They looked like Italian gangsters." Harsh coughing and retching overtake Dad. I pick up the water bottle and place it near his lips.

Italian gangsters? What the hell are Italian gangsters doing here? The throbbing in my head increases.

"What do you mean?" Dylan asks.

Dad coughs again. "Like in ***The Godfather***."

I'd laugh if not for the grave situation and my dad's coughing. ***The Godfather?***

Dad must notice the look on my face. "What do you want me to say? The one had kind of an Italian accent. The other sounded like he was from a big city. Somewhere like that. Tough guys."

It doesn't matter who they are. They don't have the right to mess with my family. All of our personal belongings, the documents for the ranch, whatever we had left of Mom—everything is lost. The security we've always known is gone, replaced by something cold with sharp claws that are scratching at the walls of my life, tugging me this way and that, like a demon about to possess me.

"This is going to raise big questions about Tanner to the authorities," Dylan says. "He's going to get himself killed—and the rest of us with him."

I get his point.

"Almost did," Dad says. "It'll be trouble and more trouble."

Hell yeah, it'll be trouble.

"What're we going to do?" Dylan asks. "We'll look suspicious if we don't report this. But we need Tanner's side of the story."

"Who says we won't report it?" Dad says. "We'll make the call. Only it'll be a different story… until we have Tanner safe at home."

The sides of my lips lift. I like the way he thinks. "We won't have to call. You can see this mess from miles away."

And what if these gangsters return? By bombing the house, they've shown their strength and are capable of even more. But by not reporting it, we'll show we won't hand Tanner over. That whatever war they've started, we're in the game.

"There was an old switch in one of the back rooms that was malfunctioning," Dad says. "We could use that as a story. Or… maybe someone left the gas on at the stove without properly closing it."

"That might lead to more complications. More investigations," I say. "I think we just let them do whatever they do and keep quiet." The last thing I want is for Sawyer Parker or investigators to start suspecting us of anything. "The ranch house was huge—there could've been a thousand and one problems in there. We tell them we don't know what happened." I look at Dylan and Dad, who nod their agreement.

It's the easiest way out. Pretend we don't know anything.

"Dad?" I continue. "You were out doing routine checks on the horses when the house blew up, and thankfully Dylan and I already have an alibi. We were birthing calves."

They nod again. I briefly think of Destiny, glancing back in the direction I left her. Now she's involved in this without any say in the matter. I don't want anything happening to her.

After about half an hour, Sheriff Sawyer Parker, his deputies, firetrucks, and an ambulance barrel up the long driveway, rolling dust and gravel.

Here they come.

My heart hammers—I want everything to go as planned.

"What the hell happened?" Sawyer tears the sunglasses off his face as he exits his patrol vehicle beside the shed.

He takes in the damage, and I've never seen the sheriff look this shocked. He removes his hat, his face paling before he shakes his head and turns his attention to Dad with his hand extended. "Malcolm. Christ."

"You're telling me," Dad grumbles from his place on the ground, taking the handshake before releasing a rattly cough.

My stomach sinks at how defeated he sounds. It's something a son never wants to hear from his father. But the old man is tough, I'll give him that. I have to be tougher now.

Sawyer curses under his breath, shaking his head again. "Shit, I'm so sor—"

"I think we're way past ***sorry***," Dad mumbles.

Sawyer's walkie-talkie blasts as he takes out his pad and pen to jot down whatever notes he's about to take. "What can you tell me?"

"Your guess is as good as mine," Dad grunts. "Don't rightly know."

The sheriff turns to me. I fake a confused expression and try not to look at the burning house. "Don't know what happened, Sawyer. We saw the explosion from up in the hills. We're birthing calves."

"Anyone else in the house?"

"No. Thank the good Lord."

I wait, hoping he'll go back to town. The men who did this are on my hit list now, and if I give away my thoughts, I'll be behind bars in no time. We won't trust anyone to deal with our problems. We'll deal with this in our own way… like always.

Sawyer examines Dad's wounds. "What happened to you, Malcolm?"

"I was going to check on the horses when the house blew. Instead, the force threw me into the ditch."

After a moment, Sawyer directs the paramedics. "Take Mister Caldwell to the ambulance. Get him to the hospital."

He joins his deputies to collect evidence, take pictures, and make reports. I'm hoping our statements are enough and they find nothing. The sooner they declare it an accident, the better.

Even though Sawyer hasn't said anything, I can tell what he's thinking from the silent but firm look of suspicion crossing his face. ***"You're lying, son. And I'll be watching you. I'll sure as hell be watching."***

As Dad leaves in the ambulance, rage seeps through my every pore. It's been quite a while since this part of me kicked in. Whoever these men are, they won't get away with hurting my father, burning my house, and threatening my family. I'll keep them safe. The next time someone comes onto our land, they'll meet lead.

Italian gangsters—we'll see about that. ***Fuck 'em.***

"C'mon. Let's check on the girls," Dylan says beside me. "They've been up there a while."

We ride the wind. Along the way, my attention is caught by

something or someone, bloodied and ragged, tied against the old shed on the hill. At first, I think I see things—I blink several times before I gallop up to the shed to check it out.

"Holy hell!" I dismount and run to the man. Dylan and I untie him as his bloodied, swollen face greets mine. "Tomas?"

"Mister Caldwell." His voice is hoarse, and his teeth chatter.

"What happened? Who the hell did this?"

"I—" He stops, catching himself.

"You need to get to the hospital," I say.

"No, no. I can't." Tomas gasps. "My wife—she'll stitch me up. How's your father? Is… is he—"

"He's alive," Dylan says. "He's on the way to the hospital."

"Thank God," Tomas breathes out.

I stand and look over to where the Big House once stood. "You saw everything? You know who it was? The ones who did this?"

Tomas goes rigid. "It was a bomb."

The beast inside me bangs on the cage. "Can you tell me who it was? A description?"

There's hesitation there, clear as day. "I don't… recall."

"You're lying, Tomas," Dylan calls him out immediately.

"He threatening you?" But I know the answer.

"I'm sorry, Mister Carter, but yes." His gaze finds mine as he shakes his head. "All I can say is that he's a hitman looking for your brother. But I told him nothing because I don't know where Tanner is."

No one does. Since the fallout with Dad, it's been silence between Tanner and the family. Until now. He sent a literal bomb home and blew up our entire lives. All without taking a step onto the ranch.

Damn my kid brother.

"This hitman," I draw, my stomach churning. "He was in the SUV?"

Tomas's eyes widen, and it's all the answer I need before he swallows. "It was him."

I swipe a hand across my face. "You should attend your wounds."

He nods, swallowing over the lump in his throat. He's pale and barely able to stand, using the shed's wall for support. "I'll be back to help you track that dog. Just let me get stitched up first."

"You'll take the next few weeks off," I command. "I'll call you later."

His eyes widen. "I can't take time off. I have work—"

"If you're worried about pay, it's covered."

"I can't abandon Mister Caldwell. I owe him everything," Tomas pleads.

"You'll only cause Uncle Malcolm more pain if you die," Dylan adds.

Tears roll from Tomas's eyes, and I know there's more to the story. Dylan and I glance at one another, waiting to push him until he's ready.

"I owe you all," Tomas says after a long pause, his lips quivering.

I push my hat up with a finger. "Maybe the other way round?"

"We just want you to go home and rest," Dylan says.

Tomas chokes out another sob. "Thank you."

The praise almost makes me laugh. "Tomas, don't tell the sheriff anything regarding this matter, you understand?"

"You don't have to worry about me, Mister Carter." He dry chuckles. "If the deputies show up at my door, trust me when I say it's not about the bomb. They'll be bringing ICE for my ass."

I want to laugh but can't force it out of my mouth at his dark humor.

"You need help going down?" Dylan asks as Tomas limps toward the path.

"I've been through worse crossing the border," he cackles.

I shake my head. "Message me when you get home."

"Si."

When Tomas is out of sight, Dylan and I mount our horses.

Dylan eyes me. "I suppose we have a lead on who these guys are."

"Yeah," I grumble, my mind going to what to do next. Once I set my mind on something, I act. Which has caused me trouble in the past. But I can't mess up now. There's too much at risk.

Dylan turns his horse. "Let's get back to the girls."

We gallop up the hill and across the fields until we spot three figures huddling together on the grass. Relief washes over me. I'm glad they're safe, glad they didn't see Dad getting hurt or the Big House burning close up.

For the gangsters to attack at the time they did, they must've been watching our every move, knowing Dylan and I were out in the fields. A shudder goes down my spine. I'm racking my brain for a way to ensure no one else gets hurt in the crossfire when the time comes. God knows who and what's next. I can't risk losing anyone. ***And I won't.*** Even if it means shackling them to my wrists.

Especially ***Doctor Destiny Hart.***

I'm not going to tell her about the danger ahead. It's the last thing I want her to deal with, especially when I just got her back in my life. I won't lose her. She and my family are the most important things.

But myself? I can't promise that. I don't know who I'll become when I find these men, but it won't be good.

Chapter 10

DESTINY

I don't know who's alive and who's dead. It's impossible to explain, but every minute that passes is heavy.

What if they're all dead?

Helpless, I stand, watching the events unfolding below. The once-beautiful valley is a smoky mess of darkness, the heavy smog drifting for miles. The stench of ash invades my nose, and everything inside me wants to jump into action. Plummet down to the fire to find Carter. To help in any way possible.

Was it an accident? Or if it wasn't, who would do something like this? That's the big one—what kind of enemies does this family have? And what could they possibly have done to deserve having their home destroyed?

Thundering hooves barrel toward us, and the sound makes my heart race. I barely see who it is amid the smog. Tears well in my eyes as I make out Carter, my hand going straight to my mouth as I choke back a sob.

He's alive! And Dylan, too!

The galloping horses match the pace of my heartbeat. The animals and men are covered in sweat, blood, and dirt, but I breathe a sigh of relief for the first time since the explosion.

They're alive.

The men dismount, looking ragged. Their breathing is labored from the smoke inhalation, and their eyes are wild. I've known Carter a long time, but I've never seen his eyes like this—more animal than man.

"Your dad? Is he—" Lara chokes out. "Carter? Is your dad alive?"

"Hey. Hey." Carter attempts to soothe her. "He's alive. Just bruised up. They're taking him to the hospital."

Relief pours through me as I halt a few feet behind everyone. Juliet and Lara hug the guys, but I'm at a loss for what to do, longing to fling myself at Carter, but knowing I'm the outsider.

"What happened? What's going on? Who was that?" Juliet rapid-fires at them, her blue eyes flashing.

I'm frozen in place, pathetic, like a teenager who doesn't know how to respond.

Dylan kisses his sister's forehead. "It's going to be okay, kiddo."

I don't know if I believe him. They know something—it's all in how Carter's hands tense, fingers curling into fists until they turn white. "Do you have any answers?" I ask.

"We're working on it." Dylan is vague enough to give me all the verification I need. They know who did this, but they're not telling us.

Carter's eyes pierce mine. His deep gaze reaches my soul, and I almost break down at his ragged, desperate look. He's barely keeping it together.

A painful lump forms in my throat, choking me. I can't speak because I want to cry for the man before me.

We overestimate strong people and how much pressure they can withstand. We think the strongest can take on the most because they often take on the responsibilities of others who won't or can't. But that's why the most vital people need more comfort when things start to crack—even if they stubbornly say they don't.

"Uncle Malcolm was outside when the house exploded," Dylan says to wide-eyed looks of surprise. "He was lucky. Blew him into that drainage ditch behind the house."

Glancing down, I rub my sweaty palms on my jeans, trying to come up with anything helpful to say. A shudder falls over me, but my arms still ache to hug Carter and tell him everything will be okay. Even if that's a lie, he can allow me to shoulder some of these responsibilities he's holding. I know he's going through a lot, trying hard to be strong, but he doesn't need to. I shake away all the suspicions I have for the moment and hold his gaze.

"Carter?" I whisper his name, and that seems to do it.

He clears his throat and glances around at everyone else. "Excuse us for a minute."

Dylan takes Juliet and Lara into his arms, and they walk to the horses, conversing in hushed tones.

Carter looks at me. "Come here."

My breath hitches. Not able to control myself, I fly into his arms. He grunts at the impact of my body but doesn't push me away. Instead, he wraps his arms around me and holds me steady. The smell of smoke is on him, soaked into his clothing. "I thought my heart was going to stop," I manage to choke out.

He runs his hand in soothing circles on my back. "It's going to be okay."

It breaks me more that he's trying to reassure me, though he's the one suffering. I cup his bristled, scruffy cheeks between my palms, making him look at me. I let the past fade for the moment. "What happened?"

"Not quite sure," he whispers.

"Do you know who did it?"

He blinks slowly, and a flash of dread returns to his face. "Not yet."

"But—" I widen my eyes. "Look at you."

"I'm okay."

I say what's on my mind because he needs to know. "No… you're not okay. You don't have to be okay right now."

"I'm okay, Destiny. Just let us handle it."

"And if you can't?"

It's like he reads my mind. "I'm not going to let anything happen to you."

There's an intensity in his gaze, in how his jaw clenches, that makes me shiver. As we stare at one another, it's almost like a magnetic pull, especially for me, knowing I almost lost him. I want him to kiss me.

He pushes his hat back and twines his fingers in my hair before slamming his lips across mine.

I'm greedy for his mouth and touch as he holds me against his hard body. I moan when our tongues brush, and we taste each other, fueling me with heat. His kiss is skilled, with a bit of aggressiveness that sends tingles rocketing through me.

It's an odd moment to be turned on, but nothing like a brush with death to ignite a spark. Literally and figuratively.

"Much better," he breathes against my lips.

I register that he's cupping my ass, bringing me closer. My boots bump his, my hips meeting his rough denim-clad body as his touch reminds me we're both alive—very much alive in each other's arms. I pull his neck and direct his mouth over mine again. ***You need one more kiss.***

He groans and deepens the pressure. The raging pulse of his heart against my chest proves he wants this. The chemistry, the pull, is all still there.

This will end with us crashing and burning, but I can't stop it.

"You have no idea," he pulls back a fraction, his eyes piercing mine, "how much I've dreamed about this."

The confession makes me achingly aware of every hard inch of him. Tightening my arms around his neck, I pull him closer and kiss him as if I'm starving. ***Because you are.***

I pull away after a few beats, breaking with a breathless gasp, but he holds me in place, not allowing me to wiggle free. It's the adrenaline, the fear, all of it combined, rushing in on me. I want him, but I can't forget everything that's happened.

I'm kissing my ex-boyfriend. The man I swore I'd never allow to hurt me. Again. ***Again, damn it!*** I'm opening my mouth to say something along the lines of, ***I can't,*** when a band of horses and riders gallop over the hill toward us.

"This isn't over," Carter says lowly.

Fuck.

Slowly, he lets go of me and pulls me behind him as a man with a graying beard and pointy nose pulls his horse up beside us. Dylan, Lara, and Juliet walk over, and I notice them boring holes into Carter and me out of the corner of my eye.

"Good God Almighty, what happened?" the man asks. "We saw the fire and came straight away."

"Damn, we heard it," one of the other men chimes in, resting his wrist on his saddle horn. "Smelled it from miles away."

"We're checking into it, Sam," Carter says. "They took Dad to the hospital. Sheriff Parker has his men down there."

"How'd Mister Caldwell survive that blast?" Sam nods toward the carnage. "I know your pa is tough, don't get me wrong, but—"

"He was outside when it happened," Carter addresses his ranch hands, taking on the role of leader. "Okay, boys, I need you all to stay with the heifers. We have some business to attend to with the family, to say the least."

They all agree in unison, giving curt nods and tipping their hats.

"Everyone else, come with me," Carter commands, nodding at Dylan, Lara, and Juliet.

And me?

Timidly, I shift on my feet, pondering what to say. "I'll stay and watch the heifers, too, then?"

"You stay with me," Carter calls back.

Electricity runs through my veins as he stretches out a hand. But I hesitate. Despite his lips, his hands, my attraction to him that I can hardly control—whoever did this, whatever happened down in that valley, isn't over. Taking Carter's hand means I'm in this. I open my lips to say everything I feel, but his eyes harden.

"I won't let anything happen to you," he says again.

I believe him. Biting my lip, I force my feet into motion and slide my hand into his large one. He gently tugs, then pushes me toward one of the horses before I remember something. "Oh, wait–"

"I mean what I said," Carter says. "Mount up."

"I know." I huff, rolling my eyes at his caveman-like behavior. I forgot how demanding he can be when it comes to what he wants. "I need my vet bag."

Carter hands me the reins to our two horses, then gathers my things and returns with them.

"If you need anything, Sam, please come find me." I mount my horse as Carter takes my items with him onto his horse.

"Will do. Thank you, ma'am." Sam tips his hat before Carter moves his horse forward, and I follow.

We walk across the grassy meadows and down the hills into the valley. I can't wrap my head around what's happening, and the mystery plagues me. I've never been a fan of being on the outside, and even less so in a dangerous situation.

My gaze travels to what remains after the explosion, a chill racing over me. What used to be a grand ranch house has been reduced to ash. Some spurts of fire are still being put out by firefighters, who are shooting blasts of water as smoke curls everywhere.

It's like a crime scene.

Unable to stand the sight anymore, I focus on Carter's broad back—which doesn't make things easier, as the memories of our kiss rush back.

I can't believe we did that. We were high on emotion and not thinking straight, that's what. It means nothing. I'm not going through that again, no matter how he makes me feel. And the more I think about the explosion, the more complicated everything gets. I understand Carter wants everyone safe, but I can take care of myself back home. He can't just order me around.

This leads to my next question. "Hey, where we going?"

He doesn't respond, just continues to lead the way, past what's left of the house and around the winding road. No matter how far we go, I smell the smoke, its stain on my skin. I'm uncomfortable, and Carter's silence isn't helping. I vent my frustration by nibbling on my bottom lip for a while. "Carter, where we going?"

"We'll stay at The Mansion until we figure this all out. Juliet and Dylan live there." His voice is distant, far off, and if he's anything like me, he's replaying the incident in his head.

I don't care who lives there right now—I only want to wash up and get outta here. Once we arrive at the stables, we cool the horses, unsaddle them, and care for them before we climb in Carter's truck to drive up to The Mansion.

Inside the house, Lara and Juliet rummage in a hurry, searching for medical stuff, while Carter and Dylan crash into chairs in the sitting area off the main hall. They waste no time diving into the next steps of what they should be doing while I awkwardly stand out of everyone's way.

"Damn it." Carter sighs, raking his hair back.

Dylan bounces his boot on the hardwood floor. "How are we going to find Tanner?"

"I have no idea." Carter leans and rests his elbows on his knees. "Though one thing's for sure. He's getting his ass whooped when we find him."

"What about the gangsters?" Dylan asks.

Gangsters? I mean, the explosion looked straight out of a crime film, but how the hell did they get involved with gangsters?

"I'm sorry," I cut in brashly, and they turn to me. Carter's face is hard as stone, but I don't let it move me. "The explosion wasn't an accident?"

"We're trying to figure it out," Dylan responds carefully.

"But you're sure gangsters did it?" ***Just saying it sounds ridiculous, boys.***

Carter rubs at a spot on his neck. "We're not sure of anything. We've already seen how far they're willing to go to find Tanner. Right now, we can only ensure everyone's safety—our priority. We'll watch out for them. We'll check the heifers in between." He turns to look at his cousin. "I'll leave you in charge while I check on Dad. That work?"

Dylan nods.

I rub my lips together. All right… if men blew up the Big House, and these guys are gangsters, things will get ugly. Do I want to be caught in this crossfire? Can I stand by Carter's side and take that on when I have Storm to protect? Again, with the harsh truth. ***You shouldn't be here.***

I've heard of cases where people have gotten involved with gangs. They show no mercy and wipe out entire families; anyone close to their victim without blinking an eye. Not only that, but they get away with it, get dirty cops on their payroll to fit their needs—shit like that. I can't get messed up in this.

"Why're you standing in the hall?" Lara makes me squeak in surprise. Then, she takes control of the house, plopping a laundry basket next to the men. "Strip, guys. Clothes need to be washed."

They kick off their boots and pull off their socks. My eyes widen when Dylan goes for his belt, and I avert my gaze as articles of clothing hit the basket. I presume Dylan is still in his boxers, so I peep to see if opening my eyes is safe.

He's flashing a mischievous grin at Lara. "More?" She sighs, and he sniggers. "Hey, you're the one demanding we strip, Miss Bain."

"Come on, Dylan. No time to waste." Lara looks at Carter next with an arched eyebrow. "Let's go."

His eyes meet mine. His hand reaches the back of his shirt and pulls it over his head.

My brain tells me to look away, but I can't. Especially not

after our kiss. Not as his piercing brown eyes hold me hostage, flashing and dancing with heat. It feels like the room has gone up a hundred degrees. I'm struggling to level my breathing.

Once his shirt is off, I can't believe how much he's filled out. He was muscular when we first met, but now his chest is more defined, his waist trim with a six-pack of abs. He reaches for his belt buckle, and I don't look away this time.

Do Lara or Dylan feel the tension in this room? I certainly hope not as Carter drops his jeans. He doesn't try hiding the bulge in his black briefs while he bends to gather his clothes and tosses them into the basket. He slicks his hair back, and every move he makes is about to take me to my knees.

Lara bustles around the room, and I finally snap out of my daze.

"Dylan, can you prepare something for Carter? You know?" She gestures like she's drinking, and it's well understood by Dylan, who quickly nods. Once he's out of sight, Lara tips her chin toward Carter and me. "I'll get you two a change of clothes. But make sure to throw all your dirty things in here. Destiny, that includes you. Chop, chop, we don't have all day."

It hits me that Carter has nothing besides the clothes on his back and whatever soiled things he left in the cow fields. I ache for him all over again and can't help but turn to look at his grim expression. He must've just realized the extent of the loss as well. His mind has been so occupied with his father and keeping everyone safe that he probably hasn't thought about the damage done to his possessions. All his things. Every keepsake he's ever owned, blown to bits. I can't imagine what he's going through.

In my dreamlike state, I begin to unbutton my shirt.

"Destiny?" Carter comes over and takes my hand, bringing me back. "Didn't you hear her?"

I blink a few times. "What?"

"Lara said she'll find something for you to wear—she'll bring it to you in the bathroom."

My cheeks heat. No, I didn't hear her say that. I guess I

spaced out since I've been running all night and day without sleep. Just as I register how exhausted I am, my eyes grow heavier. "O-oh," I mumble. "Right."

"Although I'd love to see you stripped bare—" He chuckles darkly and shakes my hand in his. "I don't feel like beating Dylan to death for looking at what's mine."

"I'm... I'm not yours," I bite out and pull my hand away. Even if the words make my stomach flip and everything inside me weaken, they aren't true. "Not anymore."

"Keep telling yourself that," he murmurs.

"I kissed you, but that doesn't mean you get to claim me like one of your horses."

He chuckles. "That's not what you are to me."

"I don't want to do this right now." But, of course, some part of me does. I want to figure out what's going on between us and what it means, but it's hardly the most pressing matter.

Dylan returns before Carter can say anything else. He puts some space between us, and Dylan gives me a curious look before he holds the drink to Carter. "Whiskey?"

"Thank you." Carter takes the glass. "I'll show Destiny where the bathroom is."

Dylan nods. "I'll find Lara."

I follow Carter down the hall, trying to look anywhere besides his butt in his briefs. Finally, he takes a right and opens the first door for me with a smile. "Here we are."

"Thank you." When he doesn't leave, I raise my brow. "A little privacy, please?"

"So long as you let me know when we're having a conversation."

He really is pushing it, isn't he? "There's nothing to talk about."

"All right." He shrugs and closes the door, separating us.

It's strange how obedient he's being, but I'm too tired to wonder why. Right now, I want a hot shower, some food, and to sleep the rest of the day away. I need to process. ***Badly.***

After turning on the shower, I kick off my boots and socks. I've barely released the button of my jeans before the door opens. I squeak, almost entering cardiac arrest, and whirl my head around. "Carter," I hiss. "Are you insane?"

He shuts the door and locks it with a devilish grin. "I had to put my whiskey down so we could talk."

Are you serious?

I cross my arms across my chest. "You do know I'm about to shower?"

"Seeing as how you were eye-fucking me ten minutes ago, I figure I might shower, too," he says with a wolfish grin. "Don't think I didn't see you. You look at me the same way I look at you. The same way we've always looked at each other." Then he dares to cross his arms and lean against the door.

"You're seriously going to watch?"

He grins, and there's a challenge in his eyes. "If you let me."

We're playing a dangerous game, but I realize he needs a distraction, and I can't say I don't, either. It's mostly because I'm stubborn. But what happens when the game goes too far?

I steady my hand and unzip my jeans.

A million thoughts run through my head, electricity buzzing in the air. I wiggle my hips, and my jeans hit the floor. I skim the buttons on my shirt, my gaze finding his.

A small part of me is trembling, but another part wants to tease him. Punish him. My fingers move slowly as I unbutton my shirt, then pull off my T-shirt revealing my black cotton bra with a red bow in the middle. My nipples harden, and Carter practically moans, not even trying to hide the growing erection in his tidy briefs.

Every inch of me tells me I need to make it clear that nothing will happen and I should kick him right out. But he's at least a couple hundred pounds of pure muscle. Carter could do whatever he likes with me, and I couldn't stop him. ***Wouldn't stop him, either.*** It's all lust, real and raw.

But is it possible to keep it that way? Not to feel anything deeper for him?

"You're overthinking," he says. "I know that face."

I arch my brow and lie. "You don't know me like you think you do." My heart slams as my clothes puddle onto the floor, and shower steam fills the room.

I slip out of my bra and, without thinking twice, drop my arms. At first, I don't dare meet his eyes, choosing to stare at his tight abs. But then, curiosity gets the best of me, and I slowly look up, wondering what he's thinking.

My God, I wish I didn't, as I find his impatient eyes dancing over my breasts—his Adam's apple bobs.

"Fuck," he drawls. "You're beautiful."

Unconsciously, I press my thighs together, feeling my pussy clenching.

He glances down at my panties. "I bet you're fucking dripping for me."

When he steps toward me, all hell breaks loose. He hauls me up and sets me on the counter by the sink, slamming his mouth on mine.

I whimper, spreading my legs and wrapping them around his waist.

He presses me close as I buck against his stomach. My nails dig into his back, making him groan as he nips my bottom lip.

"You have no idea how often I've thought about this," he rumbles. "Wanting you."

Again, I let the reminder play in my head. This isn't anything that's going to work out. It's just two consenting adults needing one another in a crazy, heated moment. He's not in the right headspace to make any serious decisions. We're just in a moment—a fucking good one, but it'll pass.

"This doesn't mean anything." I give him a taste of my no-nonsense tone. "It can't mean anything."

"The hell it doesn't," he growls.

My lips part, but my voice is stolen as he seals his mouth

over mine. I wonder if my words angered him because his mouth becomes more aggressive.

Damn him and how he's rocking his hips—I can't help but give in to the sensations he's arousing. In my mind, I tell myself this is a one-time thing. We can have sex, so long as I don't get attached.

I wind my arms around his neck and pull him closer. He cups my ass, pressing down on me while I wind my thighs upward and rub my soaked pussy all over his stomach.

How long has it been since my body burned like this? ***Too, too long.***

Carter's mouth takes mine, his fingers gripping my ass, and I open my thighs wider for him. I grab his silky hair and pull him closer, closing my eyes and blocking the world out. The pain of our past. The confusion of today. The chaos. I shut my mind up and decide to let my body have him.

There's a knock on the door, and it breaks whatever spell we're under. I gasp, my face feeling drained of blood. I scramble against his hard body and push him away.

What the hell are we doing?

"Destiny?" Lara calls from the other side of the door, followed by another soft knock. "Are you in there?"

"Yeah." I wince at how it comes out as a squeak when Carter brushes his finger across one of my nipples.

"Is—" Lara trails off, and I almost want to beat Carter, who grins at me. I swat his hand away. "Is everything okay?"

"Just... just dandy." ***I almost die.***

"I'm leaving some clothes here on the shelf by the door. I think they'll fit you. Let me know if you need anything else."

"Okay." I don't dare make another noise or move until I hear Lara walk away. Then, once the coast is clear, I glare at Carter. "Out. Get out. Get out now."

"But—"

"Out." I point at the door, nudging him. When he doesn't

move, I have no choice but to shove his solid body with both hands. "I mean it."

"Okay. Okay." He pauses, holding the doorknob and glancing back at me. "But—"

"You still got it, Carter, I'll give you that. You touch me, and I turn weak. But I don't forget… I never forget."

"Listen, I—"

"What?" I grumble. "What do you want from me? You want to fuck right here in this bathroom? Fine, let's fuck. But that's all it'll be, and you've only got yourself to blame for that."

He looks like he's toying with the thought with flared nostrils. I don't talk like this to him, I never have, but it feels good to have some ground to stand on. To find strength now that his hands aren't all over my body.

"This isn't over."

If he says that one more time… But before I can manage a reply, he leaves.

My fingers tremble as I slowly bring them to my bruised lips.

God, what have we done?

SPOONS CLINK AGAINST CERAMIC BOWLS, FILLING THE dining room as everyone sips their tomato soup and downs grilled cheese sandwiches. Despite my gurgling stomach, I suddenly don't have an appetite, but I pick at my food to show my appreciation for the effort.

"We're in danger, aren't we?" Lara breaks the silence first. She looks annoyed, which I don't blame her for as she flashes her green eyes around the table. "We're sitting ducks, waiting to be taken out by the bad guys, aren't we?"

"That's not going to happen," Carter says.

I'm not convinced I understand the nature of these ***bad guys***, but I'm with Lara in wanting information about what's next instead of sitting around waiting for another explosion.

Juliet puts her spoon down and pushes a strand of hair behind her ear before staring at her brother with wide blue eyes. "Are we in danger, Dylan?"

"Don't worry, kiddo."

"But... what if they come back?" Juliet's voice breaks. "What then?"

"They could come back," Carter butts in. "But Caldwells don't run."

"But Dylan and I are McClintocks," Juliet whispers. "And Lara is a Bain."

The rest of the room erupts into laughter.

"We'll be waiting for them," Carter adds. His firm voice settles the confusion, and the clatter of spoons on ceramic takes over once again.

When the table is cleared, Dylan and Carter resume positions in the living room with a bottle of whiskey while Juliet and Lara sit at the dining room table. I gobble my chocolate cake, my open ears taking in the guy's conversation.

Unable to rid my nagging thoughts, I turn to Lara, sitting next to me and try to speak around a bite of cake, "Who's Tanner?"

She takes a sip of her coffee. "Carter's younger brother."

Everything comes together in a flash but in a terrifying way. I get it now. Carter's brother has something to do with the gangsters. "Ah, yeah. I remember Carter mentioning him. I believe I saw some pictures, too."

"They don't talk much about him after what happened." Lara cuts into her cake.

Something happened?

"What do you mean?" The suspense kills me. And frankly, I'm tired of being the only one in the dark. I'm not family, but I'm here. I deserve answers. "What happened?"

Lara presses her lips into a thin line for a moment. "I don't want to dive too much into this story, as it's not mine to tell, but I think you have the right to know. Tanner is the reason you're here, after all."

"Really?"

"He had a heated argument with his dad and left the gate open when he stormed off the ranch. The bull got out. Bred the young heifers. Flash-forward to now. Here we are... and here you are."

"Why're those men looking for him?" I ask. "I don't understand."

"I don't know." Lara shakes her head. "He must've gotten messed up in some big trouble."

"Yeah." I nod in agreement, even though ***big trouble*** is the understatement of the year.

After scrapping the last bit of chocolate frosting into her mouth, Lara gets up before glancing down at me. "You should get some rest, darlin'. Why don't I show you to a room?"

I open my mouth, ready to tell her that it's not necessary, that I need to get home to my parents and Storm when Carter steps in.

"She's staying in my room."

You can't be serious!

"Lara says I can stay with her and Juliet." Why am I saying anything? I'm getting out of here. This isn't my crazy—why should I stick around to see how the show ends?

"No." He strides toward me, and the same stubborn look returns. He's not backing down. "You're coming with me."

Chapter 11

CARTER

This woman brings trouble to my door… and to my heart.

My father is alive but in the hospital. The Big House is blown to bits, left in a pile of ruin, and you'd think seeing your ex after years of being apart, feelings would fade.

Except when I look at Destiny, it's clear. I'll never get her off my mind nor out of my heart.

Her light footsteps pad behind me as we make our way to the bedroom I'll be occupying until I figure out what to do next about the men hunting my brother.

I'm grateful Dylan and Juliet opened their doors to me, though this house also belongs to Dad.

My cousins lived with us at the Big House when they were growing up—my aunt left them with my mother—before Juliet and Dylan moved here to The Mansion when they were older to give everyone more privacy.

"This place is nice," Destiny says behind me.

"Dad had it built for his brother before he left Wyoming," I explain, looking back at her. "Now Dylan and Juliet live here. They call it The Mansion because—"

"Because it is," she finishes with a laugh. Even with how tired she is—and how tired she is of me—she still looks around with wonder. And her laugh is genuine. Pure. I love that about her.

"How do they not get lost in here?"

"I got lost once," I admit with a chuckle. "I was about five or six."

"You?" she asks in disbelief, matching my pace. She bats her lashes a few times. "I find that hard to believe."

"My brain developed over time. Took a while, though," I tease back. "But when I was a kid, I thought the only way out was through a window, or else I would die inside. Stuck for eternity."

"Did you actually jump out a window?"

Grinning, I push my hat back and show her the nick on my forehead. "I jumped out the window after I broke it with a chair. Fell right into the shrubs."

"What?"

"It was barely anything, but Dad was so angry I thought he would bust a blood vessel."

Destiny's expression softens when I mention Dad, and I love how she never gives me pity but rather understanding. "Your dad is going to be okay, Carter."

"I hope so. He's stubborn, and I hope he'll be no different this time."

She rubs my shoulder, her palm warm and comforting against my shirt. "I hope so, too."

After getting my dad taken care of, I need to regroup and find my brother to ask him what the hell is happening. Tanner always liked adventure but isn't the type to get involved with a gang.

I open the enormous spare bedroom and flip on the light. It's decorated in earth tones with a fireplace and a huge slate-blue rug on the hardwood floor. I stand in the doorway as Destiny takes it in.

"Wow, it's beautiful," she breathes out.

I shut the door behind us. "You can spend the night."

She frowns. "Carter, no."

"You were up twenty-four hours straight. I'm not letting you leave. It's sleep… that's all." I lift my hands up.

"I need to get back to the clinic. Doc Jones is expecting me. What about a nap instead? It's only, what… around two or three?"

"You don't have to worry about Doc Jones." After all, what if this is the only second chance I'll get with her? I'm going to make the most of it. "I'll handle him."

But I've forgotten Destiny hates being ordered around or saved like a damsel in distress because she turns on me, crossing her arms. "Excuse me?"

I stare at her, mentally cursing myself. Everything I'm doing is to keep her safe—and the safest place for her is here with me, considering she's in our world now. "Destiny—"

"Zip it. I said I need to return to the clinic, and you're telling me you'll handle it? Did I ask you to?"

My situation worsens when my cock stirs at how feisty she is. ***Shit.*** I'm in a state of exhausted confusion, and all I can think about is how hot she is. "I didn't mean it like that."

"Just who the hell do you think you are?" she throws in my face. ***Your man. I've always been your man.*** "First the ***mine*** comment, and then the bathroom? I don't need you to handle anything. I haven't needed you for a ***very*** long time."

I bite on my tongue until the taste of metal fills my mouth. The last thing I want is to fuck up my chances of winning her back. But on the other hand, I'll keep her safe, no matter what.

"Look," I try again. "It's for your protection, so don't misunderstand."

"Protection?"

If my dad were here, he'd shake his head at me. I'm always messing up when it comes to Destiny Hart.

"What the hell, Carter?"

"I didn't mean—"

"Do I look helpless to you?" She takes a step toward me. "Do I look like someone who can't take care of herself? Is that the kind of woman you want? Someone you can save? Someone you can throw around and make demands of? Tell me, have I ever been that kind?"

When she's done ripping me to shreds, one hand on her curvy hip, she takes another step toward me with an expression I'm familiar with. Her dark eyes captivate me—I never tire of gazing at what my heart beats for. I'd give anything to have her in my arms again. In my bed again.

Electricity buzzes in the air. If she touches me, I'm done.

The scent of her bodywash—vanilla and musk invade my senses, making me drunk off her. Having her close without holding her and reminding her who she belongs to is tormenting.

"I know you can handle yourself." I close the last space between us and take her chin between my thumb and forefinger. "You're the toughest, stubbornest, and most intelligent woman I've ever met. I know you don't need saving, but that doesn't mean you can't rely on me because of what's happened in the past."

Hurt flashes in her eyes, and I know she doesn't believe me. But I can't focus on that. I've fucked up in the past, but it doesn't mean I can't make it right going forward.

She rubs at a spot on her chest, her gaze flitting away. "I guess I am a little tired."

Good. "Okay, then… how about we talk about everything later?"

Slowly, her eyes lift to find mine. "Just a nap?"

I hold up a hand in promise. "Yes, ma'am."

She twists her lips, considering me. She's an intelligent woman for not believing me. "But afterward, I'm leaving, Carter."

"We'll talk about it."

Her nose flares. "Damn it. I'm tired. If you keep this up, I'm moments away from socking you."

"Fine. Get under those covers." I shake my head, remembering how she gets mouthier when exhausted. "Make yourself at home. I'll be back, so don't wander off."

She shoos me away and climbs into bed. "If I get lost, I'll smash the window and take a leap of faith that a shrub will save the day."

I laugh.

"Mmm," she murmurs, and she's drifting off.

She may think she's defying me when dishing it out like she does, but she's forgotten how much I enjoy a challenge. A smile tugs at the corner of my lips as I shut the bedroom door behind me. I don't have anywhere to go, but I want to give her time to rest before we hash out our differences.

I walk to the fence that separates the pastures from the yard and take in the evening air. I need it, just a few moments of quiet. Then, holding my breath, I turn to look at the Big House. It's strange to see where the huge house once stood is now nothing. My home is gone.

The memories flood me again, and everything hurts all over.

Atlas.

I say his name in my mind, letting the anger course through my veins at what his presence means. How dare he come onto my ranch and endanger the lives of my family.

I fixate on the open space where my home once stood majestic, built by my grandfather. Every holiday celebrated with our loved ones. Every family dinner together. All of Mom's possessions… all of our stuff, too. Gone.

Everything comes crashing in on me. My fingers dig into my palms until they become numb.

Atlas… I'll be waiting for you.

I won't back down, nor will he get away. It's going to be his death or mine.

My mind reflects on another time I had to choose something like is. Unfortunately, that choice cost me everything back then… and led to prison time.

If Atlas won't yield, will I end up there again?

An hour later, I enter Viola Memorial, where Dad's admitted. A stretcher zooms past me, and a shudder runs through me. Things could've been so much worse. I swallow the lump in my throat as I walk through the pale hallways until I find his room.

Fluorescent lights greet me, and they've got his name on a whiteboard just across from the bed he's resting in. The entire hospital smells overbleached, and his room is no different. I haven't even looked him in the eyes yet, but he'll be far from comfortable.

"Carter?" Dad's scratchy voice welcomes me. A cup of juice, a plate of eggs, toast, and a sliced tomato sit on his tray near his bed.

"Hospitals don't suit you." I flash a warm smile and place some apples on his table. "From your niece. Straight from the cellar."

"Thank ya." Dad sits up, grimacing. "I'm ready to get out of here."

Oh no, you don't.

I draw a chair to the side of his bed and sit, briefly glancing at the metal IV stand. "How are you, Dad?"

"Ready to be discharged," he replies in a lively voice that seems somewhat convincing, and I'm glad for that, but he's still not getting out of here.

Nice try. Now that he's here, I won't let him escape. "Soon."

He releases a long breath and sinks back against the bed.

"How are you ***really*** feeling?" I ask again, and this time, I know he understands what I mean.

"Angry. I damn well should've shot those guys. I'm a kill 'em when I see 'em again. How's the ranch?"

"Fine for now. But there's no telling when those fellas will be back."

"We need a plan, son. There's no way I'm leaving this in the hands of the law. Those men asked for a fight, blowing up our home, and I'm gonna give it to 'em."

"We'll give it to them."

He searches my eyes. "And Tanner?"

"I don't know where to start. Give me time. With these guys here, we're bound to learn some stuff."

I hate to give Dad no for an answer, but I don't even know where to start looking for my brother. He never said where he was going when he stormed off the ranch last year.

"Sawyer and his deputies have been around to see me. I don't think they buy our story." Dad rests against the pillow and closes his eyes. I wonder if his muscles ache from the blast or because he's in this stiff bed and not his comfortable chair at home.

Why does my brother have to be such a pain in the neck? Danger follows him everywhere he goes. "What do you think Tanner did for it to be this bad?"

He opens his eyes. "I just hope his love for adventure isn't why we're targeted."

I scoff, knowing my brother.

"I know," Dad says. "You don't have to say it."

But I have a plan forming…

"Carter?" My father's harsh tone snaps me back. "Is everything gone?"

I consider trying to be delicate, but I don't want to lie. "Everything."

We sit in silence for a while, letting everything sink in. The only sound in the room is the faint echo of someone getting paged over the intercom. When Dad finishes eating his cold eggs, I press and hold the button that alerts a nurse.

"Get some rest, Dad. I'll come back in the morning. I need to get some supplies and head back to the ranch." As I finish, another nurse steps in to give him a dose of something, and I slip out. He needs all the rest he can get, and the last thing he needs is to worry about Tanner.

Pulling out of the parking lot, I get a sense of being watched, and I remember those devilish steel eyes inside the SUV.

I'm going to have to end that bastard. I feel it.

DESTINY IS STILL ASLEEP, CUDDLING A LARGE PILLOW WHEN I return to check on her. I'm glad she stayed.

Sliding a strand of hair off her cheek and behind her ear, I study her curves beneath her shirt, following the lines from her feet back up to her face. ***You're mine.*** She's always been mine. But how am I going to convince her? Is she ever going to forgive me?

"Storm... sorry," Destiny murmurs and drifts off again.

Who's Storm? I've never heard that name before. It better not be some guy's name, that's for damn sure.

Without waking her, I leave the room and close the door. My furrowed brow stays knitted all the way down the stairs. I'm at the last step, about to head for the whiskey bottle, when a pop from the fireplace catches my attention.

"Hey."

I flinch at the voice—I didn't notice the person curled up in a blanket by the fire. "Lara. Damn it. Don't scare me like that."

"I've been talking to you since you came down the stairs." She laughs, her green eyes twinkling. "You were staring into space."

I sink into the loveseat beside her. "I was lost in thought."

"Yeah, you were." She hunkers in under her blanket with her dark head peeking out. "How's your dad?"

"He's all right. But he has to stay there and get checked out. He's needed to do that for a while. He hasn't been right since Tanner left."

"I think he hasn't been right since your mom."

I glance at my best friend. She knows the truth. "I'll head to the hospital early tomorrow. Tell Destiny for me if she asks? I'm trying to let her get caught up on her rest. She doesn't need to be driving back exhausted."

Lara nods. "Of course."

We're quiet for a few moments, listening to the clock on the mantel and the snapping embers in the fireplace. "Doubt your dad fancies a sleepover, though," she says to lighten the mood.

"Yeah, he hates it. But he has no choice, and he won't rest here anyway. He's angry enough at what happened."

Then Lara gestures upstairs, obviously toward Destiny. "And what about her?"

"She's asleep."

Lara uncrosses her legs and faces me. "You know that's not what I'm talking about."

I stare at the rug, not sure what I should say. "I don't know, Lara."

She stands, drops the blanket onto the loveseat, and gets whiskey. She pours two fingers' worth into two glasses and hands me one. "You better figure it out, cowboy."

"Whiskey won't make me talk." We both chuckle. Ice clinks as I swirl the liquid. "I never thought I was leaving her for good back then."

"I get it."

"I fell hard. Pretty sure she felt the same. When Mom died… I meant to get home and be here for everyone. I was going back. But then…"

"I know." Lara presses her heel into my thigh as she returns to the loveseat.

I look at the glass of whiskey in my hand, then gulp every drop. I breathe down the fire as the liquid burns and warms my insides.

"But even after all these years, you'll find a way to work it out. If it's meant to be." She pauses, staring into her glass. "I wasn't so lucky."

"A relationship?" I turn to her. "In Paris? I didn't know about that."

"I thought I found love, finally." She takes a sip of her drink and keeps her expression stoic. "But I was so wrong."

"Hey, I'm sorry. But why didn't you tell me? You should've told me."

"I won't repeat that mistake. I'm done with love."

I stare into the fire. "I didn't know."

"It's okay."

"I'm just sorry I couldn't protect you like I always promised to do." Dylan and I always protected her through everything we went through growing up—friends, school, and bullies.

Lara shoves me with her heel again. "You aren't responsible for everyone and everything."

"Yeah, but—" I grin as she cuts me off with a shove for the third time. "Stop, damn it. I'm going to have bruises."

"Maybe that'll make your little chick upstairs jealous," she hisses and grins.

I chuckle. "Lara... you're going to get me into more trouble than I can handle."

"Yep. It's not easy... Love, I mean." She drifts off for a minute and sips her whiskey. "I had some good times in Paris, though. Their bakeries are top-notch. I couldn't get enough of the French Onion Soup. And the bread and pastries. And the coffee—"

I listen to her go on about her days in Paris, hoping she's moved on from her painful past.

"I'm thinking of opening a clothing store in Wind Dance," she adds. "Maybe my own line."

"You'll do well." I smile at her and get up to take another splash of whiskey from the bottle. "You've always had flair."

The night air blows against the window and seeps inside. I

stand closer to the fireplace while Lara buries herself in the blanket again.

I take another sip, feeling my chest and face heat. "Suggesting the whiskey was a great idea."

"You should get some rest. You've got somewhere to be early and want to look rested for—" Lara points upstairs and grins.

I ignore her on that. "What about you?"

She holds up her glass for me to refill, then snuggles back into her nest of blankets. "I'll finish this."

"Don't go too hard?" I tip an eyebrow at her and drop the bottle on the table before heading toward the stairs.

"Yes, sir." She releases a hiccup after her reply.

I shake my head.

I'm going to sleep in another room, giving Destiny space, but I stop outside her bedroom and press my ear to the door in hopes of hearing her breathe. But the room is quiet.

And I hope more than anything… that her heart hasn't gone silent for me.

Chapter 12

ATLAS

This damn road is darker and longer than I remember it. As I drive the country highway into the forest, my jaw ticks in irritation.

Rocco bounces his heavy foot on the floorboard behind me, and Marcello grinds his teeth—or he's working his jaw, or some shit, in the passenger seat beside me. Their tics make my frustration blow through the roof after dealing with the Caldwells earlier.

Malcolm sure is loyal to his son. It's commendable. A father who loves his child, who is willing to lie and die for him. I admire that. That's what they're supposed to do—fathers, I mean—so I've been told. I wouldn't know.

Tanner Caldwell is young and reckless, and he's fucking good at hiding. But my name isn't Lupo, the wolf, for nothing. My keen senses will find that boy and hunt him down. Humans are predictable when they start panicking. It'll be only a matter of time before I capture him and return to Chicago. Finally, back to the city, away from the miles of open space and too much time to think.

"Where're we headed, Boss?" Rocco cracks his neck and pops his shoulder right in my ear. "This place is getting creepy."

My men haven't been to the cabin I've rented yet. Instead, they've been staying at a hotel with another of my men, the one who waited to swap the Escalade and our clothes to rid the evidence before returning to Chicago. And I've been staying at the cabin for some seclusion. I didn't need too much time alone, but I needed enough to think about how to flush out a cowboy in uncharted territory.

It's where I devised the plan to detonate the Caldwells' house if they didn't tell me where Tanner was. I figured, go in with guns blazing like in old Western films. Show them I'm not here to play around. Because Don Moretti won't play around with me if I fail him.

"We're staying at a house north of here. A good place to watch for Tanner." I pull the new vehicle, a Range Rover, onto another turnoff. "We'll lie low. See if news gets to him of what happened to his family. He'll get sloppy. That's when I'll snuff him out."

Marcello chuckles and adjusts his lanky frame against the door. "That's why you're the boss."

I pass the ***Welcome to Bridger-Teton National Forest*** sign.

The cabin is the perfect for us. It sits on several thousand acres of land, with four bedrooms and three baths. There's a creek beside it, too. I found it online and used an alias to book our stay for the next few months. The woman who owns it, Connie, a realtor, is in her early fifties and lives in another city. She inherited the cabin from her dead parents—at least, that's what her owner profile says. She has another real estate agent handling the rental and assured me it was secluded yet accommodating.

Something catches my attention, moving in the shadows on the side of the road. I press the brake, then jolt to a stop. It wouldn't be unusual for bears, deer, or other wild animals to roam into the road, but I don't want anything jumping in front of the vehicle and crashing out here in the night.

A starved-looking woman is limping on the shoulder. ***That's unusual.*** She's shoeless, wearing a tattered black dress like a part of some Gothic horror movie.

Her long black hair is soaked, and there's something in her

hand. I can't tell what. I'm amazed she's not frozen, especially in these April temperatures, dressed like that.

But this is not my fucking problem, and despite my curiosity, I let off the brake and drive.

Rocco taps the back of my seat, and I see him shove his glasses up his nose through the rearview mirror. "Boss, did—did you see that? Shit, was that a ghost?"

"Are you serious? A ghost?" I sneer. Rocco kills for a living—this should hardly freak him out. We're probably all haunted by the people we kill, anyways. I know I'm going to hell, so ghosts are the least of my worries. "She's probably a lunatic."

"You never heard about the ghosts in the forests?" Marcello joins the conversation. "Some crazy shit happens here. I'm talking thousands of people just disappearing."

"She wasn't a ghost," I say again.

Marcello chuckles nervously. He seems as freaked out as Rocco and rolls up his window. "I didn't know you booked a place in the forest."

"You've w-watched those d-documentaries?" Rocco leans closer until he's breathing down the back of my neck. "I have."

Marcello scratches his salt-and-pepper beard. "There are tales of a witch who lives in these parts, Boss. I read it in a flyer at the hotel. This entire area is filled with lore and—"

"What?" Rocco gulps.

Marcello tosses a look over his shoulder. "You know this is the alien state, right?"

You'd think after blowing an entire house up, you'd know things about your friends. Like if one believes in ghosts and another believes in witchcraft or aliens. Which is nothing but bullshit, in my opinion. The frigid weather will kill that girl by morning, and I doubt she can follow us barefoot out in the wild to haunt us. Or beam us anywhere.

It's close to 9 p.m. when we roll up to the cabin. The moon is peeking out as I park, and Rocco unloads himself, quieter than usual as he glances around. ***Thinking about the damn*** *ghosts.* Marcello gets out and stretches before he grabs bags and gear from the back of the SUV.

A flock of dark birds hops in the yard nearby and caws loudly.

There's been an abundance of these odd creatures lately.

Isn't it late for them to be out? I've never seen birds at this hour. Not that I know much about wildlife in Wyoming or birds in general.

Opening the squeaky front door and stepping into the stone-and-log foyer, I turn to my men. "Make yourselves at home. I occupy all the space upstairs, so don't touch my shit. If you want to fight over them, there are other rooms downstairs."

Something's off tonight. My money, weapons, clothes, nothing is out of place, but there's a scent that wasn't here before. It's not foul—it's herbal and minty… but something doesn't feel right.

I intend to find out why.

I turn the heat in the living room up a few more notches. I'm not cold, but hopefully, my men will relax the faster I make this place homier.

"Shit, this cabin really is in the middle of nowhere." Marcello pulls off his jacket and gloves. His gaze scans the space, taking in the place he'll call home for however long this mission takes. "Any idea where the nearest neighbor is?"

"Miles away." I toss the keys and other items in my pocket—except for my phone—onto the island.

"This is where you've been staying, Boss?" Rocco's beady pale-blue eyes widen behind his glasses. He's still clutching all his things, looking like an overstuffed penguin.

Has he been standing in the living room for the past half hour just holding all his shit?

I grab the orange juice carton from the fridge and pour a glass. "You'll get used to it."

"I doubt it." Rocco lets his shoulders slump and places his

stuff in the corner of the living room. "The place looks haunted, Boss."

"Marcello, hook up the security cameras when you settle in and ensure everything's running well." Perhaps I'm being paranoid, but there's undoubtedly something off tonight.

"You got it, Boss." Marcello nods before trekking off with Rocco to unpack and set up.

I down the juice, place the glass in the sink, and fill the glass halfway with water.

"I'm going for a walk," I call. I'm still running on adrenaline from talking with Malcolm. Something about his loyalty and love for his son, his willingness to sacrifice himself for his family—it eats at me.

"You're going outside?" Rocco calls. "Alone?"

"I'll have the ghosts for company. And if you keep this up, Rocco, the ghosts might come for you tonight," I throw back, making Marcello chuckle before I slam the door shut.

I reach for a cigarette and let out a sigh. Standing in the forest, I probably look strange now in my three-piece suit.

I'll have to find hiking clothes or nature wear like the tourists wear. I chuckle at that. I can see myself now. Yeah, I don't think so.

Lighting my cigarette and unbuttoning my jacket and vest, I go to the stream. There's not much noise out here, just the gurgling water and some owls or some shit. I don't believe in ghosts, but I can see how forests create an illusion of the supernatural. The tall trees leave flickering shadows on the ground, and any sense of trails seems to vanish into the undergrowth.

God, I'm anxious to find the cowboy who killed Don Moretti's son and get the hell out of here. Unfortunately, patience has never been my strong suit. I grow bored quickly. A wolf must hunt before being hunted, after all.

I take a drag from my cigarette and face the stream. It's dark as sin out here, even with the full moon, and I'm mostly only able to hear the water flowing.

Once I haul Tanner's body back to Don Moretti, I'll be hailed a hero and handed a million dollars.

Not bad at all.

But I've been wondering more than usual lately—what happens after this job? I'm getting older and getting tired. I've never thought about slowing down or if I want out of the killing profession. My mind never let me imagine anything other.

As I pick my way back to the cabin, I swear something makes a thudding noise from my bedroom on the second floor. There's a trickle of light from the hall, and I squint up—only to see those crows land on a branch beside the window.

I'm not sure that's normal.

Upon entering the cabin, I lock the front door behind me. The cameras aren't hooked up to the security system yet, but Marcello is making quick progress.

Flicking on the light in my bedroom, I shut the door with my foot and tug off my tie. The window is open—the screen on the floor.

That window was closed when I left to pick up my men from the hotel. I'm positive.

I throw my tie and jacket onto the bed, not showing any indication that I know someone is in my room. I shrug off my vest and throw it onto the chair.

Could it be that crazed-looking woman from earlier? Did she follow us? Amusement dances in my bones at how fearless she must be. The corners of my mouth twitch. I know I have a target on my back, yet I don't think they'd send someone who seems to barely weigh more than a baby deer—what're they called? A fucking *fawn*—to kill me.

Without making any sudden movements, I lock the bedroom door to slow whoever it is if they try to escape. Each step is light as I go to the window, replace the screen, slam the window shut, and latch it.

Water droplets lead a path to the closet. I thought for sure they would've picked hiding under the bed.

My phone vibrates. I pull it out and press it to my ear. "What is it?"

"Hey, Boss—" Marcello clears his throat. "Remember that witch—"

"Oh, God!" Rocco calls in the background.

"I think she climbed into one of your rooms upstairs."

"It's handled," I clip before slamming the phone back into my pocket.

I yank the closet door open.

It's the skeletal, drowned-looking witch we passed more than a few miles down the road. She's somehow carried her battered body up here and even managed to make her way to my second-floor bedroom, through the window, no less.

Her large eyes stare back at me through the curtain of her long black hair, almost like she can see into my twisted soul. There's something unhinged in those eyes.

I flick the closet light on to get a good look.

She's skinny, her onyx-colored dress plastered to her and splattering water onto the floor. Her waist-length black hair sticks to her back and shoulders in weighted-down strands. Her pale arms and chest are covered in bruises and cuts. Her wide, almost-purple gaze holds a wildness that reminds me of some mythical beast's eyes.

And in that sense, I'm drawn to her. Curious. She's probably a runaway. A lunatic. A homeless person. An addict. An assassin. Take your pick.

And… she's cradling a box.

"Who the hell are you?"

"My n-name?" Her voice is hoarse yet feminine.

"Yeah. Your fucking name."

"I—I don't remember." She stares into my eyes and then strums her nails on the top of the battered box. "But… he called me Nine. Does that help?"

She may be crazy, but she has the guts not to cower in the face of danger.

"Nine?"

"The number I was given."

She doesn't wait for me to say more before stepping forward and shoving the box into my hands. Then she winces, putting her weight back onto her right foot. "I'll show you." And she lifts her tattered black dress and pulls the filthy thing up to her breasts.

My breath stills. Not because of her body, naked aside from her black panties—because I like my women curvy, voluptuous, and healthy-looking—but because of the branding in the middle of this girl's chest. A crescent. ***Branded. Like an animal.*** The mark is puckered against her almost-translucent complexion.

"The spirits, though—they gave me another name." She releases the fabric so that it falls past her knees again and takes the box back. Her freezing slim fingers with dirty nails brush over mine just briefly before she rocks from the balls of her bare feet, covered in mud, back onto her heels. "Raven."

"Spirits?"

"Yes." She plays with her hair. "My friends."

I've met many, many crazy bitches in my lifetime, but none quite like this. "You remind me of one of the nuns from the boy's home. And just like with her… I don't understand a fucking thing coming out of your mouth."

"Was she kind, though?" Raven whispers. "That's what matters."

I decide to humor this little intruder before I kill her. "Why are you wet and covered in scratches? Did you get into a fight with a wild boar?"

Her eyes go wide. "I must've been swimming in the stream. I think. It helps me relax. Then I went to find some dried berries or nuts for my friends, didn't I? I put their gifts in my box."

She's completely lost in her bizarre story as she puts the tattered box on the floor and opens the lid. No way she could swim in that stream. I guess she could float in a place or two, but—she'd freeze. And there are no berries this time of the year. I don't know about fucking nuts. ***She's fucking nuts.***

Inside her box are feathers, shiny coins, dried berries, and other whimsical, unidentifiable pieces. She admires her items, almost as if they're her most prized possessions before she places the lid back over them.

"Why're you here?"

Her gaze beams around the room. "The spirits led me."

"Why did you enter when you saw the place occupied by men?"

"I didn't see any of you at the time. But it's warm and inviting here. Much like you." She smiles, her long lashes fluttering over her purple-colored eyes. "What's your name?"

Warm and inviting?

This girl—Raven—is something else. She's not normal. Something's wrong with her. Especially if she thinks someone like me is ***warm and inviting.***

Ever so slowly, I grin. "Atlas Lupo. And I'm your worst nightmare."

Chapter 13
ATLAS

"We're keeping her here?" Rocco shoves his glasses higher up on his nose, then fills a pot with water, and puts it on the stove to boil. "But, Boss—"

Rocco and Marcello share a glance before staring at the woman in front of them, standing beside the island, dressed in black, with her long midnight-colored hair around her shoulders. I don't blame them for thinking she looks like a witch or an evil ghost. I think she looks like shit.

"Yes. She's staying here." I reach for the Scotch and a tumbler. Raven may be of use to me. And once I set my mind on something, I hold on to it—which means I'm not backing down until I figure out how to use her.

"Hello," she greets my men, her voice a soft melody. When they don't acknowledge her, she goes back to humming, staring out the window where two fucking crows sit on the banister. She twirls the ends of her matted hair, lost in her own world.

"Hey there, beauties," she sings. "Aren't you glad the Chosen One has been so welcoming like the spirits said he would be? He has followers and everything."

What the fuck? Chosen One?

The pesky birds puff out their chests and caw to her, tilting their heads while she giggles and limps to the porch. In her chaotic mind, they're probably having a damn conversation with her. I rake my hair back and take a seat on the barstool.

"Boss... are you sure?" Rocco waves a wooden spoon toward the porch. "Those birds are out there ***at night.*** I don't like this."

I pour myself a neat Scotch. Hell only knows how many drinks I'll need to put up with this shitshow. "Positive. Do you want her out there roaming around when you don't know where she is? Haven't you heard of keeping your enemies close?"

I'm still trying to figure this out, too. I don't know anything besides this woman's name, and that's not the part I'm interested in. But she intrigues me enough to keep around for now. So it's best to keep an eye on her.

"I don't know if she's—you know..." Rocco taps his temple with the spoon. "Right in the head?"

"She isn't." I don't hide it. Instead, I allow the alcohol to burn into my chest, precisely what I need after the day I've had.

Marcello pours a Scotch, then downs it before his lips pull back. Arms resting on the counter in front of his laptop, he studies me. "How will this all go, then?"

"What do you mean?" I do know, because I usually kill anyone posing a risk to our operations. Backstabbing and betrayal are common in my field, and I'm not going out because I trusted the wrong person. But Raven doesn't seem like a risk.

"He means, what're you planning to do with her?" Rocco removes a box of pasta and a jar of sauce from the paper bag of groceries on the counter.

"I'll use her," I vaguely answer. "And when I'm done with her, I'll kill her."

Marcello looks up from his laptop. "You're not planning to fuck her, are you, Boss? I don't want to hear that."

I snort. "Someone who looks like they're at death's door doesn't do it for me." I check the time. It's getting late, and I have many unanswered questions about the weirdo outside cooing to the birds.

"How do you know she's safe to be around?" Marcello asks.

Rocco holds up his spoon. "And how do you know she won't try to kill us instead?"

I drink another shot. "I don't." From what I figure, Raven—or Nine, or whatever the hell her name is—is not mentally here. Whatever she's gone through has left a confused, broken shadow of a woman. "But I doubt she can lift a gun, much less swing a knife at us."

She cradles one of the birds like a child in her arms and rocks it. We watch with disdain as she slowly uses her cheek to nuzzle the pest as it clicks its beak.

I jab a thumb her way. "I think disease will kill her before she can lay a hand on us."

"What about summoning something to curse us?" Rocco presses, and I'm moments from taking a bomb, strapping it to myself, and detonating it.

"Are you serious about this witch shit?" I ask.

"She looks like a vengeful spirit," Marcello interjects, not helping matters. "What's she doing dressed all in black like that?"

"You're all so silly." Raven giggles softly, airing out her dress as she returns inside. The two crows have now flown off, and there's a feather tucked into her hair. "There's no such thing as ghosts and witches."

Well, look at that, the crazy bitch makes sen—

"Not like the kind you're referring to." She gives us a bright smile. "There are spirits and magic, though."

Ah, I spoke too soon.

Rocco looks at her with a pale face. "Are—are they not the same thing?"

"No. They're not," she sings out and limps her ragged body close to us, almost like she will tell us a secret. "Thanks to the spirits, I was led to the Chosen One."

I can't spend any more time listening to this. "While we'd love for this conversation to continue, we're busy men, and you need to shower, Nine."

My use of what I presume to be her number catches her attention. The wildness dancing in her eyes fills with a void.

She blinks erratically. "I do?"

"You smell like a—a wet dog." Which is far from the truth. Her scent is a mix of berries and mint. But she does need to clean up. Her dress, arms, legs, and face are filthy. I push off the counter. "Rocco, prepare that dinner. Marcello, finish setting up the security cameras."

I don't spare either of them another look as I lead Raven up the staircase. It's odd—she doesn't seem to have a presence. I only know she's behind me because of her stupid humming. We round the corner to the guest bathroom.

After flicking on the light, I turn to her. "Everything you need is in there. You have fifteen minutes."

Raven takes a step inside. Her hand lifts to part her hair to the side, and she strokes the matted, sticky strands. "I... I don't know how to use that faucet."

I'm fighting the growl in my throat as I brush past her and turn on the showerhead. She seems amazed as water spews out, and she beams at me. "Thank you, Chosen One."

I scratch the side of my nose and turn to go. As I close the door, I see her cupping water with one hand and then rubbing it onto her arm without getting into the tub. Instead, she's smearing the dirt into mud and dripping onto the white bath mat. Then she puts her head under the water spray before shaking her hair like an animal.

Jesus fucking Christ.

I take one giant step and turn off the water. "Do you not know how to fucking shower?"

She recoils at the roughness of my voice. "Am I not doing it right?"

I start rolling up my sleeves. "Strip off that mess and get in the fucking tub."

I don't do this kind of shit. I've never taken care of anyone, much less helped someone shower. I've known her for less than an hour. So what the hell am I even doing?

I convince myself it's no different from bathing a dog, which

I have done. And I don't want her walking around looking like she does. Her eyes never leave mine as she slips her arms to the inside of the dress as if weighing to see how much she can trust me. Then she lets the dress plop and pool at her feet.

"Everything?" She still holds my gaze.

"Whatever." I swipe my tongue across my lips. "But I would."

She hooks her dirty fingers into her panties and strips them off, and they, too, pool by her feet. I don't look. My eyes catch onto her necklace rather than glance anywhere else. It's rustic-looking, and by how she fiddles with it, it seems to have significant meaning. Under the light, I notice more scars and bruises covering her body before she turns her back to me.

Something inside me clenches.

Not only is she branded between her breasts, but on her back as well, like a fucked-up tramp stamp.

Master's Ninth.

Although her skin has healed, it's a miracle she hasn't died from some infection.

As always, the unknown intrigues me... Who is this master? If Raven's his ninth slave, then how many more are there?

She holds onto the feather that was in her hair and takes a seat in the tub. I crouch, take the feather from her fingers, and place it on the edge of the sink.

Her nipples bead due to the cold, presumably, and I check the temperature before letting warm water fill the tub. Next, I take a washcloth and scrub away the dirt staining her cheeks. I rinse the cloth several times until the sheen of her porcelain skin is visible.

I scrub her neck. "Why're your eyes that color?"

She pushes her hair behind an ear. "M-my eyes?"

"They're purple."

"Well, they should be kind of grayish-blue," she says matter-of-factly. "Because... that's what color they are."

Maybe I'm colorblind. "Hmmm."

I rinse the washcloth again and gently rub her delicate collarbones and pale chest. Then, I quickly move the cloth across her breasts, not wanting to stare at her nipples.

"Here." I hand her the cloth and let out the dirty water. "Keep scrubbing." She does so as I refill the tub again. "Now turn around," I order softly.

She does as she's told, and I'm pleased to see this submissive side of her where she isn't saying some wild nonsense or the other. I use a sponge to clean off the mess caked to her back. She flinches when I arrive where the words are carved into her flesh.

"Is the water too hot?" I can't see her expression, but I know it's not the water that made her flinch.

"No," she whispers.

I rub down her ass and legs. There's not a sexual thing about this, and it may be the first time I've been with a woman naked without it leading to her beneath me.

After squeezing shampoo into my palm, I massage it into her hair and scalp. Over time, her body relaxes.

Christ, if Rocco or Marcello saw me like this, I might have to kill them.

I drain the tub two more times. The amount of dirt in her hair is unreal. I'm sure she hasn't showered since escaping whatever hell she came from. Finally, she turns her head to me, and her eyes pierce mine.

Without the mess of mud and matted hair, her face shines clearly. Her delicate nose. The fullness of her pink lips. Her cheeks are too hollow. Her long black hair only makes her lavender eyes gleam more.

"Up."

She stands, dripping water, and my eyes wander from hers to her waist, her too-thin hips, and her legs. She clutches onto her necklace and waits as I grab the towel. "When will you save the others?"

Once again, utter nonsense spews from her mouth. "Others? What others?"

"The spirits said you'll save them. It's why they told me to find you," she softly tells me, almost as if she's expecting me to know this. "They led me to you because you can save them. They said you'll keep me safe, to trust you because you're the Chosen One."

I'm the last person she should trust.

"I'm no savior, Raven."

Her eyes widen as I ruffle a towel over her hair. She reaches to grip my shirt. I don't like people touching me, but I can't say anything when she raises her head and looks at me.

"You are. You saved me."

Delusional.

Disturbed.

Demented.

Whatever hell she's gone through has made her like this, made her think the first person to show her kindness is her savior—the Chosen One. It isn't me.

"Dry your hair." I let go of the towel and pick up her disgusting dress. "I'm putting this in the washer and getting you something to wear. Don't move from this fucking spot, you hear me?"

With that, I close her into the bathroom.

Downstairs, I thrust the tattered dress at Rocco, who has just finished cooking. "Throw that in the wash, then dry it. When it's done, leave it outside my door."

"You got it, Boss." He makes a face when he sees how disgusting the dress is and dramatically holds it away from his body. "If you need anything, let us know."

I make a noise to tell him I've heard him before grabbing the dinner tray, consisting of bowls of pasta with sliced chicken on top and bowls of salads. I set the tray on the table in my bedroom, then throw open the closet, grab one of my shirts, and return to the bathroom, where Raven still has the towel draped over her head.

"You're going to have dinner, and then you go to sleep." I take the towel away before throwing the shirt over her head.

Slowly, she slides her arms through the sleeves. She brings the shirt's neckline up and sniffs it before smiling at me. "Thank you, Chosen One."

"Stop calling me that."

She hums in response before padding behind me like an imprinted animal. Her stomach growls right on time as she stops by the food tray. I slide the entire thing toward her. "Sit. Eat."

She stares at the food and drops to the floor.

I take a deep inhale. "Get the hell up and sit at the table. Sit in this chair."

She obeys, and I think she'll start wolfing the food. But she intertwines her fingers and prays. Then, when she finishes, she takes food from the fork and swallows it down as if she hasn't eaten in days.

She probably hasn't.

I sit on the bed and don't bother watching her as I take out my laptop and finish up some business details. It doesn't take long before Raven's finished everything on the tray.

"Thank you for the food. I'm not worthy, Lupilia."

"Lupilia?" Instant regret. Why am I bothering to ask questions?

"Lupo means wolf? The spirits say you're the Chosen One. Which means you're my family. Famiglia di lupi—wolf family." She comes to the bed and curls herself on the other side of me, nuzzling deep into the pillow and sighing. "We're family and tied by the thread of destiny now."

What the hell is she saying?

A few seconds later, her breathing steadies, and an hour later, I join her.

The plan is to sleep for a few hours, but by the time I wake, the sun has risen—and Raven is nowhere in sight. Her wild scent lingers on the sheets as I scramble up. Her box, her dress, and even my shirt are gone.

The fucking girl has made a fucking fool out of me.

She's not only sneaked out without waking me, but I let my guard down for the first time in—

Have I dreamt the entire thing?

Then I look at the nightstand, where the black feather is attached to a piece of red twine.

The thread of destiny.

Chapter 14

DESTINY

I scan the field of cattle in front of me.

Where the ***hell*** is that man? I need to get back home.

I've kept an eye out for Carter all morning, and it's nearing time for me to return to my part of the state. Of course, it'll be easier to leave without seeing him, but I secretly do wish to say goodbye.

"Morning, boys." Dylan tips his hat as he draws his bay gelding beside the field of ranch hands. "You all haven't been properly introduced, as yesterday was hideous, to say the least." He smiles warmly at me, baby blues twinkling, before turning back to the men. "Doc Hart, meet Sam, Bill, and Jonas." He gestures toward the men one after the other, and they tip their hats at me.

I shift in the saddle, adjust my reins into my right palm, and smile. "Hello."

"And boys, this is Doc Hart. She's our vet and the person who saved our heifers and newborn calves."

Thank you, ma'am," they chorus together.

"That was a fine job you did out here," Bill says.

I blush a little and stroke the glossy neck of my horse. I typically don't care much for flattery. Why should I be praised for saving a life? But something about what Bill said fills me with pride. Though Juliet, Dylan, and Lara were also helping with the births, my mind drifts to Carter. "I had help."

Dylan moves his horse forward, a step to disperse us. "Okay, you can get back to work, fellas. Doc Hart and I will handle things on our end."

Bill twirls his hat in his hands. "Any word from Mister Caldwell?"

"Not yet," Dylan says over his shoulder, keeping his horse moving. "But Carter is at the hospital again this morning. He'll update us."

The men nod and return to work.

I catch Dylan staring over his shoulder at me. I bring my horse up alongside his. "What?"

"Umm." He wags a finger in my direction. "Carter used to talk about a Destiny."

The silence between us hangs as he continues to stare. I wait for him to change the subject and talk about the cattle, but he doesn't.

Fine. I've got nothing to lose in telling him. "I'm that Destiny."

He grins. "Figures."

I scoff, but I'm joking. "What's that supposed to mean?"

"He's different." Dylan's gaze is on the bounding calves up ahead, but his mind is trying to figure out his cousin and me. "He changed ever since he returned from Texas. Like he's missing something, or… maybe ***someone***. Whenever Texas is mentioned, regret is in his eyes. He never said why, and I don't mean to stick my nose where it doesn't belong, but what happened between you two?"

I follow his attention to the calves, wishing for their carefree freedom without the complexities of human life. "He left me. Did he mention that?"

From the corner of my eye, I see Dylan studying me, waiting for more information.

"We dated. It was good. I wished we could've been together forever." There, I've said it.

"I don't know much about anything. About you and Carter.

But I do know that there are many things you probably weren't aware of—and maybe should know."

What's that mean?

I need to change the topic right now. I can't deal with this. "C'mon, let's check on the calves." With a bright but forced smile, I lead the way.

The first set of babies are hyperactively playing round and round, dodging away from their mother's advances. We examine more of them until we arrive at the second heifer with twins. She lies with her head down, eyes listless, and even though aware of our presence, she doesn't move, not even responding to her black furball calves.

"Something's wrong." I dismount and hand my reins up to Dylan. "Get my bag, please?"

I gently shoo away her bouncing calves. Then, when Dylan arrives, I collect the bag from him and set to work.

"What's wrong with the heifer?" Carter asks, surprising me, riding up behind us and dismounting from his coal-black horse.

I don't let my gaze linger on him.

Bill saunters up beside Carter. "Everything all right, ma'am?"

"Hopefully." I kneel on the ground beside the momma. "Has she been eating?"

Bill nods. "She seemed okay earlier."

"I'm going to give her a few things. Hopefully nothing serious. Watch her and ensure she gets a little more TLC today?"

"Yes, ma'am." Bill tips his hat. "Will do."

"When did you get back?" Dylan asks Carter, and I listen in on their conversation.

"Just now," Carter answers.

"How's Uncle Malcolm?"

Carter watches me administer the injections. "He'll be all right."

There's a long stretch of silence.

"Well, uh, okay. I'll see what the ranch hands are doing," Dylan says and tips his hat before leaving.

I nod to him and rub the fur on the heifer's rump, watching her slurp the water Jonas is serving her. "Be strong, momma." I smile. "Fight for your little ones."

After a few minutes of taking note of anything off with the heifer, I stand and join Carter. I pat his horse. "Nice-looking animal."

"This is Bandit." He slides his palm down his horse's glossy neck, and I watch the movement with a bit of jealousy. "He's my trusty steed."

"He's a beauty."

Carter shifts on his feet before his stance becomes firm. "Come ride with me."

"Where to?" I ask with indifference, not wanting to show my curiosity and a secret desire to spend more time with him.

He takes my hand and pulls me away. "You'll see."

"But—"

"Destiny? It's just a ride."

My heart speeds as his grip on my hand tightens, and a flush of heat passes through me. Then, after a moment, I remove my hand from his, ignoring his pained expression.

When we reach my horse, Carter hands me the reins, his scent invading my senses, heady like after a rainstorm. We ride across the fields, looping and weaving all over the mountainside.

"Where're we going?" I ask after a while.

"A place you'll like."

I watch his smiling face for a minute before I force my gaze away. I want to say something.

"Are they really gangsters? The men who blew up your house?" I'm busting to know what's going on around here. "I overheard you and Dylan yesterday."

He shifts in the saddle and clears his throat. "I'm not sure. Dad says a man named Atlas is their leader. I'm trying to find out who they are… and why they want my brother."

"What did he do to get them so angry?"

"We're almost there," he says ignoring my question. We round the bend, and the field opens up. "Race you to the edge?"

"Heyaaaah." I nudge my horse, leaving Carter in my dust.

He won't go down without a fight, though, and we race to the line of trees at a dead gallop before pulling up. There's a welcome relief in letting myself have fun for a moment.

"Beat you!" I call.

He grins. "I let you."

The sound of rushing water fills my ears as our horses meander through the trees, cooling down, until we come to another opening, and I pull my horse to a halt, taking in the most beautiful sight I've ever seen.

Three rivers join in an artistic congregation. In between them sit little islands. Their shores and the blue-green water glitter under the noon sun. The huge mountains surrounding us block our view of the valley, but the landscape before us is covered in green and brown vegetation, like a painter's choice of oil on canvas.

Carter dismounts and stands with his feet in a solid stance before he rocks back on his heels, warmth in his expression. "Welcome to Three Rivers, my favorite place in the world."

"Wow." I take it all in, the breeze on my face. "This is a different kind of heaven." The scent of earth and water floods my senses. The calm. The beauty. It's magical here.

I take it all in like it will be my last moment. The moment when you think the world will end, and you're asked where you'll spend your last five minutes and with whom.

Carter walks Bandit down to the river, and I smile as I angle down the slope with my gelding.

"Hey, wait up," I call after Carter. With the wind in my hair and against my face, I lose my breath and feel reborn.

"This is where I come to get away from everything," he says as we draw near to the river. He takes our horse's reins and loops them over some driftwood.

I throw a pebble in the river, hoping I can make it skip. "How often do you come here?"

"Not as much since I've been busy with the ranch and with Dad's condition."

I look forward to a detailed answer. "What happened? You know, between him and Tanner?"

"They uh... argued and said mean things to each other." Carter cocks his head, and I give an understanding nod. "Tanner said he was tired of living the ranch life. He's always been adventurous, but I think it's gotten him into trouble this time."

"Then what happened?"

"Chuck happened. Tanner stormed off the ranch. That's what I know. Now here we are, hunted by ***The Godfather*** crew, and no word from my brother since." Carter throws a pebble. It bounces across the water, creating tiny ripples.

"How'd you do that?" I look around to find another pebble and hand him a glassy flat one. "Show me that again."

Grinning, he throws the pebble, and it makes five short and fast bounces across the water.

I want to do that!

But every time I throw my pebble, it thumps and sinks. I hate being bad at things, especially something this simple.

I'm getting frustrated.

"Calm down, Little Bear. I'll show you. Keep the pressure in your palm, on the stone, and in your wrists. But, keep it loose so your wrist is still flexible."

Little Bear? I've not heard that nickname in a while. I smile at the memory attached to it but turn away from him. I don't want him to get the idea that he's wiggling his way back into my heart.

Carter steps behind me and leans around, his arms on either side of me, before taking my wrist. His touch ignites a wave of heat that spirals through me, making me giddy, and I'm sure he senses it, too, because he pauses before he removes his hands and steps away.

I'm like a spellbound deer.

What're we doing?

Shit, I can't remember. I thumb the pebble in my hand. Oh. Skipping pebbles. I glance at him, my eyes tracing a path from his lips back up to his eyes.

Snap out of this. You're here to finish your job—no strings attached.

I have nothing left to do here. The ranch hands can handle the cattle. I'll return to my life, to Storm, and forget about Carter. I've done it before. I can do it again.

"I have to get back," I find myself saying, breathing quicker. "I have a job. I have—"

"Absolutely not."

"What?" I reply to his abrupt tone.

"I said you're staying. I didn't change my mind." With his firm gaze on me, I'm all jumpy inside. I'm not about to be Carter's puppet again. Things are different now. I have someone waiting for me. Someone more important than him.

"I can't." I allow the words to settle.

The air between us goes icy.

He licks his lips. "Look, those men—they know every one of us now. For them to attack like they did, they must've spied on us. You're not safe anywhere but here... with me."

Oh, he will love what I have to say about that. "Like how you stayed with me in Texas? I'm not afraid of gangsters. I have to go. I have obligations, and you can't stop me."

"You're not leaving."

I press my lips together. I'm not afraid of him, nor will I back down. "What're you going to do? Force me? Because I've made up my mind, and I won't change it for anyone—certainly not for you." I stride to the horses, though I don't know the way back to the stables or to my truck.

Carter grabs my wrist. "Stop."

I yank my hand away.

The truth is, he's right. Going back to my life might cause

problems for people around me if the Mafia find me. I can't let that happen. Even if it feels wrong, the smart choice is to stick around to figure this out before I leave.

But I don't want to give in to the man who broke me.

I fixate on his brown eyes, searching for answers. His expression is sincere.

Why didn't you fight for me back then? For us?

I barely managed to move on after he left the last time.

My mind dances and comes up with a good story. "I need to keep things right with Doc Jones. I have student debt to pay."

Chapter 15

ATLAS

Torture.

By definition, it's the act or practice of inflicting pain. Sometimes in life, I've been both the torturer and the tortured. So it's not a surprise I prefer to stay on the giving end. But right now, I'm dealing with pain caused by my own hand. This is what I get for taking shot after shot of Scotch.

My head pounds like someone took a hammer to it as I wobble down the steps to get some water. ***Hell!*** I forgot about the creak on the sixth step, and the noise shoots through me like an explosion.

I must stop drowning in alcohol.

Since Raven left—when was that? Last night? This morning? —I'm trying to accept that she's slipped from my grasp. It's hard. It's damaging my ego.

As I enter the kitchen, Rocco looks up from his phone, and Marcello stops typing.

He scratches his bead. "Someone looks like they've had a rough time."

"Another word, and I'll shoot you." I beeline for water. I chug as Rocco slides a tray with two huge plates of much-needed eggs and buttered toast in front of me, along with mugs of steaming black coffee.

“I doubt you'll be able to shoot him without your head splitting in two, Boss.” Rocco chuckles. "Here's some breakfast for you and the wild one upstairs."

"Why're you both up this early?" I grumble.

Marcello taps at the laptop again. "It's noon, Boss."

I wince and take a coffee. "Any luck finding out who the girl is?"

"Unfortunately, no."

"How is she anyway?" Rocco's beady light-blue eyes train on me, undoubtedly waiting to keep track of the witch.

I don't want them to know I fucked up, and she managed to slip away. "She's fine." I pick up the tray. "If you need me... leave me alone."

I head to my room and shut the door with my foot. I startle when Raven throws her leg through the open window, her knee caked in mud.

"We—we need to help them." She heaves, sliding onto the floor, looking like an ink splotch in her voluminous dress.

I power through my hangover. "Them?"

She scrambles to her dainty feet. She's ripped her dress a few more times, and she's cradling some matted dark-red fur. The foul stench makes my stomach churn. There're bones sticking out of whatever the hell she's brought back.

"What the fuck is that?"

"Bunnies," she whispers lovingly. "I found them next to their mother."

"You took them from their den?"

"No, no. Their mother was killed. She was mauled." Raven shifts them from one arm to the other. "Maybe by a fox or something. Thankfully, it spared these."

Narrowing my eyes, I shake my head. "What?"

"I saved all five." She thrusts the mangled animals in my face. "Look at them."

I take a quick look. "They're dead."

"They're all alive." She giggles. "See? Look."

"I *am* looking. The creatures are dead. You carried back five dead animals. Some with their bones hanging out."

She shakes her head wildly. "How can they be dead?" She

shoves the dead kits in front of my face again. "They're here. They're all alive. They're sleeping. That's all."

"Dead," I say slower when I realize she's not seeing what's in front of her. "Blood is fucking all over your arms. They need disposed of."

She flinches and takes a step back. "We can't throw them away like they're trash."

"Then we'll fucking bury them."

Her hands shake as she places the kits on the bench at the foot of the bed. The cream-colored upholstery starts to slowly stain with the blood. I hope Connie, the cabin owner, won't mind, because I sure would.

"I don't know what's real and what's not anymore," Raven whispers, raking her long hair back before she claws at her arm.

Red marks are streaked all over her pale skin, past her elbows. I grab her wrists before she causes an infection from whatever diseases the dead creatures could be carrying.

"I don't know what's real," she keeps saying. "I don't know what's happening."

I pull her near me to stop her from thrashing and try not to get blood on my shirt.

She tries to pull away. "Why am I even here?"

"I don't know."

She takes a sharp breath. "There has to be a reason."

"Yeah." I don't know what I should do with her. For her. "You need distractions to keep you occupied."

"Distractions?" She nods against my chest. "Distractions are good."

"I'll find you distractions."

She leans back, and we stare at one another. Her cheeks are still blue-and-purple. The swelling has gone down, but it'll take a while before she's healed.

From the corner of my eye, I notice a movement from the nest of matted fur. One little brown head pokes up from the pile and wiggles its nose.

"Look," I whisper. "One is alive."

"Alive?"

I point to the stubborn creature. "Yes."

She gasps, darting to pick it up. Her face lights up. "Look at you. He brought you back," she says as if I've given her the cure to all diseases. She rocks the creature back and forth in her hand. "The Chosen One can do that. And—he's going to save all of us."

My phone buzzes, and I fish it out of my pocket to see a text from Marcello.

We found out something about Raven. Come down.

"Get that blood off you," I say to her. "Clothes are in the closet. Finish the food. Give the creature some if you want. Bury the others when you're done. The shovel is in the shed. You do ***not*** leave the property. Do you understand?"

"I came back, you know." She gives me a stern look. "In some cultures, the red cord means we're tied together. For always. I was going to return."

I don't answer; just click the door shut behind me.

Marcello is furiously typing, a cup of coffee at hand.

"What do you have?" I ask.

"I don't get why you're so intrigued by that girl, Boss." Rocco's bushy eyebrows furrow as he washes the dishes.

"Shut the fuck up," I spit out. Marcello returns to his laptop with a huff at the two of us. "Did you find anything?"

"I've pulled up some files and found a picture." He taps a few keys. "Here she is. Clementine Comet."

"Oh, wow," Rocco drones. "She has three fucked-up names now."

I rub a palm over my eyes. "Let's call her Raven because I don't think she remembers who she is."

Marcello leans close to his screen. "She's from Texas."

"Texas?" Rocco wails. "Wonder how she got to Nowhere, Wyoming?"

Marcello squints as he scans the file. "Holy shit. She graduated from high school when she was twelve. She has degrees in psychology and behavioral science. Her IQ is off the charts. And she often spends her time helping animals at a local shelter and volunteering at food banks, this says. A regular little angel on Earth."

"What happened to her?" I look over Marcello's shoulder.

Raven is smiling brightly on screen. Her hair is neat, and her clear skin has no cuts or bruises. She's happy.

Marcello pulls up a new tab and scans it. "It appears she dropped off the planet a few years ago."

Rocco dries a plate. "Any family?"

"Her mother is—or *was* a professor. Her father was a mayor. She has a baby sister." Marcello's eyes widen and meet my gaze. "They're all missing. Like... gone."

I arch an eyebrow. "Dead?"

He pulls up some documents. "They weren't declared dead."

Rocco dries another plate. "Her parents must've been bad people, and their daughter was collateral damage when something went wrong, I bet."

Marcello taps away. "I'll keep digging."

I nod and turn to Rocco. "I need you to meet the supplier and pick up ammunition. I'll text you the place."

He grumbles a string of curses but knows better than to talk back.

The sound of shoveling comes from outside, and I look out the window into the yard. Raven is dressed in a plain black T-shirt—mine—with some little shoes—ballet flats. I don't even know where she got those—and her hair is dripping wet as she buries her dead kits.

I shake my head and turn away.

This Wyoming paradise is turning into a burial ground from hell, and I can't wait to get out of here.

Chapter 16

CARTER

Well, that's the most ridiculous thing I've ever heard.

I push my hat back and chuckle like I can't believe what Destiny just said. "Student debt is keeping you from my bed?"

She gives me an evil glare like a riled grizzly. "Carter… that's not what I meant, and you know it."

I gaze at the river and the grasses growing near the bank. Then I turn back to her. The slow-moving air current blows through her hair, and her scent drifts my way, leaving a mix of her and nature resting in my nose.

She's been beautiful since I first spotted her in that café back in Texas. She was so cute and sweet I gladly went over the moon for her. She was everything to me.

And now with the sunlight and wind twining in her dark hair, seeing how strong and matured she is, she'll forever hold a place in my heart.

I'm not letting go. The choice isn't hers. Whether she wants to go along with it or not, she's my destiny.

But I think she knows that. She has to. Deep down, she remembers we're meant to be together.

She squints at me and shakes her head. Her brown eyes hold mine, and I fight back everything to not cave and take her in my arms. I need to take things slow if I want a second chance, even if it kills me.

"So... since it's time for me to return to the clinic, we better head back to the stable. Thanks for bringing me here, though. It's beautiful." She picks one of the white wildflowers dotted along the bank. Her smile turns flat, and I know she's thinking of a way out from how she's backing to where our horses are.

I open my mouth to tell her something meaningful, but she quickly stops me.

"It was nice catching up with you after all this time. I mean it. But I really have to get back to Doc Jones."

I smirk at that. "So it's not the student debt, then? It's Doc Jones now?"

She huffs. I know exactly what she means, but I can't help myself from teasing her.

"It doesn't matter, Carter." She unloops her horse's reins from where they're tied and mounts easily before her attention lands on me. "Let's go. I want to tell Lara and Juliet goodbye."

"Nope." I shake my head, walking to Bandit. "We're not going back to The Mansion."

Her brows bump together. "Where do you think we're going then?"

I fix my reins and mount, the saddle squeaking as I land in my seat. I want to live in oblivion for a while. I want more time with her to see if there's still something between us. "Somewhere private. We'll stay in one of the rental cabins."

"Carter, no. I'm not a damn doll you can carry around everywhere. I have a job and people back home who matter."

There's something about the way she says ***people*** that gives me pause. Does she have a man back home? Or is she referring to her parents? Or maybe Doc Jones again.

"All the more reason you need to stay put," I say. "I don't want my shit following you anywhere."

"I can take care of myself." But despite her words, her features soften, like she's giving it some thought.

"Let's get on before it gets too late." I click to Bandit to move faster, passing her to lead the way. Bandit nickers before I hear her horse clipping behind me. Glancing back after a while, I notice her attempting to text someone. "You're not going to get service out here. You have to wait until we get closer to home."

She doesn't respond. She keeps tapping.

"Texting your lover boy?" I call back to her.

Her fingers stop clicking as she glares at me.

I push my hat back a little. "The student loan people?"

She resumes her text, then glances ahead at me again with another harsh glare.

"Oh, Doc Jones, then?" I toss back at her.

"Texting my mother." She puts her phone into her zipper pocket and huffs. "Letting her know I'm still alive, you jerk."

I grab my heart. "Ouch!"

After a while, my truck comes into view, and I'm impressed Destiny's still following instead of having jogged off somewhere.

We unsaddle and care for the horses when we get back to the stable. Then, without much of an expression, she follows me to my truck.

I open the door with a grin. "After you, my lady."

She rolls her eyes, murmuring a curse under her breath as I place my hand on her jean-clad thigh and stare at her. She's warm through her jeans, and my palm is hot. She refuses to look at me, which fuels me to win her over even more. I chuckle and close the door before going to my side and scooting in.

I hold onto the steering wheel and stare in her direction. "Your text go through?"

She's looking out the side window. "Uh-huh."

"Your mom okay with you staying with me?"

"I told her I don't have a choice." Destiny flashes her big brown eyes my way. "That I'm being held captive by a Neanderthal and that she should send my father straight away with his shotgun."

I grin but wonder if she's being serious or not. "Damn, Destiny."

The cabin I want to stay at is pretty close, so I drive extra slow and casually place my arm on the back of the seat behind her. Ever the stubborn woman who's stolen my heart, she huffs and slides against the passenger door—the furthest away from me she can get.

Once we pull into the driveway, I lead her up the steps, my hand on the small of her back. She doesn't pull away. Satisfied that she might be coming around to my way of thinking, I grin as I fish out the keys, my gaze trained on hers. She's relaxed, even though I'm technically keeping her hostage. I allow her in first before closing the door behind us.

There's something right with having her here and away from the outside world. I'll get my thoughts straightened on what matters, and I hope we'll work through our differences.

Not to mention, this tucked-away corner of the world has everything we need. There's a well-furnished kitchen, dining room, sitting room, bathroom, but only one bedroom—though Destiny doesn't know that yet—along with a large balcony and a huge wraparound porch overlooking the water.

She'll love the fireplace, as she dislikes the cold. I built all of these cabins to my taste, and I'm proud of each of them. But I have a particular attachment to this one—the Honeymoon Cabin.

Destiny steps beside me with her hands at her sides, taking a slow gaze around. Her expression softens.

"I got you a few things." I go into the kitchen. "Some clothes from when I was out earlier. Feel free to shower and change. I'll make dinner."

"I have a change of clothes in my truck," she mutters.

"Use what I have." I pull a rainwater-scented candle toward me, light it, and slide it back to the center of the island. Then I head to the fridge. "Take advantage of me."

She might not like it when she finds out I got her an entire armload of things to show her how serious I am about her welfare.

I sound like a stalker or a crazy person, and I know it. But I don't care.

I rub my palms together and make omelets and fried potatoes when she does as she's told. I murmur a tune, and she returns just when I'm finished preparing dinner. She dries her long, wet hair, wearing one of the gray T-shirts I grabbed for myself rather than anything from the mountain of clothes I picked up for her. The shirt hits her knees, and I'm not sure she's wearing anything underneath from the outlines I admire through the fabric. Water from her hair drips onto the front, making dark marks where her nipples bead, and as much as I try not to stare, I can't take my eyes off her.

As she caresses her hair dry with the towel, I imagine her hands on me like that… soft and attentive.

She points to the stove. "You're going to burn the food."

I singe my finger on the pan instead and hiss. "Shit." I pop the throbbing digit in my mouth and suck like I want to do to her nipples.

"Are you okay?" Destiny gets in my space and takes my finger into her hand.

I try not to stare at her breasts. Try not to look at the wet places where her nipples are. Try not to breathe in her warm scent. But it's hard not to. It's ***really*** hard not to

"Let me see," she demands, snatching my hand. There's no caress as she jerks me from the stove to the faucet. She turns on the cold water and forces my hand under it. The sensation of the water and her fingers circling my wrist has me clearing my throat. After a moment, she nods. "Good. It's nothing too bad. You'll be fine."

My heart soars to hear at least she cares.

I wink at her. "Why are you wearing my shirt?"

"They were all the same size. I just picked one. The shorts were way too big. Fell right off."

"That's because you're wearing my shirt." I grin. "Yours are in the other closet."

"Oh," she murmurs, her cheeks turning a pretty pink. It's good to see I still make her blush. "I didn't see the other closet."

"I mean, that shirt looks better on you than me." I push a plate of eggs and potatoes toward her, then sit across from her and pour a glass of orange juice while she eyes what I've made for supper.

"Omelets?" she says sarcastically, wiggling on the stool at the counter.

"Yeah?"

Her brows knit as she inspects the food. "You're terrible at making eggs. Last time you made me eggs, they weren't just soggy but they were also filled with shells."

My face pinches. "Don't remind me." I feign surrender with my hands raised, thinking back to that day. She giggles, and I get lost watching her before motioning to her plate. "How do they taste?"

She samples a bite. ***God, her lips.***

"Mmm… good?"

I chuckle, not believing her. "Really?"

"I'm serious. They're good." She scoops another forkful into her mouth.

Curious to see if she's sparing my feelings, I snag some of the fluffy egg and chew. They aren't bad at all.

"You got something on your mouth, there." I gesture toward the top of her lip, but I dust the crumb off before she can wipe it away.

Destiny licks her lips, and I suck in a breath. Hell, I want nothing more than to throw her over my shoulder and haul her to my bedroom. Magnetic energy beckons me to kiss her. My cock throbs, and this is just scratching the surface of my desire.

Almost like we're hypnotized, we both lean in.

Her chest rises, straining her breasts against the fabric of the T-shirt. My breath jolts, and my jaw clenches as I attempt to regain control. It isn't until there's a rattle outside, what I presume to be a branch from the trees around the cabin, that we snap back to reality.

I sit up, swallowing the lump in my throat as I scratch the back of my neck, unsure what to say.

"Uh."

"Klutzy me." Destiny bats her eyelashes and wipes her lips as she straightens. The air grows heavier between us, the temperature upped to the hundreds. At least that's how it feels for me.

I grin. "Oh, hey."

"What?" she asks.

"You called yourself Klutzy," I point out. "You hated that name."

She picks up her fork to stab her omelet and takes a bite before washing it down with orange juice. "Mother Nature and Little Bear were way better pet names than Little Klutzy, believe me."

"It fits you so much more, though." I wink at her.

She rolls her eyes. "Funny."

The rest of the evening goes by without a hitch. She doesn't demand I take her back to Doc Jones, and I like seeing how comfortable she is around me now.

By nightfall, she's yawning, and I motion for her to follow me into the bedroom we'll share tonight—or ***forever*** if she lets me. I nod toward the bed, covered in a giant bearskin rug with loads of big white pillows. "Get comfortable while I shower."

I head to the bathroom for hot water and a bar of soap. The water pelting my aching back is just what I need. But more than anything, I want to take care of my throbbing cock if I'm to survive the rest of the night in peace.

After finishing, I close my eyes, some of my stress washing away with the minty scent of body wash. I distract myself with thoughts of the explosion, the gangsters, my brother—anything but her. There's so much going on. My entire world is changing, but even with the threat so present, Destiny is what consumes my thoughts.

I dry myself before stepping out of the tub and wrapping a towel around my waist. I grab the smaller towel to dry my hair before seeing how my guest is faring.

She sits on the edge of the bed, clicking and scrolling through her phone. I notice her stealing peeps at me. Her lips part, her cheeks flush, and I fight back a grin, knowing she's still very much affected by my body. ***That's good, baby.*** I mischievously smile as I grab clothes, sensing her eyes on me as I allow the towel to drop to the floor.

Her breath catches. I slowly dress, ensuring my muscles ripple as I drag my white undershirt over my torso, then slide on a pair of sweats. Nothing more than sweet revenge.

When I turn to her, she whirls her head away and kicks her feet against the hardwood floor, pretending to be engaged with her phone again.

I rake my fingers through my hair, slicking it back.

"And where will you sleep?" she asks, not paying me much attention.

"In here, of course. Why would you think I'd be showering in this room if I wasn't sleeping here?"

I walk to the left side of the bed. Then, without glancing in her direction, I arrange the pillows, getting ready to settle in.

"Maybe this is the only room with a bathroom?" she shoots back before shrugging. "I don't know. I've never been here."

"I'll give you the complete tour tomorrow. Now get your pretty little ass under the covers."

She gets up from the bed and comes to stand on my side. "I'm not sleeping with you."

I grin, playing along as she shoves me backward until I'm outside in the hall.

But she has another thing coming if she thinks I'm giving up. Now that she's back in my life, I'm keeping her close. ***Very close.*** I want her to know I mean to fight for us.

"Don't you want a personal heater?" I wink as I say it.

She tries to slam the door in my face. "No."

I prowl back inside with a smirk, stepping closer, and backing her up.

She glares and takes another step back. "Carter, don't you dare touch me." The table behind her jabs her in the ass as she retreats, causing her to stumble.

"Careful, Little Klutzy." I take her in my arms and press against her. My breath catches at how she whimpers, her eyes growing hazy as she looks up at me.

"What do you want from me?" she whispers.

"You know I'd never hurt you on purpose. Surely, you knew that back then." My voice cracks as I slide my hand around her nape and push my fingers up through her hair.

"Carter—"

"I know I should—" I take a breath. "Leave your life and pretend we were nothing to each other. But I'm not going to. I'm keeping you. I'll win you back. From now on, I'll keep you safe from everything, even when you get into trouble tripping over your own two feet. I'm never letting you go. Do you understand me?"

"No," she whispers.

"You will," I say before lowering my head to kiss her. Everything goes right in the world. It's like puzzle pieces clicking together.

Heat flames between us before I lean back with a groan. With my hand wound in her hair, I tilt her head to the side. I love the way she gasps before I slant my mouth over hers again. There's nothing gentle about how I kiss her this time, and she takes everything I give, lost in the moment with me.

I slip my tongue into her mouth. My cock hardens when she kisses me back. She ***really*** kisses me back.

Fuck, she's not over me.

Slowly, my other hand slides from her waist to the small of her back to nudge her forward. I run my hand over the fullness of her ass. With how close we are, she has to feel how much I want her by my bulge, separated by just a few thin layers of clothing.

Her hips wiggle, and I hoist her and sit her on the table she bumped into. I hook my fingers into the waistband of her panties, but she jerks back.

Her head thumps against the wall before she shoves me with two hands. My mouth is ripped from hers. "No. This isn't happening."

Damn it. I don't want to stop.

I fight inside.

"Carter—no."

I don't want this to end. I don't want to let her go. But reluctantly, I move back a few inches.

"Okay." I run my hand through my hair and take another step back with a nod. "Okay... Your head okay?"

She rubs the back of it. "It will be."

I pick her up off the table, carry her to the right side of the bed, and look into her eyes. "I promise I'll be on my best behavior for the rest of the night. You can sleep in peace."

I place her down, then slide into my side of the bed. I cover up with the sheet and blanket and interlace my fingers behind my head on the pillow.

Destiny remains unmoving from her spot on top of the covers. "Don't you think you should sleep in the living room? You know... what a ***gentleman*** usually does when they find themselves—"

I turn my head to smile at her. "Fortunately for me, I'm not a gentleman. And it's not our first time, Klutzy, nor is there another bed in this cabin. That's why I chose it. And I'm not sleeping on the couch."

Destiny jumps up, and her hands ball into fists. "Then should I go?"

This woman really isn't giving up on this.

I need to put an end to this conversation.

"It gets cold at night," I explain. "I only installed heat in this here room. You'll be shaking the entire night if you sleep anywhere else."

It's not true, but that gets to her. I fight back the satisfied grin threatening to break onto my face. She hates being cold and will do anything to prevent it, including sleeping with me.

I let out a sigh of contentment, wrapping myself up and making sure she sees and hears every movement. I'd love to see her try arguing with me now. But instead, she remains standing, probably pondering what she should do next.

"Fine... let's all sleep here," she grumbles. Then with determined indifference, she crawls into bed. Her breasts are visible through the T-shirt's neckline while she gets under the covers before she flashes me her black lacy panties as she turns away.

Still showing indifference, she switches off the bedside lamp with a huff.

All the blood starts rushing from my brain to my cock again.

God, this woman is going to kill me.

Chapter 17

CARTER

I've had enough.

It's torture having Destiny beside me, half-naked.

I can't sleep, though exhaustion pours through me, a haze of erotic dreams lingering in my head. My body and mind wage war with each other. The penalty for not having needs met.

I leave our bedroom, still on fire, desperate to have her.

How will I get through the day's work with her on my mind like this?

And the need isn't just to be inside her. That's peripheral compared to the lasting and intimate things I want.

I want her to look at me like she used to. Like I'm the only man for her. I want her to touch me in the erotic ways she used to. The ways that melted my bones. I want us to talk like we're on the same page, with nothing left out or misunderstood.

It used to be like that. And then I blew it.

Outside the cabin, early morning dawns in swirls of red, orange, and golden splashes over the majestic mountains.

The ranch hands are doing their day's work, but no one has time to chat. Every man is on guard, ready for another attack from Atlas. And I need to bury myself in some defense tactics. Forget about what else I want to bury myself in.

The stable it is.

I almost heave a sigh of relief when I'm with the horses. Maybe it's the fact that they won't mock me for the longing and wistfulness probably shining in my eyes to have ***Doctor Destiny Hart*** beneath me. To have her beg me for everything I long to do to her.

I grab a brush and scrape it over Bandit's neck, bringing out the luster in his beautiful black hide.

Footsteps enter the stable. "Howdy, cuz." Dylan comes over to where I'm grooming.

I continue to brush. "Hey."

"How them horses?"

"Ooh." I brush Bandit's long black mane next, smiling at my task. "Pretty good."

Dylan rocks back on his boots. "I hear your cabin is housing a plus one."

There it is. He's digging. I glance at him.

His eyebrows are raised, and his arms are folded across his chest. "That a good idea, Carter?"

I look at Bandit, but my hand doesn't stop brushing. "How the hell would I know?" I sound stupid, but the words are already out of my mouth.

"Where is she this fine morning?" There's a particular amusement in his voice. "And does she like the idea of being held hostage?"

"She's sleeping." My tone tells Dylan I'm in no mood for jokes.

"Hmmm." Dylan takes a brush and focuses on another horse beside mine. "Maybe don't mess it up this time, and it might go how you want it to."

I take a moment to let my guard down. He's my cousin, after all. "Sometimes I think she wants me, and other times—I have a long way to go to get there."

Dylan stops brushing the gray horse and grips my shoulder. "You need to take it slow. Everything that's happened, has happened so fast. And don't forget—she had a life out there before she entered yours. You can't expect her to adapt immediately."

I push my hat back and scratch the frustrating itch on my scalp. "Fair enough."

Everything Dylan says is true. I'm hard on her. I want her to forget the past and dive in with me. Start over. But that's not how life works. I'm going to have to earn her forgiveness.

"You'll have time to woo her," he says. "Don't worry."

"Yeah." But my mind goes to what her stay here means if the bad guys are watching our ranch.

"What is it?" Dylan asks. "You look like you're brooding over something."

"We need to hire some help. To protect the ranch."

Dylan is silent for a while. "Yep."

"I'll talk to Dad when I go to the hospital, but we need to jump on that."

Dylan nods and brushes some more. "I'll start asking around. Make a few calls."

"Sounds good." I nod to my cousin.

When I return to the cabin, Destiny is seated on a stool in the kitchen, talking on the phone. "And she should know I miss her, too." She listens for a second, then laughs.

I linger by the door, glad she hasn't noticed me yet. It allows me to appreciate her for a few minutes, listening to the happiness in her voice.

"Well, Storm is right, Mom. You—" Her words stop because she turns around on the stool and notices me.

There's that name again. Storm.

"Mom, I'll call you back," Destiny says as I stroll to the fridge. "Um… that was my parents," she eventually says. "I was checking up on everything."

"Oh? How are they? They used to live in Wyoming, right?"

"They still do."

"You know, I never met them," I say for conversation's sake, grabbing a bottle of water and heading over to her.

She pushes strands of her dark hair behind her ears before

answering. "Well, we were studying our asses off in Texas. There was never any time."

"I can't believe you just used our education to lie." I grin. "We weren't reading that much. We were doing ***other*** things," I say in a suggestive tone so her mind can wander back to all the sheet tossing we did—nights of hot sex that I wish lasted forever.

Destiny keeps a straight face. "If you weren't studying, that was on you. Because I sure was."

I lick my lips. "Okay."

"Yeah."

The seconds tick on the clock on the far wall.

"So… they've never left?" I'm happy to find a conversation line again. "Your parents, I mean? They never left Wyoming?"

"Why would they? They've struggled for years to hold onto the house and land. It's their home… But of course, you wouldn't know what I'm talking about. You were born into wealth."

Whew.

You're fired this morning, baby!

"That's not… exactly fair."

She swivels on the stool. "The truth isn't always fair."

I lean across the counter, my heart as sober as it can get. "You know if you have any need… anything at all, you only have to ask, and I—"

She leans back on her stool with a funny look and crosses her arms. "Who am I to you to ask for anything?" There's a pause. Then she uncrosses her arms and starts using her hands to gesture while she's talking. "In fact, who do you think you are to even suggest something like that? Are you my boyfriend? My husband? Even then—"

"I'd like—"

She rises abruptly, her face stern. "I would advise you not to say those words." She takes a step toward the door. "I'll go check on the heifers again. Attend to things that ***are*** my job."

I stand straight, my heart sinking. "I'm going to check on my dad at the hospital."

"Send my regards," she throws at me.

We look at each other for a while, neither saying anything nor backing down. But there are things communicated regardless.

I HIT THE ROAD TO THE HOSPITAL, DARK THOUGHTS plaguing my mind. How am I supposed to forget that my father is lying in a damned hospital bed?

I see Dad in Mom's place, in the ground, with all of us standing around his grave. It'll be drizzling—so cliché—just like it was at Mom's burial.

The family still hasn't recovered from her death after all these years.

What will we do if Dad doesn't recover? How do we start rearranging our lives to fit a reality where both parents are gone?

I'm not ready for that.

Fear and worry follow me into the hospital. And Doc Roland makes it worse, itching to give me a report. ***Nothing good can come from a face as somber as his***, I think as I sit in his white office and bounce my knee. He takes his sweet time, fiddling with files on his desk, clearing his throat, opening a drawer, and clearing his throat again.

I think I'll go mad. Right now.

"Doc, can you just tell me what it is? I can take it."

He pauses and looks up at me, something like pity in his eyes. He goes back to fiddling again. "No, that's not it. I'm just looking for—"

"Nothing." I slam my fist on his desk. "You're looking for nothing until you speak to me, damn it. What's going on?"

"Carter Caldwell," he scolds, then finally steadies his gaze on me. "We've successfully run some tests on your father, but I'm afraid we can't diagnose what's wrong yet. What I know is that this ailment is responsible for the malfunction of his organs, which has worsened due to his negligence to come for a proper checkup and get treatment. And then… this accident, as you call it, has made everything worse."

I stare at the doc, my mind in a haze. "But—but you said his condition isn't fatal. I don't understand. What does that mean for Dad?"

"***Not fatal*** doesn't mean ***not critical.*** We'll run more tests. Hopefully, there'll be a diagnosis soon."

Cold spreads through me. "What're you trying to say? That my father's life is hanging by a thread, and you don't know why?" I struggle hard to regain self-control, all my fears seizing me again.

"I'm sorry, Carter, but these things take time. For now, we must keep him here to ensure what's going on and how best we can help him."

"Okay." I'm done trying to understand. "May I see him now?"

He waves a hand. "Of course. I don't think he's awake yet, but you can. Don't agitate him, though. He needs to rest. Be mindful of that."

The doc's words echo in my head as I enter Dad's room. He's awake, sitting in bed, browsing a fishing magazine. But I see how worn out he is, the shadows under his eyes, how pale his skin is. "How're you feeling, ol' man?"

"Carter!" He waves his hand impatiently for me to enter. "What'd Doc Roland say? Can I get out of here?"

"You need to wait for a few more tests." My smile is relaxed, so I don't give anything away. "You'll be out of here soon enough."

"I'm tired. Exhausted with staring at the same things all day." Dad's eyes flash a little, and I'll do just about anything to keep that expression on him. Keep him fighting. Keep him from giving up. "And your brother? Heard from him?"

"No. But we also haven't had any new threats from the gangsters. The ranch is doing great. Don't worry. You focus on getting better."

Knowing Dad, he isn't comfortable here at the hospital instead of being on his ranch. It's already too much. I want to ask his opinion on hiring some extra help—a few bodyguards—and putting extra eyes here and there around home, but I'm going to have to handle this myself. Dad needs to rest. I have to run the place like my father would—without him.

I don't want to leave, but now I have to get back. There's much to do.

"Listen." I place a hand on Dad's shoulder. "I just want to make sure you're okay. And tell you we're okay."

As if on cue, Doc Roland enters with a nurse, and that's my moment to take charge.

"You'll be fine, Dad," I whisper to him before I walk to the parking lot and hit the road back to the ranch, ready to defend. Ready to attack.

Because we're going to fight, Atlas and I… and I'm not losing.

Chapter 18

DESTINY

She's studying me.

"Morning, Lara," I call.

She's sipping coffee in the rocking chair on The Mansion's front porch, her green eyes trained on me.

I've walked the entire way up the grassy hill and across the field, and now I'm panting like an overheated dog.

Lara's expression doesn't change—her eyes don't waver. "Hey there, Doc." She sits up, cradling her mug.

Suddenly, I want a cup of strong coffee, but my body will kill me if I don't drink water first.

"I was worried when I didn't see you and Carter last night," she says. "But Dylan tells us you're staying in one of the cabins? How is it down there?"

Wow! Word travels fast.

"It's beautiful." I smile, knowing what she's getting at, but I have no strength to indulge in talk about Carter's and my private goings-on. ***Or lack thereof.*** I still don't know what to make of him. "And right by the water," I add.

Lara rocks and sips her coffee, not even giving me a nod in return, still judging me.

"You—you hang out here a lot, huh?" I ask because I don't know what else to say, and I am curious why she stays over so much.

"My house is right next door." She stops rocking. "These guys have been my friends since birth. So, why not?"

Why not?

I don't know how to answer her, so I shuffle and stand around like a fool.

Lara finally uncurls herself from the rocker and stands in all of her tall glory. "Come on. Juliet made breakfast."

I follow her inside and sit at the table in the kitchen nook.

Juliet places a huge bowl of oatmeal and two slices of toast in front of me and grins. "We're fancy today."

"Thanks," I say. "It smells incredible." And it really does. I taste the cinnamon and brown sugar already.

Lara slides across from me and picks up her spoon. "Thank you, love."

I crunch my toast and eat a spoonful of oatmeal, gazing out the beautiful bay window. "You know, I envy you all. Living on such a perfect piece of land out here."

"You should see it in the fall," Juliet says. "It's my favorite time of year."

I smile at Juliet, briefly imagining the leaves changing colors —the beautiful orange, yellow, and red array. Then I turn to Lara. "I hear you lived in Paris? I've always wanted to visit."

"With my mother. Yes." She presses her lips together to make it clear this is a troubling subject. "My parents separated years ago, and I went to live with her a few times over there off and on."

I rub my palm up and down my thigh nervously. Here I am, just trying to make small talk, and I bring up the wrong thing. "I'm sorry if I'm bringing up a sensitive subject."

"It's okay." Lara adds some cream to her coffee. "Coming back here has helped with moving on."

"Anyone help with that?" I assume she means ***someone special*** when she gives me that ***knowing*** look. And I'm happy we're moving on to something juicy and light.

"Carter," she says as if I'm supposed to know without her saying it.

"Oh... Well... He must mean a lot to you, then?" I say, a bit too dryly. I hope I'm not coming off as investigative. I bite into my toast, closing my eyes, so no one will see how overly curious I am.

Lara grins and sips coffee with a nostalgic look in her eyes. "Yeah," she drags out. "Carter and I have been best friends forever."

Didn't she already tell me this out on the porch? Is she rubbing it in? I like Lara from what I've seen of her, but knowing Carter helped her through tough times when he deserted me rubs me the wrong way.

"He's too hard on himself," Juliet adds. "He works too hard. He does too much for all of us."

The two women have only hurt my brain, and I spend the entire breakfast ruminating over Carter, and the years we've spent apart.

After breakfast, Lara, Juliet, and I saddle the horses and head to the fields to see if the ranch hands need anything.

"The cows are happy." I grin at the sound of the bellows. I'm back in my element, and the relief coming over me pulls the tension out of my shoulders.

"Come on." Lara jumps from her horse and ties him. "Let's see these happy cattle for ourselves."

Once inside the field, I make my way to where the weak heifer was last seen. Lara and Juliet follow, but my heart rate increases when I discover the area empty.

"Where is she?" I make a desperate scan for the ranch hands. "Sam? You're Sam, right?" I say to one of them.

He looks around briefly before eyeing me curiously. "Yes, ma'am?"

"The weak heifer with the twins..." My panicky voice is riding. "Where is she?"

The poor man stares at me for a second, then smiles. "She's with her calves, ma'am. Come see." He gestures and walks to a fenced-off grazing area.

I sigh with relief when I see the cow grazing with her hyperactive calves. "How long has she been up?"

"All morning. She's good, ma'am." He tips his hat and saunters back to work.

Best news today.

We watch the grazing cattle for a few minutes until I sense Lara's eyes on me again. Only this time, I keep my concentration on the cattle. It's too good watching them. I'm at peace. I don't want to lose that to thinking about Lara and Carter.

"So... Destiny?" Lara begins. "What inspired you to be a veterinarian?"

"I love helping animals." I could go on, but gushing about my passion might not lead anywhere good with her.

"Okay." She nods. Then keeps nodding. There's clearly something she wants to add to this conversation.

I stiffen, preparing myself, and wait.

"And?" she asks.

I glance at her, my heart beginning to thump hard. I lick my lips. "And what?"

"What about Carter?" It's worse when her eyes don't shift from mine, and she locks onto me, expecting me to answer.

I choose the complicated way out to buy myself some time. "What about him? I don't know what you're asking." I look at my hands, then up at her again.

"He told me about you." Lara doesn't mince words. "About the two of you. In Texas. That you were a couple."

I guess we're going there.

"Well... you see, it's complicated." It's not, really. He broke my heart, and I don't know if I'll ever forgive him.

"Do you want to try again with him?" Lara stares at me, dead in the eyes.

I'm not sure what Juliet's doing, gazing off at the cows in front of her, but she's trained on our every word.

"Well—" I wring my hands. "The truth is... I'm scared." I want to tell it straight, but Lara is asking me about something

I've tried to forget. The friend she claims helped her through hard times ruined me. I push on. "I went through a lot."

It's the best I can come up with right now.

Lara puts an arm around my shoulders and shakes me back and forth a few times. "A lot might've happened I don't know about between you two... but I know Carter. He loves fiercely, and uh, the way he looks at you..." A pause lingers between us. "Don't let fear hold you back. Fear will ruin everything. Trust me on that one."

For some reason, the woman I wasn't clear on minutes earlier, is crystal now. She's trying to get me to understand something, and I'm comforted enough to admit my fears.

"It's my heart that isn't sure," I say desperately. "That's the problem."

I look into Lara's piercing green eyes, expecting her to counter my words with some witty remark. I expect her to rise in defense of the man who's her sun and moon, apparently. But she only nods, then gives me a look like I'm a half-wit.

"I get it," she says. "Well, then. C'mon. Let's head back to the horses."

What's she get?

I stare at her perplexedly, but she's already striding toward the ranch hands and the horses in her tight, expensive jeans and cute ponytail.

My head is reeling with the need for answers. "You can't just head back like that," I cry out to her, kicking at a clump of dirt with my boot. "After bringing that up," I mumble under my breath.

Both women look back at me, but I'm far from shame now. I shrug and toss up my hands like Lara had better continue.

"What do you want to hear?" Lara calls. "I already gave you the fairytale answer... follow your heart and all that nonsense."

"You think it's nonsense?"

"It is. But that doesn't mean it isn't real. You have this life ahead of you, just waiting for you, but you're a coward."

What the fuck?

I blink back my surprise. "I'm being careful because... your ***friend*** broke my heart, and I don't know if I can trust him with it again. If you spent less time judging me and actually asking me questions, maybe you'd understand why taking a risk on a fairytale with that man is the most dangerous thing I'd ever do."

Everyone stares at me.

Lara's face changes. Her lips pull into a smile that almost borders endearment.

What's she doing? Playing with me?

"You've got fire, Doc. I like it. You'll do okay."

I open my mouth, but nothing comes out for a second until I collect myself. "Were you testing me?"

"Around here, Carter's world is tough." She twists her lips. "And you're going to have to be tougher and fight. You have nothing to prove to me, Destiny." She gives a little shrug. "But you and Carter have plenty to prove to each other."

SOMETIMES FOOD CAN FIX MATTERS.

Or take your mind off of hot men—a ***certain*** hot man in particular.

I don't stop at The Mansion to visit with Lara and Juliet after we put our horses away.

I want to make lunch at the cabin so I have something to focus on before Carter and I have a talk.

Lara kept hammering on what I was feeling, and she's right.

I ***am*** still in love with Carter, and yes, I'm still angry at him for all he did. But this situation is tricky. One I can't fully wrap my head around sometimes. I'm a fool for wanting him, but then I'd be a liar if I told myself none of the love is real.

So... I wouldn't mind us talking and digging into our past.

We may not be able to address everything, but we can begin somewhere.

Carter must still be at the hospital, because he's not at the cabin, and I use the privacy his absence allows for singing in the shower with my music blasting from my cell phone.

I dress in some of the things he got for me; a rose-colored T-shirt and some little black cotton shorts that are a too short, but I don't want to rationalize all of this right now. I'm content with just letting it flow for the moment.

I pull my hair back and work my way around the cabinets. I locate pots and utensils before whipping up a pasta dish with plenty of sauteed veggies. Pineapple slices are in the fridge, a bunch of bananas on the kitchen table, and some apples, so I make a fruit salad. My singing doesn't end as I rinse a bowl and begin slicing the bananas into it.

Lunch is about ready when Carter enters, his boots sounding over the hardwood flooring.

"Wow. Something smells good." He removes his boots and tosses his hat on a chair while I arrange the fruit salad into two wooden bowls. Rubbing his hands together, he takes a seat. "What's the occasion?"

"Just a quick lunch." My voice is casual. I sit beside him and start eating my delicious creation. "How's your dad?"

Carter stabs some pasta and gives me a half-shrug, but there's pain in his eyes. "They're running some tests."

I reach out, not overthinking, and place my hand on his forearm. "I'm sorry."

He holds the fork with the pasta, staring at my hand. Then he licks his lips and roams his gaze over my outfit.

"Umm." I remove my touch, feeling tingly. "That uh—that weak heifer was up and grazing with the others when I went out to check on them. When I didn't see her at first, I thought something bad had happened, but Sam took me to her," I babble on. "They're looking good. I don't think you'll have too many more problems."

"It's like you belong here." Carter studies me after saying the words. "Like you've ***always*** belonged here."

My heart shatters. Doesn't he know everything he's put me through? And why do I keep hanging onto that like a ***fucking*** broken record? Here I am again, my damn heart aching, making me fucking mad all over again.

"What did you say?" I drop my fork and focus on him. I need to hear him repeat it because I'm going to throttle him. I swear. Then I'm going to throttle myself.

And just like I thought, he's speechless, staring at me with that damn forkful of pasta. I want to grab that pasta off his fork and throw it at him. I'm reliving the past and playing out the future we never had, the future where I live here with him. Where I belong here with him.

And the person who prevented it was him.

I pick up my fork, stab a piece of broccoli, and eat it.

On second thought, he should continue being speechless. It's the best thing to do at the moment.

"I understand a lot, Destiny, so don't mistake me for not getting you," he says sternly. "But why are you so angry with me? Why do you hate me so much?"

I could slap the words right out of his mouth.

I don't want to be mad at him anymore, I really don't. It's just that so much is on the line. So much he doesn't know about.

I squint my eyes at him. "You really want to know?"

Chapter 19
CARTER

Do you have another man to go back to? Is that it?

The question radiates in my bones as I stare at her pushing her broccoli around. She presses her mouth together as if she's fighting inner demons—or fighting stabbing me with that utensil.

A frustrated sound emits from my throat before I can stop it. "Do you really want to leave me?"

"Would you even let me?" She stabs her food a few more times and squares her shoulders. "I can't be with you just because you ***decided*** to be a part of my life again."

"Why the hell not?"

"Are you seriously asking me this?" She throws her hands up, the fork flying to the table again. "Do I have to remind you that bumping into each other was a coincidence? If I'd ***wanted*** to find you all those years ago, don't you think I could have?"

That stings, but I understand. I go rigid for the fight ahead and point at the two of us. "This, between us? It should be fucking permanent. It should've always been permanent."

"That's coming from ***your*** lips?" Her dark eyes widen. "What about the drama in your life right now?" She gives me that feisty attitude I love. "The drama between your prestigious Caldwell family and the Mafia? Or whatever's going on around here?"

"No one's gonna hurt you. I'm making sure of that."

She snorts, crossing her arms. "I'm not getting involved with all of this. Not right now."

I take a bite of the pasta and chew. "But I'm a changed man. Things are going to be different—"

"That's just a word, Carter."

"What?"

"Change is just a word. It doesn't mean anything until it's proven. I don't trust you," she whispers and licks her lips. "I ***can't*** trust you."

Her words twist in my soul. "Because I left back then? All of this hate because of that?"

"Yep. But much more. So much more." She rubs her arms as if she's cold. "You never explained what happened after your mother passed. You never returned to explain ***anything.***"

I run my hand through my hair. If only she knew the truth. But I don't want to talk about my past, let alone what I did back then. She'll hate me more than ever.

"And who's to say you won't get yourself killed with all this stuff at your ranch?" she fires at me.

I stiffen. "I won't."

She scoffs and picks up her fork again. "You don't know that, Carter."

My heart begs to clear up this miscommunication, but I can't. I can't put these problems on her, make her accept a side of me I want no one to know about. Not with all that's going on.

"My heart ***broke*** for you," she says. "But you didn't think about what you were leaving when you didn't return." She points her fork at me, another piece of broccoli trembling on the end of it. Her voice rises as she looks up at the ceiling. "But you know what? I'm not having this conversation because I can't now. I thought maybe I could, but I can't. It's just ***too*** late."

She throws her fork down, gets up, and heads toward the door. Except she's barely able to get there before I do. I block her path, wedging myself into the doorframe.

"Move, Carter."

"Pursuing you again is the first selfish thing I've done in a long while."

She rolls her eyes, then tries to push past me. When I press against her, she wiggles and then jabs my chest with her index finger. "You selfishly left without including me in what happened."

"No. No… that's not what happened."

"Look, I have to make the best choice for me now because you didn't make the right choice for us." She tries to escape under my arm. "So fucking let me go. You don't need me. You need ***your*** family. You need ***your*** ranch. This is over. This is done."

I put my hand out. "But—"

"You left me pregnant and disappeared, asshole!"

It's almost as if the world stills at her words. I think it does.

My brain goes numb.

Destiny steps backward, her chest heaving, and puts a good amount of distance between us. It's in her eyes, the truth, resting there. As if she's held on to this secret for years, and now that it's finally out in the open, she's flooded with relief. Even if I wanted to doubt her and call her a liar, her eyes tell me everything I need to know.

I grab ahold of the doorjamb before I fall. "What?"

I can't formulate words as I stare into her eyes, trying to catch my breath and make sense of everything she's saying.

There isn't a chance we have a child? There isn't a chance this entire time I've not only allowed the love of my life to escape through my fingers but our child, too?

Except the more I think about it, the more it makes sense. The reason why she wants to leave me. The reason why she doesn't want to get close to me.

Thousands of questions flood into my head.

If we have a child, do we have a boy or a girl? Where are they?

Everything spins as the room becomes stuffy—the walls

close in, threatening to suffocate me. I'm a caged animal, needing space, but my feet are rooted to the floorboards.

A part of me screams to leave, get away from everything until I can clear my thoughts. But I refuse to budge an inch, as another more prominent part of me wants to stay and listen—to deal with this. After all, if I walk away from us this time, it's over for good. And I wouldn't blame her.

A painful throbbing starts in my head, and the guilt in my gut grows.

I hate how much I've fucked up with us.

She looks at me with those piercing eyes that unman me. "So you can see why you can't walk back into my life as if nothing happened." She shakes her head, looking away. "Because something did happen, and I handled it all alone."

I deserve what I'm getting. If it makes up for the hurt I've caused, I don't mind her hating me. But watching her shut me out, the thought of losing hope, is too much. "Destiny—"

"Now I've told you. You can leave me alone," she breathes out as she goes under my arm to exit the cabin.

I don't know where she's going without her coat, shoes, and purse.

I hoist her back by the waist. "This changes nothing between us."

"Children need stability, Carter." She squirms in my arms. "Something you won't be able to provide with your chaos right now. Much less explain why her father has been missing for over ten years."

I swipe my tongue across my lips. "You said ***her***? A girl? I have a daughter?"

Destiny straightens and gives a curt nod. I know she's debating telling me more. I'm begging with my eyes.

"Yes. ***My*** daughter's name is Storm."

Destiny and Storm. I love how both names have a double meaning.

"Storm," I repeat. I need to know more about this child.

She's my daughter, too. I run the back of my fingers up Destiny's cheek, but she doesn't lean into my touch the way she used to. Instead, she fights to hold back. "Please don't walk away from us."

"There is no *us*," she answers, her voice cracking. "Not anymore."

"I know you still have feelings for me." I battle on. "I knew it from our kiss."

"Do you think you're the only guy I've kissed like that?"

I know what she's trying to do. She'd rather have us fighting than be vulnerable and open to the chance of us again.

I tighten my arm around her. "I dare you to look me in the eye and tell me you don't want me."

She doesn't tell me she doesn't want me because she can't. Instead, she tries pushing past me again. She can only take one step before I grab her around the waist and crash her against my chest.

Without giving her a chance to react, I kiss her. And she responds, both of us feverish and desperate. There's no initial tentative kiss, no buildup to the waves of desire. There's only crashing, pulling, and breaking.

I slide a hand into her hair, and she arches her back so the swell of her breasts pushes against my chest. I pull her hips against mine, and my cock hardens.

She muffles a moan, and a smile makes its way to my mouth before I slide my tongue past her lips. She accepts, and I deepen our kiss. I slip my hands beneath her shirt, groaning as I caress her soft skin when she sighs and quivers at my touch.

While one of her hands fists my shirt, the other rakes her nails around my neck. She grinds hard against my erection. The way her body fits against mine is becoming unbearable. Her erect nipples brush against me, making me shudder.

Destiny is my anchor, and I can't think of anything besides the scent of her skin and the addictive taste of her lips.

Then before I can process it, she shoves me away. Her nose flares before she storms onto the porch and grips the railing.

It must be a step in the right direction if she's not running to her truck. I'm gaining ground.

Without another thought, I open the screen door, and the scent of the water and the cool afternoon breeze greets me. It blows away heat as I stand beside her, leaning against the railing.

All around us, the sound of the outdoors drowns out the thoughts screaming in my head. Taking a deep breath, I close my eyes and focus. Once I open them, I'm calmer. Finally, I pull out the words that have been resting in my throat since the moment she returned. "I'm sorry."

And they couldn't be more accurate, especially now. She had my child, my little girl, all alone. Things we should've done together, she did alone. I missed Storm's birth and ten years of her life. Ten years of memories I could've made with them both.

"I don't want your apology." She brushes her hair back. Her eyes find mine before focusing on the lake. "You know, I waited every day for you. Everyone told me you weren't returning, but I kept waiting."

I hate what she's saying, but I force myself to listen.

"I went back to every spot we made ours, hoping to find you." Her eyes gloss over. "God, you have no idea how pitiful I looked. I kept hoping you'd come back. That you'd realize you'd made a terrible mistake like in those sappy movies we saw."

I didn't, baby, because I was in prison.

"Weeks went by," she continues when I say nothing. "It didn't take long before I began to resent you. It only got worse after I found out I was pregnant. It was storming the day I found out, a brewing storm that captured exactly how I felt. I hated you for leaving. I hated how hollow I became, but I had to live—"

I nod. "For our daughter?" I whisper.

"***My*** daughter," she corrects.

I know I shouldn't ask, but it slips out. "May I—may I see her?" I hold my breath. Destiny doesn't owe me anything, but I pray she'll let me see our child. I want to know everything. What she looks like and likes doing… the little things that make up how perfect she must be. "Where—where is she right now?"

"With my parents." Destiny sits on the bench against the cabin's wall. "Storm and I have an apartment near the vet's clinic, but we often go to Mom and Dad's. We usually stay there on the weekends. Storm has her horse there, too."

I follow Destiny to the bench. Ever so slowly, she pulls out her phone. She flicks to her albums, and I hold my breath as she turns the phone toward me.

I choke back a sob. Even though I've never met Storm, she embodies Destiny. Laughing as she rides a pony.

Our daughter.

Her cheekbones and forehead are a lot like mine. She has my eyes, and they're brimming with excitement as she grins at the camera.

Almost as if Destiny's reading my mind, she smiles warmly at the photo. "When she opened her eyes and stared at me for the first time, I couldn't help but cry because her eyes are like yours. And I knew at that moment she would be my world."

"I didn't know." I hold back my own tears. "I didn't know."

She hands me the phone, and I swipe. The more I look at Storm, the more I fall in love.

"I didn't want you to find out."

"Were you going to keep her from me forever?" More words I shouldn't say, but I have so many questions.

"You didn't have the right to know," she reminds me. "You were never supposed to find out."

Destiny gets up. She makes her way inside, though she turns to me before she shuts the door. "Love, you know—sometimes it isn't enough. And if you ever loved me, you'll walk away. This time, it's what ***I*** want."

"I won't," I tell her. I'm going to turn this around. Fate brought us together, and I'll fight for Storm and Destiny both.

"You will, especially now that your family is involved with the Mafia. My daughter is my world, and nothing is going to happen to her. You're not going to break her like you broke me."

She slams the door, leaving me with my thoughts. I run a hand through my hair as I walk to the edge of the porch and gaze over the shimmering water.

Damn. Things are worse than ever between us.

Chapter 20
ATLAS

I need a break, but I won't catch one.

My phone pings, and I glance away from the road. ***And here we go.*** Maestro Vincenzo, my boss' second in command and his best friend. I'm expecting his call.

I tap the green button. "Maestro Vincenzo."

I flip on the signal for my exit to the town of Wind Dance. It's about forty-five minutes from the cabin. I need to pick up supplies and have instructed my men to watch Raven while I'm away.

"Have there been signs of the cowboy?" Maestro Vincenzo's voice is stern. After working under him for years, I know he's not in a good mood from his tone. "What's the status of the little fucker?"

"Still hiding. Or dead."

"You losing your edge, Atlas?"

"He's the son of a billionaire cattleman in the middle of nowhere." I keep the defensiveness out of my voice. "His family are probably hiding him."

Maestro Vincenzo slams his fist on something solid. "Fucking find him, Atlas."

I grip the steering wheel to keep my cool. "Have I ever disappointed you, Maestro?"

"It's not like you to take this long."

"I certainly don't want to be out here with the cows." I humorlessly laugh. I figured blowing up the Caldwell's house would draw Tanner out. "You know, unlike in the city, where everyone has a digital footprint, there's nothing but grass out here."

There's a pause so long that I think Maestro has hung up.

"Where's this billionaire Malcolm Caldwell now?" he finally asks.

"I've put him in the hospital. His son Carter is in charge now."

The line goes dead.

Rolling my eyes, I park the Range Rover in front of the local market. As usual, my appearance draws stares as I walk in, but I scowl at them. Once I get my hands on Tanner, I'm taking a first-class trip out of this shit state.

Since I get to choose what we're eating later for dinner, I decide on spaghetti, which I'll instruct Rocco to prepare. Then I get milk and a medicine dropper to feed Raven's kit before my gaze lands on a basket-type storage bin with a lid.. I grab it, my thoughts flashing to the soggy cardboard box Raven keeps the creature in. It's starting to emit an offensive odor from whatever it's been through, and it's time for it to go. The last thing I want is for my room to smell like feces.

I throw two cans of lavender air freshener into the cart, making sure they say ***all natural***. Knowing Raven, that'll be an issue if it has chemicals or some shit like that in it.

Turning into the next aisle, I grab some lettuce and carrots. ***That's what rabbits eat?***

I grab some romance and suspense novels from a display. It's surprising what you can learn from these things. Since Raven needs distractions, maybe she'll read.

I also toss a black journal into the cart, along with some colored pens. Perhaps giving her something to focus on will keep her from spiraling out of control and murdering us all.

After I finish shopping, I drive another way back to the cabin. I want to scope out the Caldwells' ranch and see if anything's changed there.

I'm dancing with death since Carter knows what I look like. He probably has his own hits out on me now. I briefly imagine what kind of fight I'd have with a bunch of cowboys. An authentic Western standoff. What a story it would be.

I cruise past his gated spread, glancing up at where his house once stood. There's nothing salvageable.

The sun is getting low when I return to the cabin.

Rocco whistles at how much I'm carrying as I shuffle in. He grabs several paper bags. "Bought the entire store, huh?"

"Funny." I look around. "Where the hell is Raven?"

"In your room." Marcello taps away on his computer. He looks up, arching a brow, and scratches his beard. "She's been talking nonstop to that rabbit and her crows. If you ask me, she's about to raise a zoo."

"What took you so long, Boss?" Rocco puts the items in their designated spots. "I was getting worried."

"I drove by the Caldwells' place." I grab a bottle of water before sliding into the seat across from Marcello. "The place is completely gone. And not a stir from Tanner."

Marcello shrugs. "I guess he's just a big pussy."

I untwist the cap on the bottle. "Or very smart."

Rocco holds two jars of pasta sauce. "What do you mean?"

"Tanner might know this is a trick to draw him out," I hypothesize. "Marcello? Any changes?"

He groans, running his hand through his short hair. "Nothing."

"Well, keep searching." I drink the water. "The faster we do this, the faster we leave this shit place and return to our regularly scheduled lives."

Marcello sighs. "You're telling me."

"In the meantime," I say to Rocco, "make us some dinner."

"Why can't Marcello do it?"

"The last time he did, we got food poisoning," I remind him. "We don't need a repeat."

Rocco holds the jars of pasta sauce over his head for

dramatic effect. "Fine, I'll make dinner."

I take the water bottle and the other two bags to my room.

Raven turns to me as I enter, wearing only my T-shirt, with the window wide open. I don't understand how she's not frozen. Two crows perch on the windowsill, their beady eyes staring at me as if I've interrupted something important.

At least she hasn't brought bats into my room.

She smiles, stroking the kit cradled in the crook of her arm like a baby. Then, she looks up at me. "You're back," she breathes out.

I set the items out on the bed, and she admires them curiously like she can't believe they're real. She blinks a few times before placing the kit on the floor. It scurries around before stopping at one of my shoes.

"You bought gifts?" she asks excitedly.

"Necessities," I correct. I don't get anyone ***gifts.*** "Most of it is rabbit shit, so he doesn't rip my bedroom to pieces. I got a bin so you can throw away the infested one. And a journal for when you need to work out your thoughts."

Why the fuck do I sound nervous?

I pick up the journal and the colored pens and place them in front of her face.

Ever so slowly, she takes them, our fingers brushing. Her mouth curls upward. "Thank you." She picks up the kit again, adding it to the pile in her arms. "Isn't this wonderful, Starlight?"

"You named it Starlight?"

"Isn't it fitting?" She giggles before joining the birds, who seem to be waiting for her. She starts to hum to them as she sets up an area for the kit.

I sit at the table and open my laptop to reply to emails.

"Food is ready," Rocco calls after a while.

I glance at my phone. Somehow an hour has passed. I open the door for Raven, and she sets the creature into the bin before following me.

The scent of tangy pasta sauce and warm spaghetti makes my mouth water as I take a seat at the island. Raven sits beside me. It's the first time she's joined us for a meal, and Rocco and Marcello eye her. She thanks the ***Chosen One***, and I roll my eyes when my men give me an amused snicker.

Everyone picks up their forks and digs in. Everyone except Raven. She uses her fingers.

"You know we have utensils?" Marcello asks between a mouthful of spaghetti. "You—you do know what a fork is, right, Raven?"

Rocco laughs, his hefty chest puffing. "Are we about to see a reenactment of ***The Little Mermaid***?"

My lips tug upward. "You watched ***The Little Mermaid***?"

Rocco slurps his pasta. "I was a kid once."

Raven sucks her fingers. "My friend Uma taught me that eating food with my fingers feeds not only my body but also my mind and spirit."

"What do you mean?" Marcello asks.

"Each finger represents the five elements. The hand is mighty. Our fingers create a connection with the food. It enhances our awareness. We are Earth's children, after all."

"This friend of yours—where is she?" I ask.

She smiles sadly and picks up a single strand of spaghetti. "She's joined the soil. Her soul set free."

The way Raven eats as if she's rationing food doesn't sit well with me. Something about it reminds me of what I used to do as a child, starving in a boy's home.

"She's dead?" I ask for clarification.

Raven's expression is light. "The soul doesn't die, silly. She's around. Protecting and guiding me."

Eerily enough, a bird lands on the windowsill and caws. I'll be damned if that's Uma.

"So… you're saying you're… haunted?" Rocco's face pales, a meatball hanging from his fork.

"***Protected***," Raven corrects, then looks at me, her large eyes sparkling. "Do you believe in spiritual beings?"

"No."

"Hmm." Her eyes turn toward the spaghetti dish in the table's center. "I forgot to offer some to my friends. Do you mind?" But she's already going for the leftover food.

Almost as if the birds understand her, they flap their wings at the window.

Rocco shakes his head. "I'm telling you... ***a witch,*** " he whispers.

I clear my throat and continue to eat.

Needless to say, a dysfunctional group.

AFTER DINNER, I HEAD TO MY BEDROOM WITH RAVEN A stairstep in front of me. She goes straight for her kit and cuddles it in one arm, while I snap on the light in the closet and rummage through my clothes until I find what I'm looking for. I toss a gray hoodie to her. She grabs it, then wraps her creature up.

"It's for you to wear." Irritation laces my voice. I gave her the T-shirt she's wearing just hours ago, only for her to ruin it with her disgusting eating habits. By the end of the week, I'll have nothing clean. "Now, put it on."

She frowns, her lips pressing together for a second. "Why?"

Clearly she's not seeing the same mess I am. I point at the absurd number of stains on her shirt. "You have sauce all over you."

She places the kit on the bed and strips off the T-shirt, leaving herself naked.

Christ, the woman has no modesty.

Her nipples are hard with the cold air from the open window. If it's closed, the birds start clacking their beaks against it, so I have no choice but to leave it ajar for them.

When she fumbles and gets stuck putting the hoodie on, I stalk over and force her into it.

"I'm going to take a shower," I hiss. Maybe after I jerk off, I'll be able to think straight.

"Okay." She hums and walks to the window where the birds are cawing at her.

"Under no circumstances are you allowed to go anywhere outside this room. Do you understand?" I instruct, then glance at the kit on my bed. I swear the stubborn creature understands what I'm saying—its ear perks, almost like it's arching a brow at my order.

"I understand." Raven nods, playing with the hoodie's hem, then tends to her creature.

"You're never to strip in front of another person, do you understand me?"

I'm cursing myself out when she frowns. "Why?"

Of course out of everything she wants to ask me, I don't have an answer to that. I don't fucking know why. "I said so." I grab a pair of boxers and an undershirt just as two pesky birds hop indoors.

Raven giggles, holding the kit to her cheek. "You remind me of Avril."

Another name added to the mix of people shrouded in mystery. "Another one of your friends?"

"No, silly." She laughs, her body shaking as if I've said the funniest thing, before she returns to the window and gasps.

I reach for my gun, assuming we're in danger. That is, until she turns to me, her eyes brimming with excitement as she bounces up and down.

"Oh, I just remembered. It's going to be a full moon tonight."

I'm having a hard time following.

"If there's a full moon, we have to get some moon water. It's great for cleansing and—Avril was drowning in a lake when I stumbled upon her, you know."

"Raven?" I instruct after she jumps around to different subjects. "Focus."

"Huh?"

"Who is Avril?"

Raven smiles. "She's one of my sisters who also joined the soil. Avril was the oldest of us. She hated birds. She was scared of them. So her soul will never reside with a crow. But I think she's one with the wind because she always loved running."

So, she's dead like Uma. And this crazy girl still makes no sense.

Then my gaze falls on the black feather with the red twine attached. I forgot I left it on the laundry basket when I threw my vest in for Rocco to wash. Now I remember Raven saying this twine ties us together.

What was the word? Lupilia—family.

There's so much about her I don't understand. But now is a better time than ever to get some answers. Especially if I'm going to be able to use her for anything. I pick up the feather and place it in front of her. "You said we're connected?"

"Yes. The red cord of destiny."

"What does that mean?"

"It's magical. The cord can stretch. It can get tangled. But it won't ever be severed. Destiny ties us together, regardless of place, time, or circumstance. And that makes sense because the spirits led me to you. The one to save everyone."

"Save everyone from what?"

She steps back and rubs her temple. "Sometimes I remember. Sometimes I don't."

"Where did you, Uma, and Avril meet?" I set the feather on the nightstand.

Raven tenses as she strokes the kit, her breathing ragged. "They call it the Kindergarten."

"Who does?"

"M-my master... He taught me to be the perfect pet to the elites, but later, he wanted me for his own."

Christ. I have a hard time logging all the information. "Do you know who you are?"

"Raven."

"Eh, before you were taken?"

"I–I remember," she says, running fingers through her long black hair, "my adoptive father was a mayor in our town. He's not always a good man. He didn't love me like the way he loved Mother or Izzy. But it makes sense. I'm not his. My mother asked him to adopt me after they married."

Interesting. Raven does remember some things. "What happened to your parents? To Izzy?"

"I don't know because I can't remember. We were driving to our summer house. We had to leave right away. I'm not sure why. Then everything got hazy. When I woke up, I was in the Kindergarten."

Which means her father—her parents—might've been a target. My bet is her sister has probably been taken, too. I need to get Marcello to investigate her family more. "I see."

"When will you save the others?" she whispers.

I look into her hopeful eyes. If only she knew I have no interest in playing hero. I know my place in this world. The spirits have led her to a monster who will extort her only for his gain.

Not wanting to ruin this illusion for her right yet, I do what I do best. Control the situation. "We'll talk about it later."

She's content enough with the answer for now, and she smiles at me. "Thank you."

Once I get into the shower, I lean against the tiles. ***Fuck me.*** This situation is a mess, and if it weren't for Raven being the mayor's daughter, it would be best to kill her.

When I return to interrogate her, she's asleep with her stupid pet.

I look at the ceiling.

What the ***hell*** is wrong with me, and what the ***hell*** am I going to do with her?

Chapter 21

CARTER

I've missed out on so much.

Storm.

I have a little girl whose life I never got to be a part of for over ten years because of my need for vengeance. There're so many firsts I've missed with her. Her first words. Her first steps. Her first birthday. I haven't been there for any of those things. I haven't been there for ten years' worth of experiences.

And now, how am I supposed to win over not only Destiny but our daughter, too?

For the first time in my life, I'm walking a thin line to ensure I get everything right.

My thoughts move to a darker place. There may be no point in pushing myself into their lives when they've lived without me for so long.

Is it selfish to ask them to change everything for me? To make me fit into what already works for them?

The thoughts settle, sinking into the pit of my stomach and leaving me heavy with dread. Then, like a light switch flipped on, my heart catches up to my head. I ***won't*** live without them.

I'll do everything in my power to win them back.

The breeze blowing across the porch is just what I need to calm this raging fire inside me, and I'm grateful for it.

Destiny steps onto the porch with two cups of coffee and hands me one.

"Thank you." I take the cup from her. I want to be cautious.

Understanding. Not move too fast. But I can't keep from whispering, "I want to see her."

She wraps a blanket around her shoulders and leans against the railing overlooking the lake. "I know."

She doesn't seem shocked at my request, almost as if she's been waiting for me to say it, and I'm swallowing sharp needles at my next question. "Will you keep her from me?"

"I should," she says in her usual snap, but the fierceness doesn't reach her eyes. "But I realize what happened between us shouldn't impact our daughter. I won't stop her from seeing you if that's what she wants."

The breath I didn't know I'd been holding comes out in a rush. "Thank you."

"I'm not doing this for you." Destiny takes a sip from her mug. "I'm doing it for her."

I'm itching to learn everything about our little girl, so I settle with a basic question. "What's she like?"

Destiny's face changes from stern to wistful as she considers the question. She stares into the distance, and the warmest smile pulls at her mouth. "She's courageous and brilliant. I wish she weren't as stubborn as a bull when things don't go her way, though. Much like her father."

That earns a chuckle from me. ***Fair enough.*** But if Destiny thinks Storm is stubborn, then she should know what I'll do to win her back. I puff out my chest. "I think that's a compliment."

There's a look of unconditional love on Destiny's face. "She's a total sweetheart—and knows how to charm her grandparents to get anything she wants."

Grandparents... Destiny's mom and dad. Suddenly, I'm overwhelmed with the idea that they, like Destiny, believe I abandoned them all. That's just two more people I have to prove myself to. "Your parents probably hate my guts."

"Well..." Destiny chuckles. "They dote on Storm, so it's helped. You should've seen Mom on Storm's tenth birthday.

Since it was her first double-digit, she got the biggest cake I've ever seen, and Dad got her a horse."

I eat up everything Destiny says, trying to learn about all I've missed, and I can't help but wonder about this alternate life I could've had. The life of a father who helped plan birthdays and taught his daughter how to ride her first bike and horse—a father who tucked her in at night and read her stories. But most importantly, she needed a father who made promises he fulfilled.

"If you like, you can hear her voice," Destiny says, placing her mug down. "But I don't want you to say anything to her just yet, okay? Not until I speak to my parents and talk with Storm."

"Yeah," I rush and gulp. "Whatever feels right."

I'm on the edge of my seat as she takes out her phone, presses the contact, then hits the speaker button. She gives me one last stern look. "Not a word, Carter."

I hold up three fingers. "Scout's honor."

Destiny snorts, probably questioning whether I really was in the Scouts, before the call goes through.

"Hi, Mom," Storm sings, and my heart fills at the sound of her voice, all cheerful and full of innocence. I bite my tongue, willing myself not to shout out who I am.

"Hello, munchkin," Destiny says, and it tugs at my heart.

"Mom! I'm ten now."

"I know. I know."

Storm giggles. "I miss you."

"I miss you more. How was school yesterday?"

"It was good." Storm babbles about her day, and with each passing second, my smile grows wider. She's smarter than most kids, maybe most people. Of course, I could be biased, but who cares. "Wait… Grandma wants to speak to you."

Destiny laughs. "Okay."

"Destiny? You okay, honey? I was worried when you didn't answer my last text," her mom scolds.

"Yeah. Sorry, Mom. I've been busy at work. I'm okay. Everything is fine."

"That fella better be paying you well out there," her dad chimes in from the background.

"Oh, for sure, Dad," Destiny says, a little sarcastically, smirking. "In fact, he's tripling my pay."

"That's wonderful news," her mom exclaims, clearly oblivious to the goad in her daughter's voice. "Well, let us know when you'll be back."

"Very soon," Destiny says. "Let me finish up here. Kiss Storm twice for me."

"I will," her mom says before the line goes dead.

My head spins, and I swear I'll never forget that voice. It'll forever rent space in my head, a reminder that somewhere out there, a part of Destiny and me is living. I grin. "Wow."

"As I said, I'm doing this for her sake," she says. "Now... I have to leave sometime today and get back to my daughter. I'm pushing my luck with my parents. They love her, of course, but I have to get back. Maybe sometime soon... everyone can arrange to meet."

Her gaze is on me, but I stay fixated on the lake before me. I don't want to ruin this perfect moment.

"And I have to return to the clinic," she continues. "I know Doc Jones is waiting for me, and I have a busy schedule to get back to."

And what if Atlas is waiting, tracking us, and will follow Destiny? ***What if he follows you home, and I'm not there to protect you all?*** I should give her an answer right now, given what she just told me. But I almost lost my dad, and the wound is still gaping. Nothing has been fixed, and no leads have been found—the threat is real.

And that threat could take more from me.

"Still a no," I finally say.

For a moment, I figure she'll fight me. But instead, she sighs, shaking her head before walking into the cabin, tossing down her blanket, and grabbing her jacket.

"Destiny," I call after her, but she ignores me, going straight for her bag. I don't allow her enough time before jumping from the bench and snatching her keys. If looks could kill, I'd be six feet under.

"What're you doing?" she spits out.

I'm thankful for my height because even as she's stepping on my boots and struggling, it's to no avail.

"Carter, this isn't funny. I need my keys."

I'm not letting her out of my sight with Atlas out there. "No," I repeat, trying something else to discourage her from leaving. "You're going to talk this shit out with me."

"What's there left to talk about?" she snaps. I notice how she inhales sharply when I use my other hand to hold her waist, hoisting her against me.

"Us."

"There's no *us*," she maintains, though we both know it isn't true.

"The hell there isn't." That's when she claws at my shirt and goes to walk right through me. If she knew the only thing she's doing is rubbing against my half-hardened cock, I think she'd cease her antics.

Then Destiny gasps, and she wrinkles her nose. "Are you fucking getting an erection right now?"

"I'm always ready when it comes to you, baby." I chuckle, feeling a flush of embarrassment. "Now, have a seat."

"I'm going to get fired from my job, Carter. Unlike you… swimming in money, I need my job."

The remark makes me pause. I form a plan. "Your boss is Doc Jones, correct?"

"You know that," she draws out the words. "Now, give me my keys."

Rather than giving them to her, I reach for my phone on the table. She's right behind me, seeming confused.

"Who're you calling?"

"Doc Jones."

Her mouth falls open as the line clicks through. "Mornin'. This is Carter Caldwell. May I speak to Doc Jones, please?"

"Mister Caldwell?" he says after a moment, seeming to understand who I am. "Good morning. Is everything okay out there? How's Doctor Hart?"

"Everything is perfect. In fact, Doc Hart has been amazing here at Three Rivers Ranch. The Caldwell family is indebted. But we need her here for a bit longer."

"Oh?"

"There are still some complications with the cattle, and I'd like her to remain here to ensure everything goes well," I ramble as Destiny crosses her arms. "Of course, your best vet is being taken care of, and she's saving these calves by herself."

I see Destiny rolling her eyes off to the side, but she's pleased at the same time. The blush on her cheeks spreads, and I wink at her.

"Is that right?" Doc Jones asks with a chuckle. "Well, I'm not surprised. Doctor Hart is great at what she does."

"It would truly be an honor to have your understanding in the matter." I go in for the kill. "We'll generously compensate the clinic for her absence if I have your approval."

"It won't be a problem," he quips. "Thank you for letting us know, Mister Caldwell."

"I should be thanking you, Doc Jones." Then, satisfied, I hang up and turn to Destiny with a huge grin. "You can stay. And you're to give me the necessary details for your compensation."

She blinks. "You've resorted to kidnapping and bribery now?"

"Well, you did tell your parents I was about to triple your pay. So it's all a win-win. Give me the details. I'm paying for your time, and then if anything happens to the calves, you're here."

"Fine," she grumbles. She grabs a piece of paper and a pen and scribbles before handing the paper to me.

"Thank you. I'll be sure to give this to my accountant." I tuck the paper into my pocket before going to the kitchen.

She drops her coat and bag—a good sign.

I glance at her, dangling the keys to her truck on my finger. "I'll be keeping these."

She shakes her head at me.

After a much-needed second to settle ourselves, she changes clothes, and we ride out to check on the ranch hands and the calves again.

"Mister Caldwell. Doc Hart." Bill greets us, walking over and tipping his hat. "Afternoon to ya."

"Howdy, Bill," I say. "How's everything?"

"Everything's great, sir." He turns toward Destiny, who's just dismounted. "As for you, Doc, the heifer you took such a shine to is still just fine."

"Yeah?" Destiny's face lights up. "Where is she?"

Bill points her in the right direction. "They're out back with the others if you want a look."

"You go ahead and check on them," I tell her. "I'll catch up with you." Just when I think I can't want her more, can't find another thing to love about her, watching her care for the animals is the added cherry on top. Thankfully, she doesn't see me staring because she's already hustling toward the animals like the compassionate veterinarian she is.

As soon as she leaves, Bill turns to me. "I wanted to tell you —I saw an unidentified vehicle slowing by the ranch entrance this morning."

I go rigid. "Oh, yeah?"

"I managed to see his face before he drove off. No one I've seen before. I reckon he was spying."

I'm on full alert as I lean closer to Bill and lay a hand on his shoulder. "The meeting is tonight inside The Barn. We're going to devise a plan of defense."

"Dylan told us, sir. We'll be there."

My gaze finds Destiny.

"Look, Carter." She points to a particular set of twin calves playing in the sun with their mother. It's a beautiful sight, I can't deny it, but I'm suddenly tense. It's like I was on vacation with her, and the rest of the world faded until now.

The holiday is over. I'll have to do whatever it takes to protect my family.

But for the moment, I force myself to smile and watch the calves. Seconds tick by until I'm faced with another reality. Destiny is a part of this now, and we need to go.

"They look great, Destiny." I place a hand on her lower back and guide her to the horses. "I'd like to stay with them longer, but we have to go."

"We just got here." She takes her horse's reins. "Is everything okay?"

"Afraid not," I murmur, unlooping Bandit's reins. "I'll tell you later, but we have to go right now."

We mount, and in no time, we're racing back to the stable. Every few seconds, I look at my surroundings, paranoid of lurking danger.

Dylan comes out of the venue, The Barn, wiping his hands on an apron, as we pull our horses up near the stable. "Hey. Everything okay?"

"Bill said he saw someone spying. It could be those guys."

"No doubt," Dylan mumbles as we dismount and walk the horses inside the stable. "The men will be here at eight. I have whiskey ready." He chuckles.

"We're going to get these fuckers." I untack the horses, then we lead them to their stalls.

Once we get inside The Barn, Destiny gasps, her eyes veering up the posts and beams of the huge structure. "Whoa, this is nice."

"Welcome to The Barn." Dylan smiles, and Destiny gives my

cousin an impressed look. He extends his hand with a smile, indicating the room's rustic yet modern look.

The once-rough wooden walls have been smoothed to create a warm setting but still maintain their whiskey-barrel decor. The vaulted ceiling with wooden beams does wonders for opening the space, and round tables with pressed white tablecloths litter the room when there's an event going on. My favorite part, one that's been a hit for everyone who's used the place, are the chandeliers—carefully tiered layers of antlers with bulbs mixed in.

Dylan smiles warmly. "This is our restaurant, event center, wedding venue, bar, and catering facility."

"Dylan's the manager here," I explain with pride as he disappears into the kitchen. Staring at Destiny, I can't help but drink in the sight of her as the light shines in her hair, all glossy and rich. She fits into my world as if she's the missing puzzle piece. For a moment, my mind drifts to a happier place, and I briefly imagine marrying her here. We're dancing, her in a white dress, string lights above us, with music playing in the background.

After the dust settles, I'm bringing her and Storm back where they belong. With me. At Three Rivers Ranch.

"I didn't know it was this—" She trails off.

"Extravagant?" I fill in. She sits at the bar, and I pour some whiskey for us. "Yeah. Dylan knows his stuff."

"I never knew you Caldwells were this—"

"Rich?" I grin, knowing how much talking—or rather, bragging—about money aggravates her, but I love teasing her, and I can't help it.

She rolls her eyes. "Carter."

"What?" I grin cockily. "It's the truth."

She has this moody expression, but as I look at her, she starts to grin. "Okay, well… now that I have a daughter, and I'm old and tired, I've changed my mind about money."

I start to say something sarcastic, but her words catch me off guard, and I snap my mouth shut. Never thought I'd hear that coming from her.

I salute her with the glass of whiskey. "And I'm going to show you how to put money to good use. We're going to turn this situation around." I swallow the drink and let out a breath of air at the burn. "Let's finish up here—then we plan."

The kick on the door startles Destiny right out of her seat. Instantly, my priority is to protect her, and I jerk her away from the stool and place her behind me.

I'm ready for battle…

Until I realize who's standing there.

Chapter 22

DESTINY

"I'm back!"

"Dad?" Carter shouts. "What're you doing?"

Mr. Caldwell saunters up to the mahogany bar top and pours himself a whiskey. "Surprised?" He gulps down the shot. "Howdy, Doc." He tips his hat to me. I'm staring at him with an expression of a goldfish. "Heard about your services, ma'am. Thank you for helping with the heifers. I don't know how my son would've managed if you weren't here."

I'm about to speak when Dylan reenters the bar area. "Uncle?" Dylan steps behind the bar, shaking his head. "How'd you get here?"

Carter butts in. "Dad… what happened?"

"Doc Roland says I have a heart arrhythmia and pneumonia. But I can't be lying there because of an illness when my ranch and family are at risk. I pulled out the IV and left. They tried to stop me, but I'm way too stubborn to be put down."

"Put down? Dad." Carter watches his father, then laughs and gives him a manly hug, both of them slapping each other's backs.

Dylan pours Mr. Caldwell another drink. "Good to have you here, Uncle Malcolm."

Everything inside me wants to mention this is a terrible idea, and typically doctors know best, but the way Carter stares at his father like he's needed him this entire time keeps me from opening my mouth.

"Same," Mr. Caldwell answers and lifts the drink in salute.

"What'll you do about this condition of yours?" Carter asks.

Mr. Caldwell pulls a brown paper bag from his vest and pours the contents onto the counter. Pill bottles pour out and bounce all across the bar. "Backup. Look at all of this medication." He shakes the bag empty. "I have unfinished business to settle. When I'm done, I can go back to the hospital. I'll live long enough to kill these bastards who blew up my house and tried to take me out."

Mr. Caldwell's dark blue eyes are devilish, but Carter gives him a doubtful look. "How'd you get home?"

A broad, tall, older man with gray hair and a mustache enters through the main doors, and I begin to recognize him. "I brung 'em."

Carter smiles. "Mister Jenkins?"

"You're not the only one visiting me in the hospital," Mr. Caldwell grunts, followed by throaty laughter. The lofty man joins us at the bar and takes a gulp of the drink poured for him.

"And looky who we have here," he says to me with a smile. Will Jenkins has seen me often on neighboring ranches and whenever he stops at the vet's clinic. He's always a warm sight to see, a kind face. He tips his hat. "Howdy, ma'am."

I bow my head. "Good to see you, Mister Jenkins."

Mr. Caldwell studies me. "I didn't expect to still see you here, Doc."

Where to begin? ***I was taken captive by your son, then told your son about your granddaughter, and now here we are, stuck together until this insanity ends.***

I look at Carter briefly before uttering, "Well—"

"I asked her to stay until we resolve the issues with these guys." Carter saves me from an explanation. "It isn't safe out there. Bill said he caught someone spying in an unidentified vehicle."

"Hmm." Mr. Caldwell nods. "I'm gonna kill 'em."

"We're planning," Dylan says. "We're keeping watch."

"My boys can help," Mr. Jenkins adds.

"Thank you, Will." Mr. Caldwell turns to his friend. "We need all the men we can get."

My breath catches when Mr. Caldwell's gaze lands on me. "Doc Hart?"

"Yes, sir?" I choke out, worried he's about to ask me to take up arms and fight the Mafia with the rest of the bunch.

"I understand you're a veterinarian, but I'm sure you can treat an injured person?"

I swear everyone stops to listen to my answer. I glance down, hiding from the stare burning into me. Of course I can, but—I swallow hard. Carter grabs my hand and squeezes. I take a breath and turn back to Mr. Caldwell. "I'll—I'll do my best, sir."

"You need rest, Dad," Carter says. "You need to take it easy."

"Uncle Malcolm!" Juliet rushes in and throws herself at her uncle. He lets out a groan from the force of it but eases into her embrace. "We were so worried."

"I'll get one of the cabins ready for you," Carter says.

Juliet shakes her auburn head. "Uncle Malcolm will stay with us at The Mansion. It's big enough for an army."

"Seems like a better idea." Mr. Caldwell shrugs. "See ya around, Will." He leaves with Juliet dragging him by the hand.

"Okay. Let's go," Carter says to me, and I turn to face him.

I never know what we're doing or where we're going, and it's starting to get on my last nerve. "Where we going now?"

"We're going to run and get some supplies, then get back here for the meeting." Carter makes his way to the truck, and as I scramble in, he throws me some glances. "You okay?"

"Obviously not." I raise my brow. "Your father wants me to play doctor to you guys. What if something serious happens to you all?"

"It might not come to that."

He can't be serious! It's going to come to that!

I glance out the window, going right into my headspace

that's spinning with worry. The mountains and trees fly past as the truck speeds up. I rest my head against the doorframe and let the breeze blow against my face to calm me down. Birds fly past in pairs as I count the trees closest to the road. Finally, after what seems like a long while, Carter eases up on the speed, rustling me from my panic.

"I know you weren't bargaining for any of this." He sounds serious. "There's a lot going on around here, I know."

"You're telling me." That this situation is more than what I bargained for is the understatement of the century. Unexpectedly running into my ex and the father of my child was enough. Being attacked by bad guys and roped into a defense scheme is a whole other level of unexpected.

"Hey, I want you to hear something," he says excitedly.

"What?"

How can you be this calm?

"Just listen." For a few seconds, Carter messes with the stereo, then turns up the volume as a song starts playing. A guitar strums through the speakers, and he starts singing along. ***"She was a hearty heifer who needed some help... Armored cows... "***

"What's this?" I try to make sense of it all. "Armored cows?" I know whatever Carter is doing, he's doing it to make me laugh, to take my mind off the situation back at the ranch. If I could give him any credit, it would be that he always knows how to shift my moods.

"Yep. You heard me." He chuckles. "Armored cows. I think my second cousin wrote this song."

"Well, can't say that I've heard it before." I pick my words slowly. "But... I like it," I say for his benefit.

"She will fight for her rights or diiieeeeee," Carter sings on, being silly. "I thought since we're getting into defense mode, we might as well amp ourselves up a bit. We'll arm the cattle."

I bust out a giggle. "Carter!"

Our laughter fades as the song ends.

Soon Carter parks the truck and pulls the keys out of the ignition in town. He turns toward me, and we lock gazes, electricity flowing between us. There's always going to be that pull.

He grabs my wrist and hauls me to him as he leans across his seat, eyes smoldering into mine. I study his expression before dropping my gaze to his lips. He licks them wet. We draw closer, and I hold my breath. Our lips are almost touching now. Our breaths mingle. Our heat feeds off one another.

Everything is still so real. He left me. He never came back. I raised our daughter alone. I'm still hurt. But there's more to it now. The way he's fighting for his family. How his entire face changed when he heard Storm's voice. His need to protect me, even when I wish he wouldn't.

He kisses me, his lips soft and warm. He nips my lower lip before brushing his tongue against mine. It sends desire rocketing down my spine to between my thighs. Heat washes over me as he pulls me closer, exploring my mouth with his and brushing my neck with his large hand.

When we break away, we're both gasping. My cheeks burn, and I turn away. My eyes fix on a big sign in front of the drugstore, but I'm not taking in the words. Instead, my mind drifts—my heart pounds.

"Hey." Carter grabs my hand, but I pull away.

We can't do this.

He reaches his hand to my chin, and I stare right into those dark eyes, fighting my conflicting emotions. "I'll make it right, Destiny."

I don't even realize tears are falling until I feel his wet thumb against my cheek. My heart is beating so loud in my ears, I bet he can hear.

We gaze at each other, locked in a moment of wild intensity, until he opens the door and steps out. "C'mon, before this truck explodes."

Chapter 23

CARTER

A black Range Rover with tinted windows parks beside my truck, and the passenger gets out. The hair on the back of my neck prickles like the wisest cur dog around.

He's not from around here.

I eye him as I go around to Destiny's side to open the door for her.

A dark-haired guy about my height gets out of the driver's side. His steel eyes are sharp and focused. An aura of power emanates from him, sending warning chills down my spine. He stands tall and proud, locking eyes with me.

Gray eyes I'll never forget.

Here we are. This is him. I sense it, and when one of his men says something and mentions the name—*Atlas*—I know for sure. He smiles in response, then his gaze drifts to Destiny as he adjusts his shirt cuffs.

I take her hand and pull her behind me.

The man stares at me for several seconds before he grins at Destiny. "Bellissima."

I clench my fist, giving him a look that says he best silence himself before I do it for him.

"What?" he whispers with a smirk.

"Are you Atlas?" I grit out.

He places a hand in his pocket. "I see you know me."

Watching how calm he is makes me want to rip his throat

out. I almost lost my father because of this— "I know what you did." I burn to leap at him. Crush him.

He leans forward and flashes a dark smile. "And I know you… Carter Caldwell."

"What do you want with my family?"

"Your brother," he answers with ease.

I doubt Atlas is dumb enough to pull anything in broad daylight, but— "Even if I knew where he was," I drone, "I wouldn't tell you."

I'm not scared of him, but I need to talk our way out of this situation and keep things under control. We don't need extra battles. I stare at the strange man dressed in his dark suit. There are so many stories hidden behind his gaze. I catch a flicker of light in his eyes, but the rest is darkness.

"Why're you looking for my brother? Because that stunt you pulled at my ranch won't be repeated."

Atlas taps a finger on his chin, exposing a wolf tattoo on the back of his hand. "I hear your father survived. Such a waste of… ***explosives.***" He rubs his forehead, feigning disappointment.

Destiny holds on to me, pulling me against her. Right on time—because I'm about ready to tear out of her grip and beat this man to a bloody pulp. My breathing accelerates, anger hitting the prison walls of my mind.

"And that brother of yours," Atlas brushes invisible dirt from his shoulder, "the mischief that follows him… is catching up to him."

"How's that?"

"Don Renaldo Moretti—my boss. His son was killed."

My blood thickens. Tanner wouldn't kill anyone. "My brother—did he kill this man?"

"The Don asks for Tanner's head on a silver platter." Atlas licks his lips. Not in a nervous way, but like he's salivating. "And I've been ordered to deliver it."

"Not while I breathe."

"Caldwell… I won't quit. The Don won't quit. The family

won't quit—and there are more of us than you can imagine."

"You won't touch my family."

"If you don't hand him over… you'll be destroyed." His gaze snaps to Destiny. "And who might you be, signorina?" His slight Italian accent oozes off his words like melted butter, and he reaches to grab her free hand and kisses the top of it.

I'm ready to end him right now, but Destiny snatches her hand away and pushes between us. "We have somewhere to be, so would you mind moving out of the way?"

He stares at us for a while before he presses his lips together in a condescending way and moves sideways, making a motion for us to precede him.

I'll kill you, Atlas. You're asking me to choose between handing over my brother or risking the lives of my family? Then I'll choose you. I'll kill you.

"Carter," Destiny says. "Let's go."

She starts to move past Atlas, but I take her hand and stand my ground.

"This was… fun," he calls as he walks across the parking lot. "See you around, Caldwell. Sometime ***really*** soon."

Without another word, I get Destiny back into the truck. I watch Atlas from the side mirror—he's turned around to watch back. He smiles again before walking across the street.

Damn it. What's Tanner gone and done?

"We need to get home." I have no other words. I can only spare quick glances at Destiny. My head is a mess, and my emotions are exploding. Looking through the mirror, I locate the men again. They're heading toward the tourist area.

"Maybe we should still get our supplies?" she says. "Just grab them and get out of here?"

I nod, too full of adrenaline to say anything. We head into the store for our things and return to the truck, roaring toward the ranch in under twenty minutes. I'm on edge the entire time, glancing in the rearview mirror. Destiny pulls out a pack of candy—I don't know what kind it is, Jellybeans or some shit—

and places it between her thighs as if waiting for the right time to open it. I guess she stress-eats or something.

My mind is frazzled. "Why'd you pull me away back there?"

Destiny pauses as she's about to open the bag. "It was getting out of hand."

"You think I couldn't take him down?"

"He was taunting you," she says, brushing her hair from her eyes.

"Did you hear what he said about Dad?"

"I heard."

"Then why'd you pull me away? That guy is psychotic." I scratch the back of my neck, the anxiety inside me building. "And asking me to hand over my own brother? Like hell, I will. If he wants war, he's going to get it." I grip the steering wheel and accelerate.

"You might beat one or two of them if you fight, Carter, but then what? They'll send more men. And what if they kill you?"

Why does she have to be right all the time?

A heavy silence fills the truck. Guilt picks at me.

There are too many responsibilities… too much for one man. "I promised never to leave you again, didn't I?"

"Yeah," she drawls. "Because you already did that, cowboy."

The moment the words leave her mouth, pain crushes me. I cast several quick glances at her, not wanting to bring anything else up, but it's looking like it's going to happen anyway because I start yammering, "You know, getting that call when Mom died—it shattered me. I wasn't thinking about anything besides getting home that day."

Destiny turns her face up to the roof. I'm not sure if she's annoyed or what. I keep going, unable to stop. "When Dad told me that drunk driver killed her, I never intended to stay away from you. I got caught up in my grief." I wrench the steering wheel. I want that to be enough reason for leaving Destiny because I'm not ready to explain the rest. I don't know how to do that.

I mourned my mother's death in a prison yard, which shouldn't have been. I know that. Bullies, fights, solitary confinement, sick bay, and near-death experiences were all served hot to me over those years in prison. And I don't want to share that with Destiny. I can't deal with her disappointment in me.

"I have reasons, Destiny. I'm just not ready to talk about them." I glance at her. "But I got a second chance here. I don't want to lose you."

She stays quiet.

I wish there was a way to fix the past. If only there was a magic button I could push to zap me back in time. A tight knot forms in my chest, making it hard to breathe. I take my eyes off the road for a few seconds. The wind lifts her hair, and for a second, I long for my burdens to be as light.

Does she hate me? She never shies away from telling me how she feels, so why isn't she now? "Can you say something?"

She tosses some of the candy at me with a scowl, and I swerve a little trying to dodge the colorful objects pinging me. "How's that? Cause that's about all I've got for you," she says, but the shake in her voice says otherwise. "Until you're ready to talk about your reasons and what made you break my heart, I don't want to discuss us. ***There's no us.***"

"It's complicated."

"I don't give a damn. I don't care about this family drama, this danger with the Mafia, and whatever the hell Tanner did."

I'm trying to figure out what to say without sounding like a broken record. She's right. What right do I have to ask for more until I tell her everything?

Damn it!

Turning back to the road, I take a breath. Three Rivers Ranch comes into view as I take the turn, speeding onto my family's property.

Pickup trucks swarm the parking lot of The Barn. Pulling

closer, I notice regular guys from the neighboring ranches with guns walking about.

"Hey, Carter." Dylan walks out of The Barn with a grin and a cocky stride as we get out. "Recruits. We have backup. Will came through more than expected."

I heave a sigh of relief and tip my hat back. "I'd say."

Lara and Juliet run up to us and help with the supplies, heading with Destiny to The Mansion.

"Hey," I say to Dylan. "We met Atlas. He parked beside us. He says if we give him Tanner, he'll leave us alone. And if we don't—" I spot Dad at the stable, brushing his favorite horse. "What's he doing down here? I thought Juliet had him under lock and key at The Mansion."

Dylan snorts. "He's Uncle Malcolm. Even my baby sister can't keep him down. You know how he is."

"But he's not supposed to be here." He's ready to fight, to take back the pride he lost when Atlas took his home. I understand that desire for vengeance just like anyone else, but he can't do this, and it's my job to remind him of that.

We walk over to him, and Dad dusts his gloves on his jeans.

"Dad, what're you doing? You're supposed to be resting."

"I can't lie up there in bed. You know nothing you say is going to change my mind." He returns to the stable to a brown-and-white mare standing in some crossties. He brushes her gleaming coat, and there's kindness in it.

We follow him, and I pick up a bucket of water and refill the mare's water pail in the nearby stall. Looking around, I realize all the other horses have already been tended to. "How long have you been here?"

"Oh… a while. I wanted to groom Lucy. That's why I left her for last." Watching Dad brush the mare, I decide not to pester him. Lucy was Mom's horse.

"I'm going to assemble the men." Dylan nods at me, then heads inside The Barn.

"We'll be right there," I say after him.

"The love of a good woman…" Dad brushes slowly, dragging that brush in long, slow, precise strokes. "It's rare. Special."

I make no expression to give away anything. I need to figure out exactly where he's going with this. Best to just let him talk.

"Destiny, huh?" Dad gives me a raised eyebrow look. "I remember you mentioning a Destiny a couple of times." He nods slowly, telling me he somehow senses what's going on.

"Dad." I throw him a look of caution to leave matters alone.

"Son, one thing I know about second chances is that if you let it slip away, it's gone. When I met your mother, she wanted to go to college. Same place as you." ***I never knew that.*** "I was scared she'd change after meeting other men and seeing the world. You know life out there isn't like here."

I nod, listening.

"I threatened to break up with her if she left me." Dad stops brushing and presses his lips together in a tight line for a moment. "I said she had to choose between school or me." He works his jaw. "We fought and separated. I missed her." He starts brushing again. "I knew it was my fault. But my pride wouldn't let me apologize." He stops again. "In the end, I realized it wasn't me who mattered—her happiness did… And you know what I did?" He pauses. "I left everything here and followed her."

I never knew that, either.

"What about the ranch?"

"Your grandfather was my age then. He told me to go after her. Just like I'm telling you. If I hadn't gone and told her, I would've lost your mother. This is your second chance," he says with a stern nod.

"Dad." I shake my head at my crazy family.

Do I want his advice? ***I do.***

Do I want to tell him everything that's happened between Destiny and me since she got here? ***Yeah.***

Do I want him to meet his granddaughter? ***More than anything.***

But Destiny burns cold and hot so often I might never get the chance. "C'mon, Dad, let's get going. It's time for the meeting."

I collect the brushes and buckets, and we head over to The Barn, where my neighbors are waiting to start planning. Again, I'm pleased with the turnout. We should definitely be able to achieve something with these numbers.

"Everyone, may I have your attention?" I wait as all heads turn in my direction. "The Caldwell family has come under attack, and it's time to fight. We must protect each other, our jobs, our neighbors, and all our lives on Three Rivers Ranch. These guys threaten our way of life, and we'll have to take them out."

There's silence for a few beats and then a couple of nods as understanding sinks in.

"These guys blew up our house. They'll be back. They're looking for my brother. He got into some trouble where they're from." I don't give away what Tanner's suspected of. "We won't give in. We'll show them we're boss here."

The faces of my neighbors are focused and intense, precisely what we need.

"We're here for you, Carter," one of the ranch hands calls.

"We always will be, sir," another says.

"Thank you all." I signal Dylan to step up and take over.

"Will the leaders of each group stand, please," he says, and they do. "We'll divide the teams into A, B, and C. The ranch hands are Team A. The backup team for emergencies is Team B. Family members are Team C. C for Caldwell." He grins over at me. I can tell he's trying to support me and keep the morale strong.

At the end of the meeting, walkie-talkies and ammunition are shared, and everyone gets each other's cell numbers for when we do get service.

We're a rough crew.

Are we ready for the fight ahead?

Chapter 24

DESTINY

I ***have to get out of here.***

My mind is made up. These cowboys are going to get themselves all killed, and I can't play around with the damn Mafia and get murdered in the crossfire. Not when I have a daughter to protect.

Where the hell has Carter put my truck keys? After rummaging beneath the couch cushions in the cabin, I head to the bedroom to check his nightstands and under the mattress. When I find nothing, I look in the closets. Desperation fuels me, but it's also a nice distraction. My mind continues to replay our conversation about Storm and Carter's reaction, how he longed to hear more of her voice.

Did I do the right thing by telling him?

I move to the kitchen and throw open all the cabinets. No keys. Shit. ***Carter!*** A new kind of energy takes over, charging me hyperactively to win this competition. Fine. I'm up for a challenge anytime. Try me.

I search everywhere. They're likely somewhere, just watching me in silence. I wipe the frustrated sweat from my forehead, cursing Carter's successful attempt to make my life difficult. Again!

Needing to think, I slump onto the sofa and allow my tired shoulders to rest. My fingers try to massage the throbbing headache from my forehead. Okay, what I need to do now is calm down. I take a deep breath, stretch my arms, and close my eyes. ***Think like him. Where would he hide keys?***

The bathroom—of course!

Back in Texas, Carter's secret safe place was the bathroom ceiling. I've never quite figured out why, but it is.

Fortunately, like his Lone Star apartment back in the day, the ceiling in this cabin is made up of wooden planks—which he could have easily cut out and fixed back. I pull a chair from the kitchen and position it carefully in the middle of the bathroom. Standing on the chair with my feet evenly spread, I tap the planks, listening to their sounds, and the moment I hear a weird rattle, I know I've found his hideout.

Who's smarter now?

I push the plank, and it gives way. Sticking my hand into the newly opened space, I grope around until I land on my keys. ***Ha!*** Carefully, I return the board.

Let's see how he's going to stop me from leaving now. My smile doesn't waver as I pick up my bag and head to my truck—until I stop midway through the door, staring out at the moonless sky with hesitation. Even though I don't want to admit it, his logic makes sense. Nothing can follow me home if I don't leave. But if I stay and get hurt in this madness, what then? That's not good for Storm, either.

I struggle, one foot out the door and one foot inside. If I stay, I'll never get this chance again. Carter will bury the keys and give me no chance of finding them.

I have to go.

Determined, I activate the flashlight on my phone and make my way to the truck, placing one unsure foot in front of the other. A shiver tickles my arms and the nape of my neck, leaving a weird sense of warning behind like I'm being watched, and I find myself glancing back at the door. A chill fills my body, goosebumps spreading.

My phone buzzes, and I unlock it to see a message that the money Carter wired has hit my account. Nice. This will help with some of my loans, take care of Storm, give a little extra for Mom… But looking at the figures, a sudden pang of guilt for leaving stabs through me.

I need the money for sure, and let's say it's Carter paying me for the work I've done and for putting up with him. But deep down, maybe I'm just running away.

Except I have a daughter and responsibilities I need to return to. I can't risk my life by staying here.

I bite my lip, fighting more guilt. My legs move on their own, bringing me closer to the truck. It's now or never. Memories and moments with Carter flood my mind again, but I fight them. I fight the safety and warmth he gives me because I can't possibly trust him right now, not after the meeting with Atlas. And even if I sound like a broken record, like a bitter woman incapable of forgiveness, the situation made me this way, and I have to get home to my child.

Gripping hard on the keys, I speed up, reaching for the handle and inserting the key. This is it; no going back. I open the door.

Suddenly, I sense a presence behind me before an arm grabs tight around my waist. Fear takes hold of me, and I struggle to break free, clawing, kicking, and shouting.

"Where do you think you're going?" Carter leans into me, invading my senses. A chill runs down my spine, making me shudder.

Shit! I turn in the circle of his arms. "Look," I bargain. "I—I have to get home. I can't be a part of this."

"You're going to lead them to Storm. Your parents." He collects the keys from my hand and hoists me across his shoulder. The swiftness takes the breath out of me. "You're going to lie low until we end this."

My moment of victory slips out of reach as I struggle in frustration, but I remain suspended on Carter's shoulder, kicking hard and panting.

Why did he have to find me? A minute more, and I

would've been out of here, on the road to my daughter and parents. An exasperated sigh leaves my lips as I fight to get off his shoulder.

My hair, falling into my mouth, makes speaking even harder. "Let me go!" I screech, spitting out hair and pounding his back. "You can't do this, Carter. You always think you're right, but you're not. I'm going home where I need to be, and you can't stop me."

"Watch me." He snorts when I start thrashing again. "Destiny, stop. I don't want to drop you."

At that, I start flailing even harder, trying to get myself free as the world sways and spins from looking at it upside down. Just when I think maybe he's letting me down, I feel a sharp sting on my ass.

"Did you just spank me?" I ask, horrified.

Rather than answering, he chuckles and carries me inside. He releases me once we're in what I believe to be the bedroom, and I fall backward onto the mattress.

Instantly, I bounce up and push his muscular chest with a scowl. For a moment, Carter stumbles back, giving me a confused expression, but his eyes never leave mine. I swear the temperature between us rises.

I've never felt so frustrated. "You can't do this," I scream at him.

"Well, we'll see about that."

I still at his words. For as long as I've known Carter, he's always been passionate about what he wants. But this? Holding me captive? "You're infuriating!"

"Maybe, but that doesn't change the fact that I'm not letting you leave. You're not ignorant, Destiny—you know this is smarter. It's the best way to keep everyone safe."

"Did it ever occur to you that I might want to leave so I can get as far away from you as possible?"

His face twists with pure disbelief. "Your mouth says that,

but everything that's happened between us since you got here says otherwise. And frankly, I'm tired of the merry-go-round."

The words startle me, and nothing comes out when I open my mouth.

"You want me," he says. "And I want you."

"Carter," I whisper.

"Please, for once, stop fighting me," he breathes out, his lips inches from mine as he takes me into his arms. He looks so determined but also scared. "Trust me."

Then he slams his lips onto mine, almost as if we're making up for lost time. I push his hat off, and we fall back on the bed, him on top. I wrap my thighs around his waist and breathe him in, his warm, leathery, rough scent overpowering my senses. I want to drown in him.

He pushes my hair out of my eyes, and I arch my back as he runs his fingers through it. In response, he slides a hand around my hips and presses his own down into mine.

At the taste of his mouth, my body succumbs to the inevitable. I tilt my head to the side, giving him more access, and wrap my arms around his neck, pulling him closer. I moan as a shiver rakes over my body, heated desire pouring through me. I feel him smiling into our kiss before he passes his tongue across my lips. I readily accept the intrusion, and he deepens our kiss by tilting his head and kissing me like I've never been kissed before.

I gasp as he nips my earlobe, grasping at his hair as he licks and bites my neck. He groans at how I rake my nails down his back and grind against his hard erection.

"Carter," I whimper lowly when he pulls away.

"Is this what you want?" he whispers against my lips.

"Don't make me say it," I lament. "Not this time—"

"When I'm done with you, baby, you'll understand what you mean to me," he murmurs before licking the delicate skin of my throat. "I'm going to make sure everyone knows you're mine

—starting with my number-one doubter." He nibbles my ear. "You."

"Oh," I cry out, tipping my head back in response to the sweet jolt of pleasure he's arousing. My pussy clenches at his possessive tone, my heart beating wildly. I shift, searching for the best way to grind against his straining cock, feeling myself drench with arousal.

He leans back, and pride shimmers in his eyes as he stares down at me. "You have no idea how long I've dreamed of us together again. I'm going to show you just how much I've missed you."

I shudder at how he says it and swallow, trying to find my voice as I grind against him like an animal in heat. Reasoning is impossible now; my body refuses to listen. "Then show me," I demand. I place one of his hands over my breast, making him knead me, cursing all these layers of clothes between us.

I kiss him, moaning into his mouth. He slides my shirt over my head and skims his fingers across my belly and between my breasts.

"Oh God," I whisper.

Clothes start to be stripped off as we touch one another, reacquainting ourselves. Finally, he undoes my bra, staring at me as if I'm a goddess. Although we've done this countless times, his gaze still embarrasses me. I've aged. My breasts and stomach have stretch marks from carrying Storm. But Carter looks at me as if I'm perfect.

He takes me in his arms, sucking and kissing my nipples. With each passing moment, I grow wetter, my juices making me sticky. I want my jeans off. My fingers go to my fly. "Help me."

Carter pulls off my boots and jeans, and I wriggle, pulling off my socks too. He kisses my inner thighs, making his way up to my hips. My palms tingle. I run my hands through his hair and smile at him. He's always been good at knowing what I like, and my heart begins to skip at the thought of his mouth on my pussy. The ways he used to make me come repeatedly burst into memory.

I moan.

Wanting more, wanting everything, I shift against the mattress. Carter stands and slides his fingers into the waistband of my panties. He pulls them off, dragging me to the edge toward him.

He slides his fingertips up and down my thighs, kissing and licking my stomach, everywhere besides where I want, and I groan in frustration.

He grins, pushes my thighs open, and settles on his knees on the floor. Then, gripping my hips with his strong hands, he pulls me down until his mouth reaches me.

It's like a light bulb flash—lightning zaps me at his contact. I've never needed anything more in my life. When he begins to fuck me with his tongue, it's all over. I can't remember how often I stammer his name or what language is coming out of my mouth because I lose control of everything and surrender to the mounting pleasure pulsing through my clit. My body quivers from each orgasm that hits me.

My thighs are shaking, my mind is spinning—and I'm not getting enough even though I could pass out each second.

"Fuck," he groans. "I'm going to fucking ruin you."

I whimper, heated at his dirty words. I arch up, thrusting my pussy into his mouth. He flicks his tongue over my clit and plunges two fingers into me, hitting a spot that makes my mouth part in a silent scream.

He continues to lick and suck as my knees close, keeping his head locked onto my pussy. I'm bucking my hips to the rhythm of his tongue and fingers, and he reads my body well like always. He knows what I like before I do. My heart skips, and I need him more than ever.

"Carter," I whimper as I part my legs. "I need you."

"You need me?"

"Yes. You—your cock," I answer breathlessly. "Your cock inside of me."

He stares at me, his breath stilling at my declaration, before he looks up at the ceiling, murmuring several curses.

"Ruin me, so I know no one else will be able to satisfy me besides you," I whimper.

He chuckles darkly. "Yeah?"

He stares down at me, seeming to take in everything. His face is right at my open, bare, and throbbing core, his eyes the most intense I've ever seen.

I wiggle a bit, blinking several times. "Carter, hurry up."

"Stay," he commands, then gets up and goes to his nightstand. "We should be more careful this time around."

I lean on my forearms and watch him remove his clothes. His erection is hard, and my greedy eyes take it in before I meet his gaze. He holds up the silver packet and removes the condom before sliding it on. "I don't want to give you more reasons to hate me."

I shake back my damp hair. "I don't hate you."

He returns to the bed and takes one of my thighs in his hands. "I'm not taking any chances."

"Ugg." I cover my eyes, embarrassed but not really sure why.

"Open your eyes. I want you to watch."

He opens my legs, grinning, and rubs himself against my already-soaked skin. He plays and teases me until I can't take it any longer. I scuttle back onto the bed, and he follows.

He's already huge, but my pussy clamps hard on the intrusion, even with how wet I am.

"Fuck," he praises as he slowly pulls his cock out, and I can feel the emptiness as I push myself upward to coax him into filling me again. Then, almost as if he can read my mind, he slams back in.

I love this—love him taking me this way.

"God, I want you," he says, sliding into me again.

A sweet wave of pleasure erupts in my core, making me arch my back. He pulls out and thrusts in again. My body shudders. He picks up pace, and another orgasm builds as he repeatedly hits the right spot.

I push closer to him and meet his thrusts with more force. "Yeah, right there." I buck against his hips and wrap my thighs around his waist, holding him inside me.

He groans and leans close to my face. Our eyes lock. As he kisses me, I moan into his mouth, then land back on the mattress.

Waves of pleasure hit me. "C-Carter pl-please."

I'm desperate. My body aches for more. His heat, his body, his thrusts—everything is driving me crazy.

"You want more, baby?"

I nod.

"Say it. Tell me you want me."

How am I going to say that? I can't even control my breathing. Then the tears follow, and I want to kill myself. But if I don't come again, I'm going to die from need. And I do want him. I do want this.

"I-I want y-you," I say, tears streaming down my cheeks. "I fucking want you."

Why the hell am I crying?

I clench around his thickness.

He groans, rocking into me as he takes complete control. He drives deeper and faster. My moans get louder as I start begging him to fuck me. I'm riding his hips to the best of my ability, swallowing more of his cock as guttural groans slip from his mouth.

"Carter," I whimper. He continues to thrust, making me clench harder and driving me closer to my impending orgasm. He slams into me, twisting my hair and gripping my ass until I finally can't take it anymore.

The sounds of my drenched pussy as his cock shoves into me throws me over the edge.

"That's it," he groans. "Take all of it, baby."

I'm trembling beneath him, and he keeps rocking his length into me for a few moments until he comes.

Once I've caught my breath, I muster the courage to look up at him, wondering how he feels about what we've done.

I see—adoration. Satisfaction. I also see some fear flickering there, and I swallow the lump in my throat.

He discards the condom, then goes to the bathroom and returns with a washcloth. Sitting up, I watch as he spreads my legs, and my breath hitches when he runs the cloth over my inner thighs. I smile when I see what he's doing. "Thank you."

"You never have to thank me for taking care of you. It's my job," he says. "You need water?"

I lick my lips. "Yes, please."

I live the emotional high in the heat of the moment, my mind shut off. And I'm thankful for it.

He returns with two bottles of water. Taking one, I chug the entire thing.

"So?" Carter says. His water bottle is empty, too, and he looks anxious.

"Yeah?"

"After—" He trails off before he rolls his wrist. "This?"

I lick my lips. "We're going to have to figure it out."

Immediately, my eyes fall on his thickening cock. It's like a switch has been turned on again, and the question is, how many rounds we'll be able to make it through before we can't go again.

My mouth waters at the sight of him. He grins at me—almost challengingly, as if he can read my mind.

"Did I do this to you?" I ask breathlessly, reaching to take hold of him. I bat my eyelashes as something animalistic rises in me.

He laughs, low and deep. "What do you think?"

"Possibly. Yes." I giggle. "I didn't realize how pent-up you were. I need to take care of it, then, hmm?"

"Greedy?" He asks against my lips as we tumble back into bed.

One of my hands finds its way into his hair, and I tug him closer. He presses his lips against mine. His kiss is powerful, his tongue gliding across my lips before I moan, our tongues meeting in an erotic dance.

Unlike before, when our kisses were desperate, as if we'd slip from one another's grasp, this is the opposite.

Sexy.

Slow.

Seductive.

I'm sure I stop breathing as he shudders, a growl escaping from his throat. My nipples bead, and I'm wet for him again.

"I'm going to fuck you all night," he murmurs.

I shudder at his promise. His gaze lingers on my breasts before he captures a hardened bud with his lips. I writhe in pleasure as he sucks my nipple into his mouth.

I look at him through heavy eyelids. "I want you."

His hand slips between my legs and touches my pussy, and he alternates between my nipples, making sure both are hard and sensitive. As his fingers work inside me, I feed my breasts to him, wiggling on the mattress.

I cry out because I can't take any more. "I need you. Please. Fuck me, Carter."

"Soon," he murmurs against my mouth before resuming what he was doing. "When you're coming again, it'll be around my cock. You need to know you're fucking mine. You understand?"

I gasp at his words and open my thighs more.

He presses against the entrance of my pussy, and I watch in a daze as he slowly teases my wet flesh without the satisfaction of entering me. Finally, he glides against me until I'm trembling and shaking.

"Come here." He holds out a hand. "Get on your knees."

I shakingly do as he asks, and he looks at me with dreamy

eyes as I come up. A hiss escapes his lips when I wrap my hand around his cock and give it a few slow pumps. His hips jerk forward against my touch.

Grabbing the base of his cock, I take him into my mouth. The salty taste of his precum is on my tongue, and I moan like I'm drinking cold water on a hot day. Like I'm relieved to have him in my mouth finally.

He moves, making me take another few inches of him. His large hands tangle in my hair, and he holds me still for a few seconds.

I bob my head to take as much as I can into my mouth, showing him how much I want him until I'm gagging. It makes him hiss. I work him with my hand and my mouth, jerking him off and caressing his balls.

Carter lifts my head to stare at him. He swallows, not saying a word until my lips meet the tip of his shaft. He groans, further fueling my antics as I work at a pace I know he loves.

He pulls my hair back, trying to take control of my movements. "You're so fucking hot."

I take a deep breath through my nose at his compliment before pushing him further down my throat. I fight against my reflexes. My throat tightens around him, and a string of curses spew out of his mouth.

I let my lips move up and down his shaft as his eyes close. His forehead draws together, sweat running down his face. His cock twitches in excitement as I continue. I would usually be a little embarrassed about my lips slurping around his cock and letting saliva drool down my chin, but I'm too wrapped up trying to please this man to care, because it's fucking good.

The wetness between my legs drips down my thighs, but the need to satisfy him is stronger than my own needs right now. I expect him to pull my mouth to his base when he tightens his grip on my hair again. But instead, his other hand cups my throat and pushes me away.

"I'm not coming in your mouth," he says in a low voice, full of promises for what remains of the night.

I begin to protest, but he helps me up and half tosses me onto the center of the bed. I yelp in surprise, holding on to the headboard for support as I wiggle higher.

"Spread your legs and let me see how wet you are."

I know he knows how wet I am, but licking my lips, I do just that. He stares at me like I'm the center of his universe.

Then he settles between my legs and licks me, bringing me never-ending pleasure. He feeds on me, and before I can process it, my knees jerk up and hold on to him, keeping him locked there.

Carter murmurs what sounds like muffled curses as I thump my heels against his upper back, bringing myself closer to his mouth. "Put your fingers inside of me. Fill me up."

He slides two fingers into my pussy as he continues to eat me out shamelessly. I clench hard onto his fingers, almost making me come right there. Next, he swirls his tongue around my clit, making me hypersensitive, then thrusts into my core, his nose hitting my clit and sending pleasure coursing through my body like wildfire.

I arch off the bed, thrusting into his mouth to the rhythm of his fingers, getting lost in his touch. The world could burn for all I care, so long as I have him inside of me.

I'm close. So close, and I need to come more than I need my next breath. My pussy clenches around his fingers.

He moves up and rains kisses on my neck, then he reaches into the nightstand and rips open another condom packet before rolling it on. Then, kneeling between my legs, ensuring his eyes are locked with mine, he enters me.

I gasp his name, full and stretched.

We stare into one another's eyes.

"Look what you do to me, baby," he breathes.

He's huge as he hovers over me, plunging into me. I was always in love with his power and strength when we made love, and right now, it reminds me of the first time when we lost our virginities to one another.

I look into his eyes, holding me captive as he continues to stroke his cock in and out of my pussy. He's on a mission to make this night memorable. Quicker and faster, he pounds into me, each thrust making my breasts bounce.

He hits a spot that makes my head thrash to the side. His hips angle to allow his pubic bone to hit my clit, and I claw at his chest. He sucks on my bottom lip, stealing my breath away.

Another orgasm creeps up on me. Finally, I open my eyes to see his jaw clenched, his skin glistening with sweat.

"Come on, baby, give me all of it."

"Carter," I gasp, my muscles tensing.

"That's it," he coaxes.

I swallow, parting my lips as the pleasure overwhelms me.

"Rub your clit for me. I'm going to fuck you so well you won't be able to walk straight. Now that I'm in you, you're mine. Do you get that? You aren't coming on anyone's cock but mine."

I nod, completely wrecked. I just need that push once more.

"C-Carter, yes, baby."

He brushes my hair off my face then thrusts into me.

"Yeah," I cry.

He works hard, making the bed creak. I whimper from the assault of pleasure, yet I force my eyes to open and stare into the darkest eyes I've ever seen.

He fucks me so well that I can't think of anything besides him.

The wet-smacking sound fills the room as I arch my back. He travels his hands across my curves before raising my legs and hooking them around his waist, making me hold onto him as he rides me.

And then he hits a spot that makes me lose it.

Instantly, the tidal wave crashes down, and I'm moaning out his name. My eyes close, and I think I'll never catch my breath again at how intense my orgasm hits me. He tightens his grip on my hips. I'm going to be sore tomorrow!

"One more." He strums my clit, and it's enough to set us both off. He follows, groaning my name, too. He comes hard. I'm mesmerized by the man above me. He's beautiful as his body tenses, his cock flexes, and he pulses inside me.

I'm so exhausted I can barely keep my eyes open after a while, and at some point, he shifts us and tucks the blanket around us before I drift off.

I WAKE UP.

Fuck.

Okay. My brain is back in charge.

Sex isn't going to change my mind about staying. It can't.

I'm resting on Carter's rising and falling chest, and the moment I move an inch, he mumbles and pulls me closer.

Waking in bed next to him is all I've ever wanted. But my heart breaks at the realization I can't stay right now no matter how much I want to. My daughter needs me. I'm her protection, and I must keep her in my sight. No one can understand that until you've experienced it—when all your nerves and brain cells scream for you to have your baby in your arms. Carter and I had some fun, and in the heat of the moment, it meant something, but right now, all I can think about is my daughter.

Of course my dad is with Storm, and he'd lay down his life for her, my mom, and me, but I still have to get back to them.

Reluctantly, I roll to the other side of the bed, trying not to disturb Carter. Lying on my back, I stare at the ceiling and think about what's happened between us.

Fantastic sex, that's what… just as good as it used to be. In a perfect world, I'd snuggle next to him and see if he were ready for another round. I imagine our life together if he'd never left. We'd have a family breakfast, making memories with Storm while having coffee and eggs. We'd be a real family.

A part of my brain knows that with a leap of faith in each other, we can still be that. But right now my chest aches. I must go before this gets any harder.

I'm older and wiser than last time. I can go about this sensibly. I have obligations. I have a job and a daughter to take care of. I need to get back to reality before we make future plans.

Trying not to rock the mattress, I sit up. If he wakes, he'll talk me out of leaving.

After slipping from bed, I put on clothes and pick up my keys from the dresser. Looking in the mirror, I attempt to fix my hair, pulling it into a bun. It's messy, but it'll do. I don't need to look put together. I'm on a ranch, after all. But the one thing I can't hide is the glow on my face.

Damn it. I'm fucking radiant.

Closing my eyes, I relive the moments of passion from last night, and I can still feel him between my legs. I grip the dresser, trying to control myself from jumping back into bed with Carter. Yet, every inch of me yearns for him.

"Goodbye," I whisper to his handsome form as I open the door and slip outside.

It's a crisp, dewy morning, and I take a long, cleansing breath, letting the cold air fill my lungs.

I start the truck and zoom off, leaving behind a cloud of dust. I don't look back because I know one last glance will make me waver. Instead, I fix my eyes on the road and focus on getting out of here.

"I'm sorry." My voice breaks, but I don't turn the truck. I accelerate instead. I spend the next two hours replaying my time with him, going through every what-if. What if I trusted him again? What if we gave this another shot? What if he was right and leaving was a bad idea? What if something terrible is going to follow me home?

When I pull into my parent's house, all the fear and anguish leave my body. I can't wait to see my little girl.

"Mom!" Storm shouts as she quickly dashes toward me from the porch, her long ponytail swinging.

I ready myself with a broad smile and catch her in my arms. "I've missed you so much." Wiping the tears from my eyes, I kiss her and give her bear hugs.

She smiles. "I missed you, too."

"Everything all right?" my mom asks as she steps onto the porch, drying her hands on a chicken-print dish towel. My expression must be twisted into something only she can read—the kind of stress a mom can catch a mile away.

"I'm fine. Just tired. Thank you for looking after Storm." I kiss my daughter on top of her head, and she rolls her eyes. "I'll drop her off at school and head to work. The office is hectic today." This is to avoid the following few questions I know Mom will ask.

If she knew I was at Carter's place, she would give me the third degree. If I stay here any longer, she'll read the truth on my face. She's always known when something is up with me. Even when I was younger, I could barely hide anything from her. She would know when I was sneaking out or when I was sad or hurt by something. That's why I have to get to work straight away. She's going to find out eventually. It's inevitable. But it's better if I tell her on my own terms rather than getting bombarded with questions right now.

As far as she knows, I was out making a call at a nearby ranch, and that's it. Completely professional.

"Well, do you have time for a cup of coffee?" Mom looks at me with eyes just like mine and her granddaughter's. "Storm doesn't have to be at school for another twenty minutes."

I should say no. I should say I have to run an errand or something, but it's been a while since we've had coffee together, and I crave peace with her. I need to clear my thoughts and keep my face from giving everything away.

"Umm. Okay. Sure." I breathe deeply.

In the kitchen, I sit at the island while she pours me a cup, the smell of the fresh brew filling my nostrils. Trying not to tap my fingers on the counter, I take the cup from her hands and take a sip, burning my tongue in the process.

"Slow down, now. What's got you all riled up?"

"Nothing. Just not getting enough sleep."

She reaches and pulls my chin up with her long slim fingers. "I think they've been working you too hard."

"We've had a lot of calls lately. There's a lot of livestock around here, you know."

"I just wish you weren't working so hard. You hardly have time for yourself. Or time to meet someone."

"Mom—"

"I know, I know. I'm just saying maybe you should think about getting out there again. I know there are some eligible men. Somewhere."

I hold in a laugh. "There are?"

"If you'd like, I could arrange something—"

I shake my head. "No thanks, Mom. And I should really get going. Storm won't mind getting to school a little early, and I do need to get to the office."

"All right. She has a math quiz today. She made some flash-cards, so make sure she goes over them."

I smile. She's so good with Storm. Sometimes I don't give her enough credit. "Thanks, Mom. For everything." I lean over and give her a big hug.

"Of course. And are you sure you're all right?"

"I'm fine, Mom." I let go of her and walk into the hall. "Storm, you ready?"

"Coming, Mom!"

"Don't forget your flashcards." I take one last sip of coffee. "Thanks for the cup of joe, Mom. I'll call you later this evening."

Her eyes narrow, and something tells me she knows I'm only giving her half-truths, but she doesn't push it. "Okay, honey."

Storm appears as I pick up my keys. "See you later, Grandma!"

"Good luck on your quiz, sweetheart." Mom comes out on the porch and waves at us as we drive away.

Storm leans back in her seat and looks out the window. Glancing over at her, I realize how much she looks like Carter. They've got the same chin and brown eyes with flecks of honey. They hold their shoulders the same way. It's amazing.

The image of him lying in bed beside me enters my mind, and I push it back out. I don't need thoughts like that while my ten-year-old sits beside me. Even if it is her father.

Her father.

Carter needs to meet his daughter. ***Am I ready for that to happen?*** I don't know how it's going to go. Is he going to want to be in her life? Bring her to the ranch? Spoil her rotten? I think he will—but what if he doesn't? Or worse, what if he makes her love him and then disappears like he did before?

It's the uncertainty that's scaring me the most. But it's going to happen now that Carter knows about Storm. And hopefully, he sees how much of him is in her, just like I see it.

But Storm doesn't know her dad. So when she's asked about him, I've always told her the same thing; he's been gone since before she was born. And that's that.

I know it bothers her, growing up without a dad, especially when the annual father-daughter dance at school comes around and all her friends go with their fathers. I remember telling her I would gladly go with her, and in her sweet, good-natured way, she shook her head, saying, no, Mom. Let's stay home instead.

But I know deep down she would've loved to go if she had a dad. She'll only get more curious about him as she gets older. And I do want her to know Carter, even if it's just to meet him so that she can put a face to his name.

I shake off the thought. "You ready for this quiz, kiddo?"

Storm looks over at me and smiles. "Yeah, I'm ready.

Grandma stayed up with me last night going over the times tables, and I'm pretty sure I have all of them memorized."

"Okay. Nine times six?"

"Fifty-four."

"Good! Is that right?"

Storm laughs. "Yes, Mom, that's right."

"That's good."

Storm turns to me. "Mom?"

"Yeah?"

"Why were you gone so long?"

"I had to go out to a ranch for a call. You know this."

"Yeah, but you were gone a long time."

A pinch of guilt hits me. I did ***try*** to get back to her sooner. "I know, and I'm sorry."

"Can you take me with you on the next one?"

"Don't you like staying with Grandma and Grandpa?"

"I do! I miss you, that's all."

"I miss you when I'm away too. But don't worry; we'll have some time to ourselves now."

"Okay. I'm sorry you have to work so much." She looks out the window again.

Maybe she could accompany me next time I go to the Caldwell ranch. After their family drama has cleared up. Carter could meet her.

"Tell you what… maybe you can come with me when school's out."

Storms perks up. "Really? You mean it?"

"You have to be on your best behavior, though."

"I can do that! Yeah!"

Hopefully, by the summer, all the gangster business will be finished, and everything can get back to normal. Storm pulls out her phone, and I turn on the radio, listening to the day's news and the forecast. My mind keeps going back to Carter, but I force myself to shut out the thoughts. I'm heading into the office, where I'll be so busy I won't have time to think about anything.

I drop Storm off at Jackson Elementary and take a long, dusty ride to the clinic, startling Megan with my entrance.

"Doctor Hart," she says with a tone laced with surprise. She snaps her gum. "You're back."

"Yeah. I'm back," I drag out like a zombie. "How's it been around here?"

"Fine. Nothing too much. There was a stray dog someone brought in. She had nine puppies within an hour of getting here. They stayed for another day so that we could make sure they were all healthy. It was pretty exciting."

I needed that bit of news. "That's good to hear. Thank you."

"There are a few appointments this morning, but not for another thirty minutes."

"That'll give me time to get caught up." As I try to hurry to my office, she clears her throat. I turn to her with a strained smile on my face. "Yes, Megan?"

"How was it?"

"How was what?"

"You know… the Caldwells' place. Were there gold statues, an infinity pool, or a garage full of Lamborghinis? Stuff like that?"

"A what pool? Megan, the Caldwells have a nice place but aren't extreme about their wealth. They have a lot of cattle and a lot of land."

"I would love to see it."

"Maybe you will someday."

"And what's the family like? Are they stuck-up? Most of them are. At least, most of them are on the shows I watch." She picks up a magazine from her desk. "Like this family of billionaires in California." She flips through a few pages until she finds what she's looking for and holds it up.

I'm not in the least bit interested, but I glance at the article and nod.

"They own an island off the coast of Mexico that they use for parties. Do the Caldwells have an island?"

"No." I roll my eyes. "They don't own any islands. They're ranchers." I walk past the reception desk, feeling like I'm going to lose it. Holding the door to my office open, I turn toward her. "Oh, and Megan? If you get any calls from the Caldwells, tell them I'm not here."

I sink into my chair, my tired shoulders drooping as I bury my head in my hands and sob. Why am I such a mess? I clean my face with nearby tissues, dabbing the tears dry and forcing myself to get it together.

A knock sounds. "Oh." Doc Jones furrows his brow as he opens my door. "But I thought—"

"How's the office?" I interrupt, feigning an excited-to-be-back smile. "What did I miss?"

He studies me for a moment. "Work. Tons of it. It hasn't been easy without you."

Good. I'll throw myself into gear and forget Carter. I send Doc Jones a fierce expression. "I'll begin right now. What patients do we have today?"

I'm going to push Carter and that hot sex out of my mind. ***Right out of my mind.***

Chapter 25
ATLAS

The truth isn't what you see but what you make of it. There's no such thing as a whole truth. In the end, it's ***he said, she said,*** and who tells a more convincing story.

There's only one other method. Who can ***pay*** for the story to be told their way.

For me, it doesn't matter if there is any truth or not. It's about winning the game I was saddled with. Nothing more. I was told to bring the hunted to Chicago, and I'll do that.

It's been four days since our encounter with Carter and his little signorina in town, and I'm itching to try something new. A surprise attack, if you will.

Everything about how Carter stared at me, the challenge in his eyes—and that little bit of fear—has me ***bouncing*** inside. Maybe the game officially started between us when I bombed the house, but meeting the big dog around the ranch was all I needed to set things into motion for us.

I walk downstairs from my bedroom and call out to Marcello, "Find anything?"

"I'm working on it, Boss," Marcello mumbles and chugs coffee as if it's water. He massages his temples with a frustrated groan. "The Caldwell family doesn't have any social media presence… for whatever reason."

"It's not like where we're from, where everyone posts every hour as if their lives depend on it," Rocco points out, grabbing the pot of coffee. He pours me some before glancing around. "Where's Raven?"

Rather than answering, I open the blinds to the kitchen window that overlooks the backyard. She is wearing one of my finest cashmere sweaters with one arm around her ***bunny***. She's walking barefoot over the twigs and grass, and the crows are rowdy as ever, cawing and hopping around her.

In the time she's been here, I've come to accept her bizarre behavior. It's almost inconspicuous at this point.

"She's collecting rainwater," I inform my men. She'd been in my bedroom chanting before I allowed her to go into the pouring rain and place some buckets out for her water. I needed a break from the chanting.

"Why?" Marcello asks, looking up from his typing.

"Something about its healing powers. I don't fucking know," I murmur. The more I try to understand her, the more confused I am, so I let it go. I can't possibly figure Raven out and execute my plans against the Caldwells simultaneously.

"As long as she doesn't put rocks under my bed and slather honey on my food again—for ***healing properties***—I don't give a shit," he grumbles, straightening his back and grunting. "Fuck, I still think I have back pain ***because*** of her."

Rocco shudders. "I bet she's going to make tea with that rainwater."

"What if she uses it to brew the coffee?" I ask sarcastically.

"Please don't give her ideas." Rocco glares at a stray cup of coffee on the counter, and my lips curve upward momentarily before I take a sip and watch her.

I paid a fortune for that sweater. Now it's her dress, hanging to her knees, and covered with twigs and who knows what else. Her long black hair is unkempt and wild, like the rest of her. She bends over, showing the curve of her ass as she puts the kit down to explore while she gathers water from the bucket.

Her witchy purple eyes find mine, almost as if she can sense me. They're intense and intelligent, like they hold a knowing, much like Carter's eyes, which I've already grown to hate. So full of honesty.

Both are people who seem to do no wrong. All that righteousness and light goes against my own colors. Because I have this thing inside me. This black spot. It started small, but it's grown over the years into something all-consuming, like cancer. With each life I take, each person I break, I feed it. One day it will take everything from me, I imagine.

Raven is good, and the fact she sees something in me to admire makes me cringe. So why can't I just get rid of her?

She smiles, and I take another sip from my mug so I don't have to respond. Her smile haunts me. It's a smile that should never be directed at someone like me. I start to think about all the things I could do to break her, to make her look at me the way everyone else does, but the thought of something hurting her—even myself—turns my knuckles white around my cup.

Something strange stirs inside, and I pry my eyes away from Raven to look at Marcello. "Have we found anything new on Miss Comet?"

"I'm still researching." Marcello places his coffee on the counter. "You have me hacking the entire internet, Boss. I'm up to my ears."

I don't say anything. It's his job. He's good at it. And I need the information.

Samuel is—or *was* if he's still alive—a mayor in Texas. Though his records look clean, some digging has revealed his family's true colors. As for Raven's adoption, we found the records were forged and found a secret bank wiring we can't comprehend.

I sip the last of my strong coffee. "Keep digging."

"It's hard researching two people at the same time, Boss." He sighs. "However, I was able to dig into her medical history, and let me just say, the list is extensive."

Marcello is so dramatic. I turn my hand in a circular motion. "Meaning?"

"She's been in the psych ward a few times," he drawls. "She escaped."

None of that surprises me.

"Well, shit," Rocco muses, his eyes wide.

"She's out there talking to birds and collecting magical rainwater," I remind them. "A psych ward isn't news. Give me something else."

"I'm no genius, but I wonder if that's the ***Kindergarten***?" Marcello air quotes the last part. "And in case you're wondering, I have no idea why she was institutionalized. Shit is kept tighter than a virgin."

"If anyone can hack it, you're it," I schmooze, leaning onto the counter. "Now, what about Carter's girl?"

"Doctor Destiny Hart," Marcello uplifts his voice before changing the tab on his laptop and turning it for us to see. "She's a veterinarian. Her office is close by. The receptionist, Megan, told me she's returned to work. She gave out information without batting an eye. The people around here ***really*** need to learn about security. I bet they don't even lock their doors at night."

"Like the entire state of Wyoming," Rocco goads just as Raven comes in through the door. She sets her pet down, and like every time it sees me, it perks its ear and gives me a judgmental look.

I scoff. "Doctor Destiny Hart? That's her name? Sounds like the name of a Barbie doll or some Saturday morning cartoon."

"Good morning," Raven chirps, shuffling in with a bottle of rainwater and pouring it into a pot. As usual, she's humming that odd tune of hers. We watch as she turns on the burner, then adds some peppermint and lavender oil she requested from Rocco when he went to the farmers' market. Next goes in the foraged goods.

Her eyes are bright and wide, like the only thing she could ever ask for in life is being able to forage with a damn kit in her arms. "Does anyone want tea? It's full of the moon's energy. Which is great for healing."

"Will it heal crazy?" Rocco murmurs just loud enough for me to hear.

Rocco and Marcello chorus ***no*** in unison.

"So… we need to do something to ramp up our mission," I change the subject before we're forced to drink the tea. "We need to flush Tanner out and get the fuck out of here."

I barely avoid the stupid kit that's decided to sit between my legs. I do a hop-step and almost crash to the floor, muttering a string of curses.

"Like their ranch wasn't enough?" Rocco lowers his voice next to me as I cross my ankles and lean across the counter again. "We almost sent the papa six feet under, and that didn't flush the fucker out."

"That's because there's no death toll," I say.

"Don Moretti has sent more men for your disposal," Marcello informs me, looking up from the laptop.

"It seems he's getting impatient." Rocco snorts.

What the fuck is going on?

"And the men are awaiting your command. They're set up in a warehouse on the north side of Wind Dance, but they're starting to draw attention."

No shit.

I wonder why Maestro Vincenzo didn't inform me of these updates of Don Moretti's?

"What's the Don proposing I do with all of these recruits?"

"We need a holding place of our own." Marcello taps on the keys for a moment. "And listen to this—there is such a place. An abandoned asylum that might work for our needs."

Raven's hand slows as she stirs her pot of whatever-the-hell tea she's making, but she doesn't look up.

"It's like you're setting us up to get haunted on purpose," Rocco groans. "First her. Now an asylum? Please tell me no one died there. You know what? Don't tell me anything. Why's it all going down like this?"

"You're about to find out since we're going to look at it," I say. "Sounds like just our place."

Rocco's eyes widen. "We are?"

"We are," I affirm. "Meet at the vehicle in ten. Raven, go lock up your pet and get dressed."

Her lips form a pout. "But I haven't had my tea yet."

The scent of mint and earth fills the air. It's not entirely repulsive, either.

I shrug. "Then bring a travel mug."

When Raven does as she's told and takes her pet with her, satisfaction rolls through me.

"She's coming with us?" Rocco groans for the umpteenth time today.

I check my phone for any missed messages. "I don't want her running off."

"She's the one who told me about the place," Marcello says, not meeting our eyes.

Now my men are speaking with Raven? And she's helping us?

"What?" Rocco makes the sign of the cross. "No. I'm not going, then."

Marcello rolls his eyes. "Get a grip, man."

"Do you want some tea?" Raven asks Rocco as she returns to the kitchen in her long black dress. ***We've got to get her more clothes.*** "It'll steady your nerves."

He shudders. "Fuck, no. Boss? I don't like this."

I shake my head and lick my lips. "How do you know about this asylum, Raven?"

She takes a long sniff of the tea. "I passed it on my way here."

She doesn't say anything more, and I glance at Marcello.

"I pulled it up on Zillow. And Google. It's remote, and it's even for sale."

I motion for everyone to get up. "Let's go."

The drive to the abandoned asylum is an hour from Wind Dance and the cabin, and I still can't get used to not seeing any traffic and how long the drive is to anywhere. I count maybe three trucks total while Rocco drives.

As we get closer to our destination, Raven fiddles with her dress. She spent the first part of the drive in la-la land, watching the landscape pass us by with wide, consuming eyes. But now she's stopped humming and seems lost without her crows or kit.

What's her relation to this asylum? Was it where she was hiding before we found her? I take a moment to study her before the building comes into view.

The asylum is located off a secondary road, gated, and nature-claimed.

It's worse than I imagined. But it's secluded, with tall security gates around the perimeter.

We prepare to move in. I walk with the same unruffled poise I've had most of my life while Rocco and Marcello keep to my sides. Raven follows.

The front door is almost unhinged and one side falls off with a loud bang as we enter the building. There's a strange mix of disinfectant and mold in the air, filling my nostrils and making them sting. My gag reflex kicks in, but I swallow the urge and push on. Graffiti covers the walls. Papers and old medical equipment lie on the floor. Some of the tile clinks lose with each step we take. Most of the cabinets and beds are toppled over.

My gaze catches on how Raven glances at one closed-off room. Without missing a beat, I kick the door open.

"Oh, hell fucking no," Rocco curses, shuddering. "I have to get out of here."

He tries to take off down the hall as I examine the room, but Marcello follows me, dragging Rocco in with him.

Unlike the other rooms, this one's not as run-down, but the entire scene is eerie. Raven remains stuck at the doorway, a whimsical look returning to her face.

On the bed, one side of the mattress appears to have dried blood on it. Bones lie in one corner, and messy handwriting covers the four walls. Random numbers, names, and nonsense are scribbled across them upon closer inspection.

"Yeah, I'm out." Rocco rips from Marcello's grip. "I'm not staying for whatever-the-fuck-sacrifice happened in here."

Marcello grabs Rocco by the collar when he tries running. "What happened to being brave?"

"Not w-when it's a d-demonic dwelling."

"These bones are to ward off evil, not welcome it." Raven giggles before making her way inside, shoving past me. She turns to us with a smile. "The spirits led me here when I left the Kindergarten."

"Spirits?" I ask slowly, trying to understand how she can stand in a room with a bloody mattress and seem entirely unmoved.

"The souls guided me," she answers, taking a seat on the bed and brushing her feet back and forth on the floor. We all go quiet.

I pinch the bridge of my nose. ***Why can't life be easy for once?*** All I need is that damn kid.

Rocco shudders, turning white. "I have goosebumps."

"Same." Marcello chuckles, showing us his arm.

"We need to check out the rest of the place," I say to Raven. "Will you be okay alone?"

"Oh yes. The malignant won't touch me here." She nods as if she's making perfect sense, and I place a finger to my lips to tell her to stay quiet.

As my men and I look around, an idea pops into my head. "As creepy as this place is, it's right for us. No one will notice us out here."

"You're g-going through with this?" Rocco stammers, his beady eyes bulging. "Boss!"

"The building seems stable enough." I shrug as I rub at the growing stubble on my chin. I light a cigarette and take a deep pull, smiling. "And it's a, umm, it's a perfect place to have some fun with Carter's little signorina he's so protective of."

"We're going to kidnap his woman?" Marcello guesses.

"This way, we'll know for sure if the Caldwells are hiding Tanner," I articulate. "Hopefully, Carter will turn in his own brother for his girl."

"And lucky for us, her apartment is nearby," Marcello points out, eyes twinkling merrily. We stare at each other, letting the plan sink in. "I'll message the recruits about the location, then move our shit from the warehouse to here. I'll prep the security cameras, too."

"I guess I'll call in some people to fix the fences outside," Rocco says before practically running outside. "I'll stay out here."

I tsk at him before making my way down the grimy set of stairs, thinking of my brilliant plan ahead. I've fought for my place in this world while Tanner and Carter were hand-fed with silver spoons. They have another thing coming now. Once the dust has settled and I lay Tanner's head on a matching silver platter to those spoons, I'll finally live the life I've earned.

I take a deep breath, feeling a sense of newfound determination.

It's time to hunt.

Chapter 26

DESTINY

You know when your day starts well, and everything is flowing, but there's something—nagging at you?

That's today.

"Why hello there, little one." At my words, the Labrador retriever we've been treating for the last two days lifts his head.

Peanut cautiously wags his tail, which is enough to widen my smile—this is the first tail wag I've seen since he came in. But when I bring out the syringe, he whines and tucks his tail down again, breaking my heart. After years of this, you'd think I'd be used to it, but no.

"I know. I know," I coo, hoping my voice is enough to calm the pup. He flattens himself against the exam table as I administer the shot, whining but remaining still. I can't help but feel proud of his ability to endure the pain, as most puppies would be crying or even trying to bite. Turning to his owner, I smile. "He's such a sweet pup."

Mrs. Beatrix, standing in the corner of the room with tense, folded arms, gives me a beaming smile. "Oh, thank you, dear. He's very docile compared to his two-year-old brother, Bingo. That boy will chew just about anything. And he teaches Peanut to do the same. I don't even know what to do with them at times."

I laugh and shake my head as I discard the syringe. "Yeah, but we love them. Now, that should do it. He'll need to continue his antibiotics for the next few days, but he should be fine."

"Thank you so much, Doctor Hart." Mrs. Beatrix lets out a heavy breath, then grins as Peanut gets up, bounces to me, and licks my face.

All animals are important, but something about dogs leaves my heart melting. I'll never tire of them.

"Aw, Peanut likes you. Usually he's quite shy and doesn't allow anyone but me to pet him. My little demon."

Almost as if Peanut can understand what his owner is saying, he barks before scrambling into her arms, ready to leave the scary vet's office. They curl into one another, and the image burns into my mind. I file it away with all the others—a plethora of happy pets and their owners.

It doesn't take long before Megan comes in with another patient.

"Mornin', Doc," the older gentleman greets me.

Megan smiles as she passes me the file on Casper before exiting. I skim through the file, rather impressed that the white feline is almost sixteen. I deduce these two must've been together for a long time. I point toward the examination table. "Can you please put Casper on the table?"

"Okay," the old man warbles, looking nervous. "Here you go, Casper."

I reassure him, smiling, as I examine Casper, a rather chatty fellow who seems relatively happy and healthy. Then, after giving his owner a note for what he needs, I send him on his way. "Just continue to feed him and show him love."

"You're amazing, Doc." Then, with Casper safely contained in his carrier, the man waves me goodbye with the largest smile on his grizzled face.

I exhale, muscles relaxing—that was my last scheduled appointment for the day. Though it's a tough job, it's rewarding. But my body still feels out of place, and I can't figure out why. Maybe because things were nonstop chaos at the ranch, and now, with everything settling into normalcy, it's hard to adjust. Not that I'm expecting a bomb to go off at any minute, but I do feel on edge.

Will I ever get back to feeling normal?

After I say goodbye to everyone at the clinic, I go to my apartment down the street for a quick shower. I need to head to my parents' to pick up Storm, and I want nothing more now than to fall into bed and snuggle with my daughter when we get back.

I take a hot shower, letting the water pull out tight spots along my shoulder blades and neck. Once I jump out, I head to the kitchen and brew a fresh cup, tapping the counter as I wait for the drops to fall into my rose-gold coffee mug, anticipating how good it will taste.

I remember to check my cell as I get dressed—I have many missed calls and messages from Carter. My heart flutters that he's still trying to reach me, but I resist the urge to read or respond. I can't think about Carter right now. I've got to learn to forget about everything that happened with him and find my routine again.

Instead, I call my mother, who picks up on the first ring. "How was work, honey? Anything exciting?"

"Hi, Mom." Her enthusiasm brightens my mood. She's like a ball of energy and always makes me smile without even trying. "I'll tell you about it during dinner. I just got off and ran home for a shower. Going to finish my coffee and be right over."

"Storm got a gold star in school today, but I'll let her explain."

I inhale my creamy coffee and do a little internal dance. Nothing like the perfect cup of coffee. "Okay, I'll see you all soon."

"Drive safe. No texting and driving," Mom scolds before the line dies.

Shaking my head, I stare at my phone, the small circle over the message icon tempting me to check what Carter has said.

Giving in, I read the first few messages. I'm floored by how much he misses and wants to see me again. Loneliness creeps into my heart as I glance around my quiet apartment.

I do miss him. I miss Carter. I even miss the ranch.

Tempted to hear his voice again, I swipe to the dial pad. Just as I'm about to click, loud splintering sounds come from the direction of the front door. I startle, dropping my phone and slapping a hand over my mouth. My heart falls to my stomach.

Loud footsteps thump into the living room, and I attempt to prepare myself for the unknown. When a masked man wearing black enters, I throw my hot coffee toward his face and dash for the door. He lets out a curse before launching himself and tackling me. I fall with a loud yelp, letting go of the mug. It shatters near the foot of the bed, cutting my hand.

"She's in here," someone shouts, and more footsteps sound near the bedroom door as more men enter. Panicking, I kick my attacker, but he grabs my legs.

There isn't a chance I can take them all on. One of the men hovers over me, then delivers a sharp kick to my side. Pain explodes over every inch of my body, and I scream.

The next thing I know, I'm being suffocated with a handkerchief. My eyes widen at the smell of strong chloroform, and I try to dislodge the cloth from my face. There isn't a damn chance I'll stop fighting. But even as I keep thrashing, my energy drains away, and all I think about is Storm.

Why did I ever think I needed more than average? Normal is safe. Normal isn't this.

As the room blurs, I can barely keep my eyes open.

"Hey, this is Carter. Leave a message after the tone." His voice rises from somewhere on the floor.

Is this a dream? "Carter! H-help."

How long have I been out?

I'm not sure where I am, but muffled sounds start to make sense. I feel as if I'm submerged underwater. My body floats, suspended in a dark void with no way out.

I fight to focus on the muffled voices.

Carter?

No. These voices are rough and brutish. Nothing like Carter's. An unknown fear grips me, making breathing hard as I draw closer to consciousness, blinking away the haze.

A loud horn sounds, and I jolt.

I'm lying on my left side, arms and legs bound, and gagged with a hood over my head. I'm in a moving vehicle. Maybe in the trunk? I've been abducted!

Hopefully my parents will come looking for me or call the sheriff when I don't make it for dinner. Thank God Storm is with them.

I take a deep breath, willing myself to calm down and think. These must be the Mafia men. I can still see that man's cold gray eyes, and the threats he made without saying a word.

Carter was right.

At least with him, I would've been protected.

My heart pounds so fast I'm scared I'll go into cardiac arrest.

I inhale deeply, trying to slow my heartbeat. I get a whiff of coal. ***Are we on the outskirts of Wind Dance?*** There's only one coal mine near here. If that's the case, we should be making a right turn coming up.

My suspicions are confirmed as the vehicle slows and turns right. I think. I fight the trembling taking over my body when I guess where we're heading—the abandoned asylum. I've heard lots of ghost stories and rumors shrouding the cursed place.

Killings.

Murders.

Cults and sacrifices.

Are these men planning to kill me?

The panic has me drifting, my memory playing with me of years ago. Suddenly I'm outside the café I worked at in Texas. Masked strangers standing around me in a circle. A hand on my throat. The coldness of the dumpster they threw me in.

The walls of this trunk are closing in.

I spent years repressing the attack, and the nightmares faded over time. I thought I buried the fear and was safe from anything like that happening again.

I was wrong.

My stomach roils. The panic leaves me nauseous. But I'm not that girl anymore, and I have someone very important—someone who means the world to me—willing me to fight.

My daughter.

I need to think of a plan and give myself a chance at survival. From what I remember of the photos of the asylum, it's a giant brick building. Maybe I can escape and hide in one of those rooms. Escape plans for every scenario I can think of flash through my mind until the vehicle comes to a stop. The door up front opens, and my body goes rigid.

"Boss, we've arrived," a raspy voice says.

"Take her inside." This voice is menacing and dark.

The trunk opens, and I'm dragged out. My legs are untied, and I'm walked beside them. When I hear echoes of footsteps on the tiled floor, I know we've entered the asylum. I thrash around but still can't control my footing. The temperature drops a few degrees inside, goosebumps break over my flesh, and a coldness seeps into my bones.

Despite my struggling, I'm pushed onto a chair and tied to it. The hood is torn off, and I'm sure the man—one of Atlas's—grabs my hair and yanks. I yelp as he pulls my head, craning it back to look at him.

He pats my cheek several times. "Stay still, princess, or I'll help you stay."

I watch as he leaves, and swallowing my nervousness, I try to calm down, glancing around at my surroundings. The place is disgusting, with shattered windows and graffiti covering everything in the room. I don't know how long before anyone returns, but I have to get out of here.

The first order of business is finding a way out of this chair. I test the strength of the ropes and curse—they're tight.

Then footsteps sound out in the hall.

"Where is she?"

The voice brings my actions to a screeching halt. I know that ruthless voice.

My worries are proven right, and my stomach twists.

"Why the face, signorina?" Atlas grins at me, and I fake courage. I scowl at him, my nose flaring. "You don't look too good."

He sits on a stool before me and spins the silver rings on his fingers. The black diamond tattoo on his throat highlights his pale complexion. I don't utter a word, and his eyes soften as he faces me. "Are you hurt?"

Shock keeps me mute, and I blink a few times. He reminds me of a wild animal. Unpredictable before they pounce. "What?"

"You wouldn't be in this situation if you weren't associated with the Caldwells." He crosses one leg over the other and stares at me. "All I want is Tanner." He lets a few beats hang in the air. "Do you understand?"

"I don't know anything about him." I probably know less than Atlas does, so I agree with the truth. It's not like it can hurt me. "I was hired to work on the ranch and got mixed up in this bullshit." When Atlas arches a brow, I match his stare. "I'm serious. I don't know anything about Tanner."

"Careful with your lies. You don't want something to happen to you," he warns with a devilish smirk. "Why don't we try again… Where is Tanner Caldwell?"

"I really don't know," I firmly state. "You can ask all you want, but the answer will stay the same."

"Are you saying your lover boy keeps you in the dark? Hides things from you?"

It's a trick question. He's trying to break me down. I scoff and lie. "Carter and I aren't lovers."

"What about this daughter of yours?" He brings out my phone and dangles it in front of my face with a wicked grin.

My heart drops. I enter fight mode.

He swipes through the photos of Storm. "I must say, she's adorable."

I rip against the restraints. "Leave her alone."

My antics make Atlas laugh. He drums his fingers on his knee. "Where's Tanner?"

"I don't know." I try again, wriggling in the ropes. ***"I really*** *don't know."*

"How do you know Carter's family?"

"Carter and I dated years ago." I make it sound like it was a lifetime ago. "Maybe the only thing you and I have in common is mutual hatred for Carter." A lie, a big one, but I try to keep my voice even. "I don't know shit about his family."

Atlas studies me carefully. "I saw him… the way he looked at you. That wasn't hatred on his part, was it?" He takes a long moment, looking deep in thought. Then he snaps his fingers. "He knocked you up and left you? Naughty boy."

I press my lips together.

"This is his daughter, isn't she?"

"She's *my* daughter," I snarl. "Look… whatever business Tanner has with you—"

"How did Carter find out about her?"

"I just reconnected with him." I want to scream. "I told you. Out of coincidence, because of my job."

Atlas brushes his hand through his slicked-back hair. "Hmmm. I suppose the red string of fate does exist," he murmurs so softly I think I hear him wrong.

Frowning, I shake my head. "What?"

"It's amusing around here, is all… Okay, you can lie all you want, but it'll only be a matter of time before he comes out to play."

My mouth presses into a thin line at his cryptic words. "What does that mean?"

"It means he's going to try saving you. You know, like the knight on the white horse. Except he's a cowboy." He pauses. "Still has a horse, though." Atlas grins before glancing at his watch. "Let's see what's more important to him. His brother, or the love of his life."

A chill shoots through me. "That—"

He cocks his head like a wolf. "Is true."

"Oh, you're way off," I say loudly, but there's a shake in my voice. "You've got to be kidding. You're going to risk everything on a girl he fucked in college?"

"You know," his eyes flash with sick amusement, "your vanilla name doesn't suit you."

My phone ringing in Atlas's hand cuts off my next words, and I stiffen, praying it's not my parents. The last thing I want is for them to be worried more than they probably already are.

He presses a button and waits. Then he clicks his tongue. "Your call dropped." He presses a few more buttons. "Let's just turn on your location and see what happens." He turns his attention back to me. "Make yourself comfortable, little lamb. This might take a while."

"Carter's going to kill you for touching me," I blurt in a threatening tone.

"We'll see, won't we?" He heads into the hall, stopping by a man outside the door. He drops my phone into his hands. "Watch her."

Pain travels in waves from the tight ropes around my hands and legs. I rack my brain, trying to find a way to escape.

So Atlas is making a deal with Carter? Tanner in exchange for me?

Shaking my head, I search the room for anything to cut me loose.

The man in the hall enters after a while.

"Hello, princess. Did you miss me?" This is the man who dragged me in here. He grins. "I missed you. I don't think I ever told you my name. It's David, princess."

I need to get out of here.

As much as he irritates me, though, I could potentially use him to escape. It doesn't take a genius to notice how he's eyeing my body. I push away the bile in my throat and bat my eyelashes at him. "David, huh?"

"You seem to be enjoying yourself." He chuckles, seeming pleased as he takes a step toward me. Just as I'm about to reply, his phone rings. Noting which pocket he pulls it from, I figure my phone must be in his other one.

"I'm busy. What do you want? Hello? Hell—" He listens, then lets out a loud sigh. "These damn phone signals." He turns toward me with a wink. "I'll be back, princess."

"Don't take too long," I purr, leaning forward in my seat.

The moment he leaves, I struggle with the ropes around my wrists. They're growing numb and swollen, but I can't stop now.

After what seems like hours, I hear footsteps again. David's back.

"Now, where were we?"

I lick my lips quickly and smile. He places a hand on my shoulder as though watching to gauge my reaction, his hot breath on my face. I remain still, trying not to break eye contact. If the plan for my escape begins now, I better start the action. "Getting to know you, of course."

He gives me a proud smile. "You're coming around."

He reaches for me, touching my cheek as his eyes wander over my chest. It takes everything in me not to bite him.

"David?" I slyly grin. "You're not supposed to touch me, remember?"

"Atlas is gone for now."

I'm twitching, ready to leave this chair and punch David in

his face. I sigh. "Aww, pity I can't enjoy myself when my hands are tied, and I'm hurting. Bruised and all numb."

He shifts from one foot to another, staring at me as if debating. I move my butt and push out my breasts, straining the fabric of my shirt. Then, with perfect timing, my button pops undone to show my ample cleavage and my red lace push-up bra with the satin bow. He groans, his nose flaring.

My plan is working.

David will decide in—

Three… Two… One…

Chapter 27
CARTER

"Fire!"

The panic-stricken voice snaps me into consciousness. My body goes on high alert as I flail on the bed, hoping to pinpoint the danger.

Shit! Wake the fuck up.

The walkie-talkie lying next to me makes static sounds as I fumble for it. "Fire at the bunkhouse! I repeat, fire at the bunkhouse!"

I tear out of my cabin and run. The blazing-bright flames light up the dark sky like déjà vu. I can't tear my gaze away. The fire eats everything it touches.

"Get the water hoses!" I dash toward the storage building with Dylan on my heels. We lug hoses out, and Dylan flips the switch, freeing an outburst of rushing water that I direct to the bunkhouse.

Thankfully the water goes a long way to putting out most of the fire before it spreads to anything else.

This is Atlas's doing. When I get my hands on him—

I catch a movement in the darkness—a figure in all black. He might've escaped notice to most people, but not to someone like me. He starts backing into the trees.

"There," I shout, motioning to Dylan.

He follows my gesture and turns the other hose over to one of the ranch hands, and we take off after the man slinking into the trees.

Once we catch up with him, I grab him roughly by the shoulder. He pulls a knife and swings it like a madman. I'm able to dodge in time, but then he double-jabs and sinks the knife into my shoulder.

White heat rips through me. "God fucking—" I grit my teeth and swing at his face, making him grunt as he stumbles backward.

Dylan kicks him with such force it sends him flying into the bushes. The knife is lodged in my shoulder, but I ignore it, rushing toward the man before he can drag himself up. I grab his shirt and deliver punch after punch, letting it fuel me until he goes unconscious.

Anger sears through me, needing to see his body black and blue. I want to be drenched in his blood before hanging him on the gateway arch as a message to Atlas.

Dylan places a hand on my shoulder and squeezes. "Okay, Carter."

I slump onto the grass, dripping with sweat, and watch the bunkhouse light up the dark sky in flickers of bright orange and yellow light.

After I catch my breath, Dylan and I drag the unconscious man to the stable and tie him inside one of the stalls. Clenching my jaw, I dislodge the knife from my shoulder, then pull off my shirt and apply pressure on the wound.

I'm ready to fight the fire when Dylan clears his throat, pointing toward the stab wound. "You have to address that, cuz."

I shake my head. "We don't have time."

"I'm not going to let you bleed out, Carter."

"Fine," I grit through my teeth, knowing he's right.

Amid the chaos, we're able to find one of the ranch hands, and he patches me up. Then we all fight the fire until daybreak.

"Move the men to another cabin," I instruct after the fire is put out.

"This can't go on," Dylan murmurs next to me. "They walked right onto the ranch."

I clench my hands into fists, then wince—they're severely ripped apart from working without stopping all night.

Dylan shakes his head. "We need to retaliate."

"We will," I promise as a truck pulls up.

"Dylan! Carter!" Juliet calls, out of breath.

Lara gets out of the truck. "Are you all okay? I had Juliet with me at my house. We didn't know."

"We're fine," Dylan answers. "Shook up, but nothing we can't handle."

Lara hands us bottles of water. "What the hell happened?"

I chug, then swipe my mouth. "Atlas."

"We knew it was bad, but—this—" Lara crosses her arms. "These Mafia—gangsters, or whatever the hell you call them—aren't going to stop."

"Nope." I finish the water. "Not until he gets Tanner."

Juliet looks around. "Where's Destiny?"

"Gone," I clip, my mood souring. I look at Dylan. "I need to speak to you. Girls, can you make sure the men are okay and help with whatever you can?"

"Yeah," they both chorus and take off.

Dylan and I head to the stable. We need answers. I don't know if our captive is awake yet, much less if he's willing to talk, but one thing's for sure—I'll do everything in my power to persuade him to squeal like a pig. And he'll confess even if I have to skin him alive.

"Get a few guys and bring them in here, please."

"You got it, cuz."

Entering the stable, I'm holding back my anger. The man is still unconscious, but he won't be for long. I grab a bucket of water and splash it on him, making him gasp and sit up. ***No peace for the wicked, motherfucker.***

He tries fighting the restraints before his gaze falls on me, and his eyes narrow. And he has the nerve to smile.

I throw the bucket to the ground. "How long have you been spying on us?"

He snickers. Without missing a beat, I deliver a punch. The man coughs and spits out blood. He throws me a smug look again, with some ***fuck you*** attitude.

I press the heel of my boot into his inner thigh. "Let's try this again." I apply more pressure. "Who the hell are you?"

"Alessandro," he croaks after a moment, wincing hard. I keep my gaze on his swollen face, struggling to maintain control.

Dylan and the ranch hands burst into the stable with heated faces, surrounding Alessandro in the stall. Everyone is ready for blood, all wanting a piece of this man who's caused us grief. One of the men lunges at him.

I hold out my arm. "Not just yet."

"Atlas obviously sent you," Dylan encourages.

Alessandro spits out more blood, showing his stained teeth as he laughs. "You might as well kill me. Because I'm not telling you anything."

One of the ranch hands punches Alessandro. "You'll talk all right."

Alessandro laughs again as I grab him by the shirt and haul him close to my face.

"You're too late," he sings, and something about his comment doesn't sit right—

I shake him. "The hell is that supposed to mean?"

"Your little princess is in Atlas's hands now."

At first, I think of the worst-case scenario. Little princess? ***Storm?***

But they couldn't know about my daughter, not when I just found out myself. But if he's not talking about her, then… The very thing I wanted to keep from happening is happening.

I throw him onto the ground. "You're fucking lying."

"He'll put her to good use," Alessandro goads. "And how I

envy him. To be the first to take that hot little body of hers... have her legs wrapped around my waist and hear her sweet little voice—"

I know what he's doing. He ***wants*** me to kill him before Atlas does.

The blood rushes to my brain, the thread holding my self-control snapping. I won't kill him... but I can rough him up.

I rush at him, my fists delivering blow after blow, and I continue to land punches until my knuckles bleed, until I'm dragged away, and I'm punching the air. Then I break free of the hands pulling at me and start all over. The man's face is swollen beyond recognition, but I don't stop. He's gasping, trying to breathe through his broken nose, gagging on his own blood.

I'm pulled away much harder this time, sweating, panting hard, my heart beating fast with every thought of Destiny in Atlas's hands.

I stand straight and look for my hat that went flying at some point. "Make sure he doesn't die before I get back."

I walk toward my truck as the men do their thing inside the stall.

Dylan comes up beside me. "He could be lying."

"Atlas saw her," I seethe. "He saw her, and I knew what he was thinking." I climb into my truck and zoom off, feeling like my heart is being ripped out.

The first stop is the veterinarian's office where Destiny works.

"Where's Doctor Hart?" I burst into the clinic, still a sweaty mess but too desperate to care. A few people in the waiting room turn toward me as I blaze up to the front desk.

The receptionist's brow furrows. "Excuse me?"

"I'm Carter Caldwell," I rush. "I'm looking for Doc Hart. It's an emergency."

"Do you have an appointment, sir?"

"No," I snap. "I need to see her right fucking now."

"Get in line," she snaps back. "She didn't show up for work. We tried calling her, but she hasn't answered."

My hand immediately reaches into my pocket for my phone. I'm greeted with a notification of a missed call and a voicemail. I press the phone to my ear. There's a lot of noise, static, and some muffled voices I can't make out.

Then, "Carter! H-help."

Her voice comes out in a desperate whisper, in a way I never want to hear again. My chest tightens, making it unbearable to breathe. I wait for more, but the line clips dead.

"Destiny?" I yell, drawing the attention of everyone in the office. I look around in desperation as more workers peer out at the noise. "Does anyone know where Doc Hart lives? This is an emergency."

"I do."

I face the receptionist.

"Megan," one of the other receptionists hisses, elbowing her.

"What?" she huffs, pushing up her glasses. "I'm worried about her. She's been acting weird. Something's wrong. And seeing how you look like you should be in the hospital—" Megan points at my shoulder—"we better look for her."

She leads the way to the exit and climbs into the passenger side of my truck. "Take a right at the corner."

Destiny's apartment is in a two-story brick building not far away.

"Stay here." I bolt from the truck, leaving the door open. I find her apartment number on the mailbox and bound up the stairs to the third floor.

The first red flag is her busted entrance.

"Destiny!" I run through the apartment. Her belongings are scattered, and a broken mug lies on the floor in the bedroom. I hesitate, refusing to accept the dawning realization, my breath hitching at the thought. She's really been taken.

Anger is replaced with a unique fear when I see several smears of blood by the mug. I run out of the apartment.

"Is everything okay?" Megan asks.

I drive her back to the clinic without saying a word before speeding back to the ranch.

No. Nothing is okay, and if anything happens to Destiny—

Chapter 28

DESTINY

David looms above me, his hot breath vaporizing over my face. "Today's your lucky day, princess."

I feign excitement and perk in my chair, knowing I'm one step closer to my freedom. All I have to do is play into David's hands.

I let out a breathy exhale and pout my lips. "How so, David?"

"If you please me like a good girl… I'll free your hands."

God? Why're men like this?

I resist the urge to roll my eyes. "How do you know I won't run away?"

He shrugs. "Something tells me you're smarter than that."

"Desperate, though," I counter, wiggling my butt in the chair.

"Listen, sweetheart… you want to keep the other guys from playing hard with you, play nice with me. You ruin your chance and things won't go well. We've got men everywhere. They'll drag you back even if you make it down the hall."

David is smart. He understands he holds power in this situation, and even if I run, there's only a slim chance I could escape.

Still… I don't let the idea burn away my hope.

He moves behind me, brushing his beefy rough fingers around my neck and down my arms. "And I'll free your legs, so you can—"

"What if Atlas returns?" I interrupt demurely in hopes of getting more information. He strokes my hair, and the lump in my throat grows. When he moves his knuckles across my cheek, I have to resist the urge to bite his hand. "The last thing I want is for you to get into trouble because of me."

"***Atlas***," he sneers, "doesn't mean shit to me. He put me in charge of you, sweetheart."

Swallowing hard and thinking fast, I smile up at David. "Well, then! I guess we should... get together." I don't know what the hell else to say, but I have to try something.

"A little slut, huh?" He chuckles darkly. "It's easy to spread your legs once you see a real man, is that it?"

God, grant me patience.

My heart pounds at the one chance of making my escape. "Well..." I force myself to giggle. "I might as well do something ***fun*** while I'm here."

He loosens my binds. I hold my breath, waiting for the moment my hands are free. The pressure around my wrists eases when the rope falls, and without missing a beat, I elbow him in the eye. He shouts. I slam my head back and make contact with his face, intending to break his nose. While he's blinded, I take the knife he has tucked in his belt and slice the ropes binding my legs. I rush out of my chair.

He fumbles for me and grabs my arm.

"Fuck you, David." Bracing myself on one leg, I knee him between his legs several times as hard as possible.

He goes down howling and rolls to one side.

Elated at how well my plan worked, I rush at him again, take my phone from his pocket, and dart out of the room with the knife. I glance around for a way out, then open my phone. Hope diminishes when there're no network bars.

"Damn it," I gasp, raising the phone, hoping to find at least one bar. I move to each corner, trying to think and find my way around the building. I cross to a window, then recoil at the cluster of men holding guns and vehicles surrounding the asylum.

How the hell am I supposed to escape?

"Where the fuck is that bitch?"

The roaring, thunderous sound echoing down the crumbling halls makes every inch of me rigid. Undoubtedly once David catches me, there'll be hell to pay.

"I think she went that way," someone calls.

"Find her," David bellows. "Find the fucking bitch."

I take off, my legs pumping. I run. And I run. All I can think about is my daughter.

The footsteps keep coming. I run through one of the corridors, duck into a back room, and shut the door. I try to catch and hold my breath against the pounding and buzzing in my ears.

The foul stench of urine hangs in the air, and a quick survey of the room tells me this is a storage unit, with a narrow staircase leading downstairs blocked off by caution tape.

Given how many men are in this building, it won't be long before they find me. I have to hurry. Slumping behind a broken medicine cabinet, I swipe back the sweat trickling into my eyes and look at my phone.

One bar!

I dial Carter's number. ***Answer, baby. Answer.*** My hands shake as I press the phone against my ear.

It sends me straight to voicemail. "Hey, this is Carter. Leave a message after the tone."

"Carter," I breathe, blinking away tears, overwhelmed with emotions, as if he's here with me. I will my voice steady. "Atlas has taken me. We're at the old asylum. I—I hope this gets to you." I sniffle, and the lump in my throat gets bigger. "If—please keep my parents and Storm safe if I don't make it. And I want you to know I never stopped lo—"

Shouting and heavy footsteps roar down the hall. There's a loud banging next door.

"Check this one," someone barks.

I race for the staircase. I'm ripping through the yellow caution tape when the door bursts open.

David's chest is heaving, his nose flaring, his bald head shining. His lips pull into a twisted smile as he strides toward me. "When I'm done with you—"

Terror runs through me, but I know he won't harm me as much as he's threatening. Atlas has put him in charge, and if anything happens to me, it'll be on him. I knock over the cabinet full of old syringes and empty canisters to give me a head start and race down the stairs.

"You can't escape, princess," he growls behind me. "But I'll play your little game of cat and mouse. If you win, you escape. If I win, I'll choke your little throat with my dick."

"I can't choke on something so small," I hiss. Clearly I have a death wish, as he yells for his men, and I slam the door at the bottom of the stairs and bolt it behind me.

They throw their bodies against the door, the bangs echoing through the facility as David's face comes into view through the small windowpane beside the door. He takes a heavy object and smashes the window before he reaches for the bolt.

I dash into another dark room, grab every piece of furniture I can, and slide them to block the door as the bellowing down the hall gets louder.

With nowhere to hide, I redial Carter's number.

"Please pick up! Please pick up," I chant. I think he does for a moment, but then it goes to voicemail again.

"Hey, this is Carter—"

"Shit," I mumble, hanging up.

Banging against the door startles me, the thumps synchronizing with the beat of my heart. I look around for another avenue of escape when the door bursts open. I try to open the window, but it's sealed.

With no other option, I face the men and race toward them. With knife pointed, I gather momentum. I approach the first man, fist strong, and I hope to scare him with a loud shout. It doesn't work. He dodges me, blocking my knife, and David throws a low swing, striking me in the stomach.

My knife flies across the floor as I go down. Pain spreads to every nerve in my body until I'm wheezing. I struggle to see past the tears blurring my vision. I curl up to ease the pain that continues in waves. More footsteps and a voice sound from the corridor, but I can't open my eyes.

"Jesus and the saints, David! She wasn't supposed to be touched."

"Rocco. Wait—" David's voice is sober, and I understand instantly Rocco is important. "It's a misunderstanding, she—"

"I don't want to hear it," Rocco cuts him off. "Shit, man, you can't keep it in your pants long enough to guard her. Marcello showed me the cameras. What if she escaped because you wanted to get your teeny-weeny dick wet? Boss is going to kill you, man."

Rocco grabs me by the back of my shirt. A shudder runs down my spine when his eyes lock with mine. He spots the phone I stole, and he lets me go so he can check what I've done.

He grins at David. "You might be able to live after all… now that Destiny's cowboy will walk right into our hands."

My breath catches as it becomes clear what he means. Atlas ***knew*** David would succumb to his lust. He ***knew*** I'd try fighting and take my phone back. He ***knew*** I'd call Carter, leaving voicemails about where I am.

"All I want is Tanner." Atlas's words ring in the back of my mind.

Coldness washes over me as I realize Carter is being led into a trap because of me.

"You'll never take Carter down," I shout. "You'll never touch—"

David slaps me across the face. So hard that my eyes water. "Shut the fuck up."

"David... you really don't follow orders." Rocco sighs before looking at me. "Lock her up and keep your fucking hands off her. ***Don't fucking touch her.***"

I try biting and lashing out, but it's no use against the group of men who hold me down. So I keep fighting, thrashing as I look at them with disgust. But I'm hauled into a dark hole of a room and thrown onto the sticky, disgusting floor. I jump up and bang against the door blindly.

After a while too exhausted to continue, I trace my hands across the wall and retreat to a corner of the room. I rub my arms as I fight back a whimper. The walls are closing in on me. I bury my head in the palms of my hands and let out a silent wail.

So stupid.

So fucking stupid.

I should've never left Carter.

I finally sit, giving in to the loss of time. The chamber's darkness dominates me. The cold gives me goosebumps. I see why patients went crazy.

Carter? Did you get my voicemails? Are you coming?

I curl into a ball, shifting closer to the wall as my lips quiver. I'll never forgive myself if I'm the one who leads Carter to his death. Or worse... if Atlas goes after Storm.

Suddenly, a little door opens, letting in a stream of light. The brightness blinds me, making my eyes squint. The voice is rough, and I'm still determining who it is. I don't dare move, trying to blend into the darkness.

"Eat up," he instructs. "That's all you're getting. And thank God we're taking mercy on you."

Mercy? Is he serious?

Staring at the plate of food, I battle the urge to eat. I'm not a dog who will roll over because they want me to grovel. I'm not that kind of woman and won't become one. I'll die with pride and succumb to hunger rather than be in their debt. With the light feeding into the room, I spot the mold eating at the walls, and there's an unknown substance on the floor. I don't want to find out what it is.

Then the big door is opened, and I'm picked up. My knees scrape the floor as I struggle. I'm carried into another room—or the previous one, I'm not sure. But this one is the cleanest compared to the other rooms in the asylum.

Atlas clucks his tongue. "Naughty girl, signorina."

Oh, God, I don't want to deal with you again.

The man who dragged me in here chuckles. "She's feisty, this one."

Atlas snaps his fingers. "Leave."

The man nods, leaving us alone.

"Fuck you!" I scream at Atlas.

"No." He grins. "I'm not interested in another man's pussy." He lights a cigarette and takes a long drag before slowly approaching me. "I don't want to hurt you."

"Yeah, well... I'm not sure your ***men*** feel the same."

His eyes pierce mine. "David's been dealt with."

"I don't believe you," I bite out.

"He's dead."

My heart skips a beat, my mind racing in all directions to make sense of his words. "W-what?"

"He's been dealt with." He takes another drag of his cigarette. "If you need proof... I can show you."

There are so many emotions flowing through me. ***Did you kill your own man?*** No, I don't want to see it.

I swallow, trying to change the subject. "Carter will come for me." I ball my hands into fists. "He will."

"Funny how you shiver while you threaten. Like a kitten who only knows how to hiss." His lips curl upward. "He'll come. He knows I have you now. And of course, he's received my... ***housewarming*** gift."

Housewarming?

"What're you talking about?" I raise my voice, angry at his calm, psychotic personality.

"The Caldwells refuse to hand Tanner over," Atlas explains with a twisted smile. "I gave them a chance. When your cowboy didn't comply, I sent another message."

My stomach drops. "Is—is that why he's not answering his phone? Have you done something to him?"

He winks. "I'm sure he's trying to find you, or… he's dead accidentally. Either way, it's going to work out in my favor. I'm not going to stop until we have Tanner. I don't care who I have to kill."

"You piece of trash." I rush at him, but he catches me and pushes me back with the hand not holding the cigarette.

"You have it wrong. I'm doing a job… You have a job with the animals, yes?"

"You already know everyth—"

"Answer."

I press my lips together for a moment. There's no use playing cunning with him. He's too good at it. "That's my job."

"My job is to find Tanner." He nods. "And I'll see my job finished."

"Do you have a family?" I bite out. "Because if you do, you wouldn't be this coldhearted."

When I mention *family*, a hint of mixed emotions crosses his face before they're replaced with the usual cold gaze.

"Being in power is what matters." He swallows hard, then smokes again. "Not some group of people who'll abandon you when you need them the most."

"Family doesn't abandon one another," I say defiantly.

"If that's how your family are…" The smoke rises around his face. "You're lucky." The look in his hard eyes sends shudders prickling from my scalp to my toes. "That's not the way of it on my end… But…" He leans closer. Too close. "You know a thing or two about abandonment, don't you?"

I don't like how he's sizing me up, reading me like an open book.

His grin deepens. "Let's hope Carter doesn't do it a second time… yeah?"

Chapter 29
CARTER

I'm living my worst nightmare.

Atlas has kidnapped Destiny.

I failed her. I promised to protect her, and I let her walk right into the hands of my enemy.

I curse at the thought, punching the steering wheel. I've scoured every place I can think of for the past hour, but I've come up empty-handed.

I zoom back to the ranch, hopefully, to get further information from the fucker, Alessandro. If he doesn't talk, I'll beat it out of him with a sledgehammer.

I'm pulling my phone out to call Dylan when I see the voicemail notifications. Something tells me I need to brace as I put my phone on speaker and click on the message.

"Carter," Destiny breathes out. I'm gripping hard on the steering wheel, thankful she's alive. ***Where are you, baby?*** "Atlas has taken me. We're at the old asylum. I—I hope this gets to you."

"I'm coming," I yell into the air.

Destiny sniffles and my heart shatters, my breath seizing at the sound of her voice. I want to hold her. Make all this go away. And suddenly, I'm plagued with regret. She didn't need to be involved in this.

"If…" Destiny trails off. ***I know what she's going to say.*** "Please keep my parents and Storm safe if I don't make it. And I want you to know I never stopped lo—"

A loud bang cuts off her words before the line dies.

Murderous rage grips me. The need to locate her overrides everything I think of doing to those who dare touch her. I shake the thoughts out of my head—dwelling on this will drive me insane. Every fiber of my being wants to call the number back, but it could somehow make it worse for her.

I floor the gas pedal, the acceleration throwing me back against the seat. Taking my eyes off the road for a moment, I locate Dylan's contact and press it. It rings twice before it connects.

"Carter? You find Destiny?"

"They have her." I speed faster. "Meet at The Barn in five."

I drive the fastest I've ever driven, swinging into the parking lot and kicking up gravel with my tires. Dylan is pacing outside when I pull up. Once he sees me, he jumps into the truck, and I fly back down the road.

"She left a voicemail." I throw my phone into his lap. I grip the steering wheel so hard my knuckles turn white at hearing her voice sounding so helpless as Dylan replays the message.

"Damn." Dylan scratches his temple. "What's the plan?"

"Kill the fuckers."

Atlas knew she was my weakness and took her. He hurt my father, and he will keep threatening my friends and family... He knows no boundaries. Why should I have any?

This is fucking war.

Dylan takes his phone out and scrolls. "We need backup."

I take a deep breath, counting to ten before releasing it. ***Mom, if you're up there watching, I need the guidance.***

"Yeah," I bite out.

Dylan presses some buttons on his phone. "I'm calling."

Nodding, I step on the accelerator some more. When we get to the asylum, the place is quiet—

Too quiet.

This place is off-limits to people for a reason. It was shut down after a mass suicide. Some said the suicides were due to the practices carried out on patients. Some blamed it on a sort-of cult leadership. Some even blamed it on the government.

Either way, it's been boarded up since they came in and shut it down with little explanation to the townsfolk. It was one of the biggest scandals to face Wind Dance back in time.

I assumed the place would be crawling with Atlas's men. Yet there's nothing but the sound of crows and the rustling of bushes in the breeze. My survival instincts kick into gear. This could be a trap.

Use your head instead of acting on your emotions.

Dylan and I lock gazes for a second, then we move. We both stop at the hedges and take cover.

"C Team, come in." A scratchy voice rises from the walkie-talkie, and I unclip it from my belt.

Pressing the button, I say, "This is Carter."

"Backup on the way. We're almost there," he informs us. "Five minutes until arrival. Over."

"Roger. Over and out." I glance at Dylan. "The men will surround the asylum, then you and I will advance fast when they do. I'm going in if they don't make it in five."

"I'll be right behind you, cuz."

It feels like an eternity, though I know it isn't because I've checked my phone every few seconds. Images of Destiny held captive somewhere in this building are replaying like a broken record. Her voice, terrified and shaky, is something I never want to hear again.

"***Please keep my parents and Storm safe if I don't make it.***"

That isn't an option, baby. You're my life. If you die, my life ends, too.

I think back to her last words: "***I want you to know that I never stopped lo—***"

She loves me?

After God knows how long has passed, the walkie-talkie crackles to life. "A Team in position. Ready when you are. Over."

"B Team in position," the other team says. "Ready. Over."

It's time.

"B Team, standby. Keep watch," I command as I move in with Dylan. It's time to get Destiny back and show Atlas what happens when you fuck with us. "A Team, advance toward the asylum."

We creep out of the woods, nodding at one another as we scout for signs of life. The asylum is covered in vines, the windows are shattered, and an ominous aura surrounds the place. Yet, there are signs of present-day life littered about as we get closer; broken bottles, food containers, and footprints—a ton of them.

I nod to Dylan, and he approaches the side door and pushes it open, the rusty hinges creaking. Inside is covered in graffiti and trash. As the lights have long stopped working, it's dark and musty as we file in and split up, guns drawn, going to find my girl.

We search each room, and a part of my soul dies when we don't find her. ***Where the fuck are you, baby?***

These men are dead if they touch even a strand of her hair.

We arrive at a flight of stairs just as the other team catches up.

"First floor's clear," Dylan says in a low voice, sweat dripping from his chin as he stands beside me.

We begin our ascension, and as we reach the top step, there's a flash of something quick running down the hall.

Bullets zing. Bright flashes light up the hallway as we take cover and return fire. The ringing in my ears is deafening…

One by one, we fly past open doorways to seek cover, then fire in the direction of their shots.

I'll find you.

Chapter 30
DESTINY

A man shouts a warning, bursting into the room, then runs down the hallway, away from us.

"Told you he'd come." I grin spitefully over at Atlas, matching his twisted grin with one of my own. "Carter is going to kill you all." I hiss across my teeth. "And I can't wait."

Atlas moves behind me, cups my throat in his hand, and pulls my head back. He stares at me with silver bullets for eyes, and I hold his gaze without blinking.

I refuse to die like this. I won't let him intimidate me.

The sound of gunshots explodes in the hall, making my ears ring. Through the noise, I make out the agonizing screams of bodies hitting the floor.

Atlas holds his position behind me, refusing to leave me unguarded. As my hearing returns and the chaos around us dies, I count the footsteps approaching us. The sound of cowboy boots on the concrete echoes through the cavernous old building.

It's a sound I've been living for.

As he slowly sticks his head in the room, Carter's face comes into view. He has his gun raised and aimed straight at Atlas's head. The sight of him sends shudders through me. He's fierce and protective like I've always dreamed of him looking when he comes for me. Willing to do anything for my well-being.

Our eyes lock. A surge of comfort rushes over me, knowing

he's here, even though I'm tied to this damn chair with Atlas's fingers digging into my aorta.

"Stop right there." Carter's voice is solid, his hand steady on his weapon. "You move, I shoot."

"No." Atlas holds the muzzle of his weapon against my temple. My pulse skips against the cold metal. "Not when I have her." He gestures at Carter and Dylan with his other hand. "Drop them."

Carter's face turns rigid, but he stays collected. He lowers his gun before dropping it and kicking it to the side when Atlas motions for him to do so. Dylan reluctantly follows.

As the men stare at one another, it's unclear who will make the next move.

I'm caught like prey between them.

Sweat trickles down my cheeks and runs into Atlas's fingers. My life flashes before my eyes in these moments that stretch like years. My mind fixates on Storm. My daughter. ***Our*** daughter. Who Carter still needs to meet.

My baby. My child. Storm. I think about what her life will be like without me. Without either of her parents. My heart shreds.

"There's only one way to save your girl now." Atlas spits the words in Carter's direction.

"And how's that, asshole?"

"Your brother."

"God damn it!"

"I'm going to shoot your ***fucking*** girlfriend in the head."

Despite the danger, a jolt of electricity pulses through me when Atlas refers to me as Carter's ***girlfriend.*** I desperately miss hearing those words, and I hope I don't die today so I'll hear them again.

"This game you're playing is pointless." Carter sounds sincere, and I sense a shift in Atlas as his fingers lose a bit of grip on my throat. He's reached an end. "Let her go. You're not gonna find the information you're after. We don't know where Tanner is."

Atlas's grip tightens again on my throat, but I don't show signs of pain. Everyone is silent for several seconds, then Atlas cuts the binds around my arms and legs.

Are you letting me go? Are really letting me go?

Carter's eyes meet mine. We're trying to read each other's thoughts and devise a plan telepathically. But of course, it's not working. All we can do is stare, paralyzed, sensing each other's fear.

Atlas grabs me with one hand, pressing the gun against my temple. He kicks the chair to one side. My mind races. I don't know what to do. Then I realize… there's nothing I ***can*** do. I'm helpless. Carter and Dylan are, too, as long as Atlas keeps this gun to my head.

Atlas begins backing down the stairs with his right arm wrapped tightly around me and his weapon trained on me in his left.

"Where're you taking her?" Carter yells as he and Dylan lunge forward.

"I'll fucking kill her."

Both men still in place. Atlas continues to back away until Carter and Dylan are out of sight. Once we're downstairs, he hurries me across the asylum. The bodies of Atlas's men lie bloody on the floor near the entry hall. It's the first time I've seen a dead person, and I'm scared witless.

Atlas stops me, keeping his grip on my arm, then bends over one of the men and starts rummaging through his pockets.

Are you robbing you own fallen man? What a heartless lunatic. Then I hear a set of keys jingling.

Atlas stands, keys in hand, and keeps urging me forward, through the front doors and out into the light. It's overcast, but the light pressing down from the gray clouds still shocks my eyes. I squint and stumble as we near the vehicles parked out front.

He clicks the key fob, pushing me toward the Range Rover. "Open the door."

I stand motionless for several seconds, afraid that it's all over once I get into his vehicle. I can't foresee a way to escape once I leave with him. And the fact he's making me participate in my own kidnapping makes my stomach tie in knots. I almost wish he'd strong-arm me into the vehicle rather than make me do it.

As I grab the door handle and pull, I pray for just one viable chance for an escape.

He pushes me into the front seat, and I almost topple into the floor for a second. He slams the door, rushes to the other side, and climbs in. The engine roars to life, and he floors it. The turf of the old asylum yard is ripped under the tires as we speed away.

As I sit, I begin to seethe. I'm terrified, but my emotions are transmuting into anger.

From the side mirror, I locate Carter and Dylan racing toward Carter's truck to follow us.

Something overtakes me, and I leap at Atlas and clench my hands around his neck. The vehicle swerves as we struggle. He manages to throw me off with a shove that slams me against the door and my head against the window.

"Stay the fuck off me."

But I don't give in. As we round a corner, I have to do more. Gathering strength, I punch the side of his neck and try hard to get my leg up to kick him.

He shouts as his body jolts to the side, and the vehicle swerves again. Then he rears back and slaps me hard, full-on across my face. I bounce, then I'm flattened to my seat with my vision blurring. My strength is draining fast, and after everything I've been through, I don't know how much longer I can keep up the fight.

Hope fades.

The world moves in slow motion, but visions of my daughter speed through my mind. Her life plays out before my eyes. I think about the day she was born. That was the happiest and saddest day of my life. I was overjoyed at the birth of my daughter, but I couldn't accept that Carter wasn't there, that he didn't know about Storm. ***He didn't even know.***

I've been cautious, refusing to open my heart. Refusing to consider the possibility of sharing our lives again. That's all I want, though. To share my life with him. To raise our daughter as a family. To rebuild the life we once had.

I want him. I want us.

I'm shaken from my thoughts as Atlas turns onto the old quarry road, the vehicle fishtailing on the loose gravel.

This road is a dead end. I assume he doesn't know this. The only place it leads is over the cliff into the quarry.

Damn it! This is either going to help or get much worse. He'll have to stop and fight—or go over the ravine.

I turn in my seat. Carter and Dylan are following us, but then they swerve and slide to a stop. Maybe not to chase us over the edge?

I try wrestling the steering wheel away from Atlas. "You're going to—"

But it's too late.

There's no stopping the momentum.

I instinctively clutch the side of the doorframe as if it will save me. But it won't. It can't.

"Carter!" I scream as the earth gives way beneath us, and we free-fall over the cliff.

Continue reading the Shotgun Mafia series, Book Two, Savage Promise! 😊

Acknowledgements

Thank you to everyone who believed in me and helped make this possible.

About the Author

Sky Coppola juggles her author career along with raising sheep and goats in rural Virginia with some crazy dogs, dreaming up her next characters. She writes action-packed wild romances where the heroes are strong, protective, and fearless, and the heroines are independent and romantic.

Enjoy them!

Readers can count on happily-ever-afters, an awesome read, and steam.

She's a lover of coffee, chocolate, and decadent romance novels from her favorite authors.

Connect with Sky:

Facebook > Sky Coppola Dark Romance Author)

Website > http://skycoppolaromance.com/

Printed in Great Britain
by Amazon

37480955R00169